Cabana Bay

by

Ruben D. Gonzales

Cabana Bay Mystery Series

Cover Art by *Teddi Black*

The Wild Rose Press, Inc.
PO Box 708
Adams Basin, NY 14410-0708
Visit us at www.thewildrosepress.com

Publishing History
First Edition, 2025
Trade Paperback ISBN 978-1-5092-6124-6
Digital ISBN 978-1-5092-6125-3

Cabana Bay Mystery Series
Published in the United States of America

Dedication

To my wife, who puts up with me.

Chapter One

I don't know why I thought joining my Uncle Manny in his entrepreneurial venture would be a good idea. I should have known what to expect when my son and I showed up at his Florida beach front motel two years ago, and the first thing he asked was, "Can you clean a toilet?"

Unfortunately, my uncle's part-time housekeeper had just quit, and he needed someone to clean the sixteen cottages in the complex. Although my mother would attest, I can't even turn on a vacuum cleaner, my uncle knew about cleanliness because he'd spent the last few years in the army as a drill instructor, where in addition to teaching young recruits how to defend our country, he taught them how to make a bed and clean a toilet.

"Moli," he still barks from time to time, "clean toilets are the secret to success."

Lucky me. All I ever wanted was to walk around all day smelling of bleach.

"Women expect to find a clean toilet when they check in," he always says. "So, I give them what they expect, and they will want to come back, you see?"

Of course, most women would never expect to find a body on the floor of their rental, like I found in cottage fourteen. I usually find beer cans and left-over pizza boxes but not bodies. Fortunately, the labored breathing of the man on the floor told me he was still alive, so I used my cell to call 911 before he became a bad statistic in the chronicles of Cabana Bay.

We have six semi-permanent residents at the motel, but most guests stay for just a week. Only a few lodgers check out after just an overnight or two, which is what the occupant in cottage fourteen planned. The McPhersons in cottage twelve had complained about noise coming from the unit next door the night before, so I stopped at fourteen first thing in the morning to check. That's when I tripped over Mr. Smith in the semi-dark room and knew the normal routine around the Cabana Bay Cottages was about to change.

Even with him face down on the floor, I recognized his lanky build and smart attire. Because there are only sixteen cottages in the place, and since year-round guests occupy six of those, it's easy to remember guests in for a week—and even easier to recall the nightly lodgers like Mr. Smith.

"What do you mean cottage fourteen?" asked town police Detective, Frank Winters, in the motel's breakfast area after he showed up to investigate. "This McPherson couple in cottage twelve reported hearing noises last night in cottage *thirteen, right next to them.* Don't you Mexicans know how to count?"

Winters always acts like a caricature of a southern law enforcement officer, complete with mirrored dark glasses and a drawl that had become a cliche for an evolving and growing Florida ethnic populace. I have the feeling he feels left out in a Florida he'd always called home but now finds changed so doesn't quite fit in anymore. Although, the bright plaid pants he wears definitely belong on a local golf course.

After the EMT unit took Mr. Smith to the hospital,

Winters came to the office to ask me about our comatose guest. It's easy to understand Winters' confusion about the missing room, since we don't have a cottage thirteen. When Manny bought the place, he reasoned the previous owner of the motel never made a profit because he had a cottage thirteen. With it associated with bad luck among many folks, he skipped number thirteen when he reopened.

Personally, I think the prior owner running a prostitution ring out of the place had more to do with it. When the cops busted the operation, they closed the place down and the city took over the property under a nuisance ordinance. After the court settled the case, the city foreclosed to recoup expenses, and that's when, as Manny says, "I bought it for a song!"

Although the previous business model for the motel ended years ago, infrequent regulars still come to the motel for the extra services. And even though half-intoxicated men think I am attractive enough to proposition, I reluctantly say we are not in social services anymore.

Before I could explain to Winters about the missing cottage thirteen, Manny entered the motel's breakfast room that shares the space with our reception desk. After he heard Winter's slur he said, "Oh, we can count, Detective, and I can count the number of cops you dragged in for backup. What do you think is happening, another Cuban revolution? You've got everyone out there but the SWAT team."

"Listen, *amigo*, I'm in charge. Let me make the staff decisions."

"Well, since you can see what you're dealing with," Manny shot back, "call off the dogs. You're scaring my guests."

"When I'm good and ready, *amigo*," Winters snapped. "So, what about this cottage number thirteen?"

"Having a cottage thirteen would be bad luck," Manny explained. He'd run into the cop before while working security at the campground next door. Winters stood short but stout, losing hair by the day. He croaked when he talked like he swallowed a frog but could handle himself in a fix, but I think he felt threatened, like Manny wanted his job.

"I don't care what cottage number," Winters said, as he glanced over the free breakfast counter crowded with baked goods. "The guy we found will be lucky to live, so I need to see his registration."

We have an online auto reservation and checkout process for guests, but if they aren't comfortable with electronics, I take care of things for them at the desk. For last-minute charges, like a late bar tab, I run their card and get everyone checked out before eleven a.m. New guests start to check in at four o'clock.

The motel's sixteen cottages are aligned eight to a side. The bar, administration office, and the owner's apartment are in the middle. Our year-round guests are located at each end of the complex in cottages one, two, three, fifteen, sixteen, and seventeen. Thankfully, I only clean their cottages once a week.

"Didn't you see his ID in his wallet?" Manny asked the detective.

"No, apparently the robber took the man's wallet and maybe some other stuff because the place is a wreck."

"So, you think this is a robbery gone bad?"

"What else?" Winters said as he inspected the

ceiling. "So, does your security system work, or are your cameras there just for show?"

"They work," I told him, "but they don't cover the whole complex."

"Don't tell me," he said. "They don't cover unit fourteen."

Manny installed security cameras around the complex which we can access on our office computer and with our phones. The cameras are concentrated on the bar, office, and apartment area, since that's where my son Ricky spends his time. Manny said the CCTV warning signs out around the complex would be enough to discourage most thieves, although for the determined, he said cameras and signs were never enough.

"We don't cover all the cottages," I explained. "We focus on the front here."

"That's just great."

Manny said, "I got the system I could afford."

"Okay, so did anyone go into the cottage and take the victim's ID?"

"No," Manny said, "we didn't let anyone in."

"How about housekeeping?"

"Hey!" I yelped.

"Moli is the housekeeper here," Manny said. "She would never touch anything at a crime scene."

"Listen, detective," I said, "when Mrs. McPherson reported a loud noise, I hustled there and knocked on the door. When no one answered, I figured the old couple were hearing things, so I left. I didn't find Mr. Smith until this morning."

"Well, someone ran into him last night," he said, as he took a croissant off the counter. "Maybe one of your guests."

"Come on," Manny said, "why would a guest do something like that? The guy was probably hammered and got robbed by someone he picked up in the bar."

"Anything is possible, *amigo,* and until I find out who, I might have to shut you down."

"What do you mean shut me down?" Manny said, his voice raised a notch. "Do you know what that will cost me?"

"I don't know, *amigo*, but unless someone confesses, that's what you can expect, and don't forget, your agreement with the city says you have to run a clean place. You could be in violation of your contract with something like this, and the city could take back the property."

"They can't do that," Manny said, his voice up an additional notch and his hands together prayer like "I've got all my retirement savings invested here."

"Not my problem, a*migo*. Maybe you should have invested more wisely."

Just before the big property boom hit Florida, Manny cashed in his retirement accounts and made a foreclosure down payment on this broken-down motel complex south of Clearwater. Knowing he'd need an additional revenue stream, he had a bar built to cater to locals and guests alike.

The little complex sits on a pretty cove on Cabana Bay. The cottages border a romantic narrow half-moon crescent white sand beach. A cute ten-foot by ten-foot open-sided palm-thatched roofed cabana fronts each cottage. If the AC in the cottage falters, guests can take refuge in the shady cabanas and enjoy refreshing ocean breeze. In the spirit of positive relations, we offer free drinks and beer until the unit is fixed.

If you sit at the bar at the right evening minute, you can watch the sun dip below the western horizon. A loud round of applause from patrons, guests, and a drumming group that meets out on the beach on weekend nights usually accompany the moment celebrating the heavenly sunset event.

"*Amigo*," Winters said, not using the term in a friendly way, "it sounds like you've got a lot to lose on this, and since you're not a cop anymore, you need to help me out, or this case might drag on for a while."

"Okay, I hear you."

"So," he said, as he licked white icing off his fingertips from the thick cinnamon roll he just ate, "what kind of stuff did Mr. Smith have?"

"I think he was a photographer," I said. "He carried in some camera equipment when he checked in."

"Did he work with one of the news services?"

"We don't know," Manny said, "you're the detective."

"Okay," he said, gulping down the last of his coffee, "give me the info on the poor guy that wasn't in cottage thirteen, that you didn't see last night, but you did see this morning a step away from eternity."

Mr. Smith's registration card contained the usual data, like fake name and what kind of car he drove. The man also paid with cash. Altogether, there was a limited amount of misinformation.

"How unusual is that?" Winters asked about the guest paying with cash.

"Last I heard," Manny said, "cash is still good at the bank."

"Is this all you got?" Winters asked, his hands out, like asking for more.

"What do you want, his blood type?"

"A real name would be a good start."

"Maybe the car rental place has more," I offered.

Winters looked at me, like he'd just realized I was in the discussion. "He had a rental?"

"He told me at registration when he had to run out to the lot to get the license number."

"Okay, we'll make a call to the rental company."

"So, how long before Moli can get in there to clean?" Manny asked.

"Hard to tell. We might be here several days, maybe a week or more, before your Moli maid can get in the cottage."

Man, I hated that reference.

My real name is Molina. That's my mom's family name, but my mother started calling me Moli when I was small. She figured a small girl with a name like Molina was a little much, so she shortened it. I liked the difference from the other Mexican girl names you hear in Latino families, like Esperanza, Alejandra, or Paloma. I mean, those names are beautiful and all, but Moli just fit me better. Then again, if I knew I was going to end up as a Moli Maid, I might have stuck with Molina.

"A week? What about my guests?" Manny squawked. "What about my bar?"

My uncle's good with his hands and he's proud of the long bar he built. He also built the tabletops in the seating area and the cabinets and shelves that hold the liquor bottles. He didn't make the bar stools, though. He said for the stools, he needed to buy steel leg stools. Stools strong enough to hold up to a crowd. Like the mob that crowds into the bar for Monday night football.

"We need to secure the place, Manny," Winters said,

"so you'll have to move out who's registered and cancel anyone coming in next week."

"Have a heart; our peak season is almost here."

I could tell Winters was thinking about the situation because he paused and crinkled up his nose, and using a checkered handkerchief, he wiped sweat from his forehead. Manny wasn't a local in town, but in his short residency, the city fathers, including the mayor, had indebted themselves to him in one way or another. He accomplished this by treating them to food and alcohol in the bar. Manny might not have been the best innkeeper, but he knew how to make friends in high places.

"Okay," Winters said, probably realizing Manny could call the mayor and put some heat on him. "You can keep the bar open and the South wing. That's the best I can do. And don't think about contacting the mayor, your drinking buddy."

"I don't drink, Frank."

Manny met Mayor Eldridge the first week he arrived in town, catching the man in a tight campaign race. With the mayor in search of an edge, Manny made a calculated campaign donation. The mayor used the unexpected cash to run some last-minute TV ads.

The mayor won the race by a thin margin and since then he treats Manny like a long lost relative, and Manny takes every opportunity to remind the mayor about his contribution.

"Listen, Manny, the Chief will back me on this. Now, we've got to get our forensics man in there, but he's out sick, so I've got to wait on him before we can gather evidence."

"Frank, come on, I can't shut down the North wing.

What about the guests already there and the ones coming in tomorrow for a week?"

"I don't know, but you're lucky I don't close down the whole place. But I'll settle for the North wing, as long as you don't let people in there."

"I've got three long-term tenants in the North wing."

"Who?" the detective asked, taking out a small notebook and writing.

"Gloria Cruz in seventeen, Doc Murphy in sixteen, and Dante Colombo in fifteen."

"What do they do?"

"You've seen Gloria in the bar, Frank. Doc's a retired physician and Colombo is the project manager on the condo project across the highway."

"He's working in town and staying here?"

"His corporation sent him down to manage the project. He's been with us for six months."

"Down from where?"

"Come on, Frank, isn't that your job? Why don't you ask him?"

"Don't worry, *amigo*, I will. How about in the South wing? Do you have long termers there?"

The run around annoyed Manny, making his ears turn red, so I jumped in, "Professor Daly is in cottage number three."

"A professor? Professor of what?"

"He teaches English at the community college, so we call him professor. He received great reviews for a book of poetry he published twenty years ago, and he has been living off the notoriety since. Nice man but he likes to drink."

"Don't all Irishmen?"

I ignored what he said about the Irish and continued,

"Señora Martinez is in cottage number two. She's from Miami originally, but after retiring, she drifted up here since it is so expensive down there.

"Then we have Lou and Marge Gigliotti in cottage number one," I continued. "They're retired too and are from New York. They moved down a few years ago. Marge is a retired Union Rep. They were living in the Oaks Retirement Community next door, but the monthly mortgage payments and the complex's HOA fees were more than their small monthly pensions and Social Security could manage, so they moved over here."

"Okay," Winters said, making another note in his little notebook. "So, do you have a list of customers who were in the bar last night?"

"The bar?" Manny asked. "Do you think we keep a guest list and a seating chart?"

"Listen, *amigo*, I need some names."

Manny's eyes bulged in anger but if he gave the cop trouble it could result in him closing the place down. By Winters' crooked smile, I figured he wanted a reason to do just that. I don't think he had gotten over Manny interfering with a campground case the year before and was just waiting for a chance for a little revenge,

Manny finally said, "Okay, the best we can do is run you a credit card tab and make a list of regulars who were here last night."

"Okay, I can start with those."

"And what about my long-term guests?"

"They can stay, but I'll still be questioning them. In fact, I need you to round up everybody and get them together so we can talk to them."

"When?"

"In an hour, outside in the bar where everyone can

spread out and be comfortable."

"Ah, Frank, you're killing me."

"Don't whine. I could haul everyone downtown. How do you think your guests would react to that? Now, get everyone together. The sooner I start talking to people, the sooner we can finish."

With the point made, the detective closed his little notebook and made his way to cottage fourteen, not thirteen. A gaggle of cops in dark blue uniforms milled about the crime scene like a flock of black birds searching for food. I always wondered why in a place where the temperature could hit a hundred in the summer, police departments still dressed their officers in heat seeking dark blue uniforms. I didn't know who in our local police department thought the color was a good idea, but I hoped whoever made that decision wasn't going to be working on our case, or Manny and I would be out of business.

Chapter Two

I got my first taste of the famous Florida heat two years ago, the day Ricky and I arrived. Being from Los Angeles, I didn't mind since I grew up only two blocks from the beach. Don't get the wrong impression. I'm not one of those tall, slim, and blonde California surfer girls. I'm short with long dark hair I mostly keep in a braid down my back. I didn't even learn to swim until I attended the police academy. Even now, I still harbor a natural fear of the seashore and drowning.

Standing there in the reception area of his motel that first morning, I didn't think I'd mind living with Uncle Manny. At the time, having just gone through a difficult divorce from a difficult husband, I didn't have many options. I was desperate to get away, far away, like the opposite side of the country, far away, so I would have put up with anything.

My dad arranged my accommodations with Uncle Manny, telling his older brother I needed a place to hide, and could I visit him for a few weeks. Dad reasoned me staying with an ex-cop three thousand miles away from L.A. would be safe.

"What about Ricky?" I asked Manny. My three-year-old son stood at my side in the motel's breakfast room that first morning. Ricky is short for Ricardo, which was my grandfather's name, but it's a bit formal for a little kid. When he's older, I'll call him Rick, like

Bogart in *Casablanca*.

My uncle's legal name is Emmanuel. It's a mouthful, so everyone calls him Manny which is appropriate since Emmanuel means, *God is with us* and infers an angelic person. Since he is tall, wide, bearded, and resembles a mean brown bear, the shortened Manny, is more fitting.

"You and Ricky can stay," he told me. "But you'll have to share the spare bedroom with the Dude."

"Who?"

"The Dude," Manny said, stepping aside and showing us the one-hundred-pound Bordeaux Mastiff, standing behind him. I think Manny settled on the name since the dog was a French breed, and he figured a high-class dog should have a high-class name, even though he can spread drool all over anything within ten feet.

"It's up to the Dude," he said with a shrug. "It's his room."

The big brown dog reared up on his hind legs, plopped plate size paws on my shoulders, and nearly knocked me over. The Dude stood taller than me and outweighed me, making me unsure about sharing a bedroom with the dog, not to mention a life. The dog, as if he understood Manny's proposal, got down and circled around Ricky, sniffing. With Ricky standing, the Dude stood eye to eye with my brown-eyed, curly-haired son.

To settle the matter, the Dude licked Ricky up his face from chin to forehead and sat down beside him.

"I guess it's settled," Manny said.

After the terms were agreed to, we settled in together amid the sun, sand, and salt, and I started to work in the cottages the next day.

Although our new home in all reality had been a

motel, Manny thought the motel label would be bad for business, so when he bought the place, he had a new sign made for the front and changed the name to the Cabana Bay Cottages.

Cute.

****

"Moli," Manny said, "better call all the guests and get them out at the bar in an hour."

"Yes, sir!"

"And better check the reservation list and work out the cancelations in the North wing next week."

"Yes, sir!"

"Okay, and as soon as you're done, I need you to go up to cottage fourteen."

"Why?"

"I need your help with this."

"What do you mean?" I asked, not sure I wanted to get involved. I mean I never wanted to be a cop, one reason why I quit rookie school, so why start now?

"I've got to get ahead of this investigation," Manny said. "I can't afford to be closed for a week."

"What about the desk?" I asked. Check-in time was approaching, and I was groping for an excuse to say no.

"Don't worry, it's only three o'clock. Put out the, four o'clock, check-in sign."

"What are you going to do?"

"I'm going up to seventeen and talk to Gloria."

Our bartender, Gloria, has been in cottage seventeen since Manny opened the place. They dated for a while, but with thirty some years between them, the relationship became paternal. He still wanted to help, so he let her stay for free in cottage seventeen in exchange for managing the bar and putting up with a kaleidoscope of customers every night. He doesn't pay her, but she's so pretty, she makes a couple hundred dollars a night in tips during the week, and more on the weekend.

Along with the free cottage and the food she pilfers from the breakfast bar, she makes out. I mean, Gloria eats like a mouse anyway. Any time we eat together, I feel like a hog at a trough. I've been trying to eat better and worked off the baby weight I put on during the nine months ahead of Ricky's coming out. With the divorce and our relocation, my psyche is fragile, and food continues to be my best friend, especially tacos.

For exercise, I try to get out and walk on the beach most mornings, dragging the Dude with me. Slogging on the beach to stay in shape is a losing proposition. On most days, the temperature soars, and the Dude starts to pant and barely makes a mile before we trudge back to the apartment. Once inside, he plops down in front of the air conditioning vent and sleeps for an hour.

I put in workmanlike days, cleaning those toilets, which makes up for missing artificial exercise. Besides, I don't plan to ever get married again, so what do I care what I look like in a bikini, although I've been told I'm pretty. My friends always said if they squinted at me, I resembled the actress from *The Devil Wears Prada* movie. Not the devil, the young star with the big smile and all those teeth.

"Why are you going to talk with Gloria?" I asked Manny.

"Because I saw her flirting with Smith last night in the bar and I need to find out what she knows before the cops talk to her."

"Who says the cops will talk to her?"

"Are you kidding? They'll fall all over themselves

trying to get to her."

Tall with golden brown skin and hair, when Gloria Cruz strutted along the beach in a bikini, you knew she used to be a runway model. Beautiful wasn't a strong enough word to describe her. Standing next to her, I felt like a warthog.

Gloria got heavily into drugs when she worked for a model agency in Miami. A friend asked our local priest, Father Torrez, if he could help relocate Gloria to a safer environment. Father Torrez runs the local Methadone center, so he called his occasional parishioner, Manny Soto, to ask if he would put Gloria up for a while, until she got her act together. Due to friendship and guilt, Manny agreed. Working with Gloria didn't seem like a job, so he asked her to stay.

Manny took her to his local AA group. Gloria has been drug-free for two years now, although she still relies on occasional tequila for anxiety self-medication. When you think about it, so do a lot of people.

"Do you think she might be involved with this?"

"No, but she has eyes around this place and maybe noticed something with this Mr. Smith."

"Like what?"

"Like did he talk to anyone."

"What are you thinking?"

"Since Smith only checked in a couple of days ago and probably didn't get a chance to make any enemies in town, I figure Winters might be onto something about the guy getting whacked by someone staying right here in the Cabana Bay Cottages."

Chapter Three

I made the calls to all the current guests and invited them to the meeting with the town police. When done, I reluctantly made my way toward cottage fourteen.

"What time did you say you found the body?" Winters asked when I trudged up to the cottage.

A cool breeze washed through the cottage's shaded porch. The wind tempered the ninety-degree Florida heat that blasted off the sand beyond the thatched cabana that fronted the cottage. Whoever built the original motel laid out all the units the same way. A seating area in front faced the beach and a kitchenette and island counter sat in the middle. A bathroom, closet, and a bedroom took up the rear of the space. However, if you entered through the door that faced the roadside parking lot, you stepped in the bedroom and might say you came in the front, not the back.

"I told you, eleven-ten," I said, avoiding a crime scene tech who maneuvered around the room taking photos.

"That's exact," Winters said. He stepped out on the porch and glanced both ways, but Manny had already disappeared into Gloria's cottage. "How do you recollect the time you found our comatose friend?"

"Easy. I closed the desk at eleven, grabbed fresh linen and stuff, and pushed the housekeeping cart this way to start cleaning the cottages. Since Mr. Smith hadn't checked out, and because Mrs. McPherson complained about noise last night, I stopped to check on him first. He didn't answer the door when I knocked, so I used my duplicate cottage key to open the door."

"Do you always carry your keyring with you?"

"If not with me, it's on the housekeeping cart."

"Are any keys missing, like the one for cottage fourteen?"

"They are all accounted for."

Nodding, Winters stepped in the unit and eyed the chalk outline where I found the nearly dead man. "We'll have to wait on the crime scene techs for verification," Winters said, "but I think someone clobbered him from behind with a blunt object." He gazed at me, like he was waiting for an answer.

I said, "I don't have a hammer or anything, detective."

"How about on the housekeeping cart? Any blunt objects there?"

"Several bars of soap and a toilet bowl brush."

When he continued, unamused by my cleaning equipment humor, he said, "How about in the workshop? I'm sure there are hammers and other blunt objects in there."

"There are, but Manny doesn't like anyone touching his tools. He's a little weird about them, especially with his drill, so he keeps the shop locked."

He nodded at me then, after he scanned the chalk outline on the floor, asked, "Did you think anything unusual when you first found Mr. Smith? Manny told me you were once a cop. What do you remember?"

"I dropped out of the police academy," I said, feeling guilty about my short try at cop school.

Although my whole family is in law enforcement, I didn't make the grade. Manny retired from the force after he separated from my Aunt Colleen. To forget about the ordeal, he took his two pensions, one from the army and one from LAPD, and got as far away from Southern California as possible, buying the rundown place in Cabana Bay.

Ricky and I stay with Manny and the Dude in the two-bedroom owner's suite between the bar and the office. The arrangement is not bad, being a recent add on, everything in the addition is new and works. There's a kitchen-great room combination directly behind the office and two bedrooms in the rear with a bathroom between. Because of the way the cove is crescent-shaped, you get a salty ocean breeze from both sides of the apartment, although with the windows open the chatter from the bar can keep you awake.

There's not much privacy to entertain personal guests in the owner's apartment, but since I kind of swore off men since my divorce, I'm okay with the arrangement.

Manny lucked out buying on the Gulf side where there are no waves.

"What do you mean there's no surf?" I asked him as I stood on the lake-like Gulf shore when I first arrived. Manny never liked the ocean and all the sun, sand, and salt. He preferred a lazy river option.

"I know, right? A beach without waves."

Lucky me.

Manny didn't spend any time at the beach growing up. As a troubled youth, with a half-dozen cops in the family, he chose a different path. Long before he wore army green or LAPD blue, a young Manny Soto became a regular in juvie court. The way my dad tells it, my uncle ran with a wild bunch that drank and did drugs. Still just a teenager, he played bass in a heavy metal band that performed at local bars where he was too young to drink. Of course, the last time he appeared in court, a judge ordered the selective service system to draft him, and a year in the heat and mess of the Vietnam jungle turned his life around.

Our great-grandfather of the Soto clan, Tommy Soto, migrated to L.A. from Texas in the thirties. The men in the Texas line of Sotos were Texas Rangers. Since then, every generation of the family tree has had at least one cop in it, not including me. I'm the family's police academy drop out and single mom sharing a room with a big dog. Learning the ropes around the place took a while, but I'm now into a daily boring routine of checking people in and out, cleaning those toilets, and second guessing my premise that a life in janitorial services might be a good career choice.

"Still," Winters asked, "what do you remember? I'm interested in your first-hand view of the crime scene."

I paused to focus on the spot where I found Mr. Smith face down on the linoleum. I didn't scrutinize the scene then, caught up in the excitement of the moment and everything. "You mean besides the fact he looked dead?"

"Besides that," he said, not smiling at my attempt at humor.

"Well, I don't think there was a struggle or a fight."

"Why do you say that?"

"I didn't see any drag marks and all his clothes were in one piece."

"That's observant. Why do you think that?"

"Someone surprised him?"

"Bingo!"

I smiled at his reaction to my assumption. Mr. Smith could just as easily have been attacked from behind, by someone hiding on the other side of the door. Or, maybe by an acquaintance, or someone he wasn't afraid of, so he turned his back on them. In fact, there were a couple of near-death scenarios to consider.

"So, I'll need the names of everyone still registered, everyone who checked out this morning, and the names of the long termers too. You can give them to me when I talk to all the guests at four o'clock."

"How about the shack crew?"

"What shack crew?"

On one side of the bar, Manny built a twelve-foot by twelve-foot open cabana beach shack that sells beach supply stuff. You can get sunscreen, snacks, drinks, ice, and little sand toys that kids like to play with. In addition, you can rent umbrellas, floats, and beach chairs. We also rent beach towels because you are not supposed to carry the fluffy white cottage bath towels down to the beach where they could get sandy.

To work in the shack, Manny hired a crew of pretty stay-at-home moms who needed to make extra money and put Gloria in charge. She's got the moms on a rotating work shift, so during the day someone is always at the beach stand and in the bar. They all take turns babysitting each other's kids when they are working. The ladies like the job because they get a break away from those same kids, and they can work on their tans. Part of the deal is they work the tables in the bar at least one night a week but no more. At least one works most nights, but two or three work on busy nights. The deal works out for all, because the shop closes at four-thirty, and except for the night moms scheduled for later, the day moms get to go home, no matter what.

I usually stay clear of the shack moms since they could all be in a swimsuit edition of a sports magazine, and I hate comparing my evolving body to theirs. "We hired a crew of part-timers to work in the beach rental shack," I told Winters. "While they are here, they also mind the bar during the day."

"I'll need to talk to everyone on duty yesterday and last night."

"Do you think a stay-at-home mom could be a killer?"

"Probably not but I still need to talk to them because they may have seen something important."

I hadn't thought about that. "What about the taco truck guys?"

"What guys?"

In addition to the bar, Manny bought a used taco truck to increase revenue. He has a contract with the Lopez brothers to man the truck, seven nights a week. The brothers are likeable, and although they pretend to not speak or understand English, they do. They are all hard workers. The four brothers work construction by day and rotate working in the truck at night. They appreciate the extra work since they all have big families to feed, and Manny lets them take home any perishable surplus product left over at the end of a shift.

The truck menu offers a variety of tacos and burritos, but the fat fish tacos are the best sellers. In a nod to the health conscious, I added salad bowls to the menu with any Mexican topping imaginable, including freshly made guacamole, which cost extra. All the orders come with an order of warm chips and a foam cup of homemade spicy red salsa that Manny makes. He claims it is an old family recipe, which is a tall tale, since no one can recall him ever cooking at home, and most people in the family prefer a *salsa verde* on their tacos.

"We've got four brothers who rotate in the taco truck at night."

"What are their names?"

"The Lopez brothers."

"What are you guys, a refugee center?"

I wanted to hit him with a smart retort about his obvious prejudice to anyone with a non-Anglo name, but I kept my mouth shut since he could very well determine the future of the Cottages.

"Which Mexicans were on duty last night?"

"Bob and Raul worked last night. Young handsome guys, not that I notice that kind of thing. All the brothers work across the street during the day and come over to put in a night shift in the truck. I don't believe I've ever seen a bunch work harder. Most of those guys work two, sometimes three jobs."

"They've got to, so they can buy those fancy jacked up cars they all drive."

The terrible characterization of hard-working people made me cringe. Most Mexican immigrants worked extra hard to make enough money to send home to poor relatives.

"Anyone check out this morning?"

"We had four cottages vacate this morning. A total of ten guests, if you don't count Mr. Smith.

"We can ignore Smith for now. He won't be leaving town for a while."

With my marching orders, I hustled to the parking

area in front of the building.

My daily routine included getting my son Ricky on and off his school bus. He had just started kindergarten, and I scheduled my time in order to see him off in the morning and greet him when he gets home in the afternoon. I had that maternal instinct. The instinct I swore I never had until Ricky came along, which surprised a good many people. Even after he made his appearance, more than a few people have said I am not much of a mother.

I was unprepared for parenthood, so my mother took charge once Ricky showed. Thank God. She basically took care of him the first two years. That gave me the strength to fight with my ex-husband. She warned me when I said I wanted to relocate to Cabana Bay. She said, "How can you take care of Ricky by yourself?"

I laughed, I mean, how hard is it to raise a kid, right?

Since then, I've found out it is harder than I imagined. I've been trying to do better, and luckily, the Dude has filled in the gaps.

The parking lot has a wide, yellow-lined loading zone area right out front where the bus always stops. This is where I share the welcome home duties with the Dude. He usually beats me there, and thumps his tail on the concrete walkway, as he waits patiently for my boy.

When Ricky got off the bus, he gave the big dog a hug, not even having to stoop, which earned him a slick film on his face. I don't feel good about Manny's dog getting more attention from my son than I do. I mean, I'm the mother who suffered through twelve hours of labor before I forced him screaming into the world. Then again, maybe he remembers the whole ordeal and is still mad about it.

****

Only a few guests check out on Fridays. Most guests are in for a full week and check in on Saturday afternoon and check out the following Saturday morning. An early Friday exit usually means people are anxious to beat the highway traffic. Or, being cooped up together finally got to them and they couldn't wait to get on the road home.

I put a list of motel guests together who had checked out of the North wing. The list included one couple, one family of three, the McPhersons, and a single lady down from Atlanta for a sister's funeral. Luckily, with the departures of two couples from the South wing, I transferred the guests in the two remaining cottages in the North wing to the South wing for the night.

I called the guests in the North wing and told them about the meeting with the cops and broke the news to those who had to change cottages to the South wing. Since they were mad about the inconvenience, I sweetened the deal and offered ice cold free drinks in the bar after the meeting. As an extra incentive, I offered to help carry stuff.

The McPhersons said they didn't need help, but the Atlanta lady said I could help her. Later, as I carried her bags, I listened to her lament about her dead sister and how she never called her, and how her sister died before she got to say goodbye. After I left her, I rushed to the office and called my oldest sister to say hello, before one of us died.

"*Aye, por Dios, que paso,* what's wrong?" my sister Alma asked me when I called.

"*Nada,* I just called to say hello."

"You never call to say hello."

"Well, I called today to say hello."

"Is something wrong with Ricky? *Aye Dios,* I told you if you left L.A. and took the boy away from his friends, it would be hard on him."

"He was three when we left. He didn't have any friends."

"Is he doing okay in school, making friends?"

"He's in kindergarten. All he does is play and make friends." I didn't tell her about his one-hundred-pound best friend dog that could eat Ricky as an appetizer.

"How's Manny?"

"Oh, he's the same old Manny."

"Oh, no, something is wrong. Did he start drinking again?"

"No, he didn't."

"Well, that's good news. Thanks for calling."

****

I made up a list of everyone who changed cottages, and all the guests already checked out, and remembered all their names. I have always been good with names. I'm like the adult nerd who remembers the name of every teacher they ever had, including all my high school subject teachers. Now, most of them were nuns. Sister Mary taught math, Sister Susan taught social studies, and Sister Charlotte taught chemistry, which made remembering their names easier. That's what made me curious about Mr. Smith, because he didn't have a name for his face. Isn't Smith like German? This Mr. Smith was more like a Morelli or a DeNero.

I wondered, with the people on the just-left list still on the road, how Winters would track them all down, much less question them any time soon. Maybe if he put out an APB and set out roadblocks on all major highways, he could keep them from fleeing the state.

I made the call to the guests with a reservation for the next week in the North wing. Five contacts and five calls. Luckily, two didn't answer, so I got to leave them the bad news in their voicemails. The other three hated me. I did mention to them that through a previous arrangement Manny made with the Pirate Cove Campground next door, they were welcome to book one of their cabins, which were similarly situated to the beach as the motel, and we would guarantee a similar price. One couple agreed to the offer, one didn't, and the other one hung up without saying more. For those who didn't answer their phones, I left cancelation messages and hoped they didn't show and expect a warm bed and soft pillow.

With the cancelled reservation business finished, I needed to go to the bar meeting, so I checked on Ricky who didn't even glance my way when I told him where I was going. Of course, the Dude barked out an okay.

I know what you're thinking, who leaves her five-year-old son alone? Well, that's the deal. When I leave little Ricky in the care of the Dude, it's like leaving him in the care of an army platoon. No one will come close to my kid with the Dude on guard. Plus, with the CCTV, I check the cameras on my phone at least ten times an hour we are separated. Just to make sure things are quiet in the apartment, unless I check at night. There is no quiet at night because the Dude snores like a freight train.

I plodded to the bar, bumped into several guests along the way, and all of them grumbled about the inconvenience. When the last of the guests arrived, the cops split everyone up and directed them to widely separate tables. Winters greeted the guests and advised them the cops would take their statements. He told them to not be nervous about the formality and to just answer the questions truthfully.

As the cops circulated asking their questions, I searched for Manny to fill him in. I found him as he sifted through credit card receipts. Gloria sat on a bar stool across from him, enjoying a tall cold drink of unknown contents. "Did everyone come out?" he asked, concentrating on a legal pad in front of him.

"Everyone."

"Did you call next week's guests?"

"I did, and I told them about our arrangement with the Cove."

"Great, thanks."

"So," I asked, "what's going on with all the questioning with the guests."

"It's standard stuff," he said, watching the cops go table to table. "At least two cops ask each guest a set of questions. After, they compare notes on the responses. If they find an inconsistency, they'll go back and ask again. If they find someone way off in their answers, they put them on a final suspects list and dig deeper."

Keeping my voice down, I asked Manny about the bar guest list from the night before. "How many did you come up with?"

"I'm working on it."

I turned to Gloria. "What about our Mr. Smith? Did you talk to him last night?"

"I told Manny, I only talked to him as much as I talk to any customer," she said. "We were busy for a Thursday night, and I didn't have time to sit and chat with a stranger."

I asked, "Did he sit at the bar and drink all night?"

"He ate an order of fish tacos and worked his phone.

He got up a couple of times, shuffled down to the beach, and he ordered another red wine."

"Red wine?" I asked. "Who drinks wine at the beach?"

"Someone always wants a glass of wine. I learned a long time ago to keep a couple of bottles of wine in the fridge for the ladies. I even got a dozen tall, stemmed wine glasses. The women love them and tip big."

I admired Gloria's entrepreneurial spirit. I mean, I enjoyed a glass of wine every once in a while, although an ice-cold beer and fish tacos are hard to beat after a day out in the sun, salt, and sand.

When Manny finished his list, he asked Gloria to check and see if he missed anyone.

"You missed quite a few," she said after a quick minute.

"Like whom?"

"You got the regulars here, sure, but they usually pay with a card. You missed the cash paying customers."

"How many?"

"Twenty, easy."

Manny paused, then said, "Okay, this is all Winters gets. It'll keep him busy for a while."

"What about the rest?" I asked.

"We're going to concentrate on the guests in the cottages. If my hunch is right, the person we want is a guest right here."

"So, we don't need to consider anyone else?"

After a pause he said, "Okay, once Gloria gives me the other names not on the list, we'll check them. Anyone out to kill someone is not going to use a traceable credit card. No, more than likely, the guy paid cash."

"Why us?"

"Winters is going to take a month to investigate this, and I can't afford to have the place half closed for that long. If this thing stretches more than a week, I'll be in big trouble. So, I'm going to find out what happened to Mr. Smith in cottage fourteen, so I can keep this place on track."

"Providing beds for people?"

"Making money."

"Okay," I said, "but a list like that will be long. Who's going to have the time to work through a list like that? I don't."

"She's right, Manny," Gloria said. "You need help."

"Help? Where are you going to find someone to help on something like this?"

"Let me think about it," Gloria said. "I may have an idea."

"What kind of an idea?" I asked her.

"Don't worry, I have an idea you'll love."

Chapter Four

After the police finished interrogating the guests, I gave the list Manny had compiled to Winters.

He scanned the list quickly and smiled. "Is this everyone?"

"That's everyone who checked out. I divided them into columns. The second list is from the credit cards."

"What are all these check marks on the credit card list?"

"Manny checked off the regulars. He figured you could skip over the regulars and concentrate on the others."

"He figured that, did he?"

"Yes, sir. He thought if you knew who the regulars were, it might save you some time."

"Isn't that nice. Well, you tell *Manny boy Soto* that I appreciate the help, but he's not a cop anymore, so I'll investigate this the old-fashioned way, and with as much time as I need." Then, creasing the list in half and pointing it at me, he said, "You got that?"

"Yes, sir." I said, pretending to dodge the pointer like it was a dart.

"And don't expect me to fret about closing down a wing of rooms. From what I hear, Manny takes in more money from the bar than all the cottage rents combined."

He got that right.

****

With cottages to clean, I grabbed the housekeeper cart and marched to cottages ten and eleven. Crime scene tape draped all over cottage fourteen and made it appear like a big, yellow-wrapped present.

I don't mind the work in the complex, even though the guests refer to me as Moli Maid, and I've over-heard the derogatory comments from people who can't tell the difference between a Cuban, a Mexican, and a recently arrived refugee from Central America. For a lot of white people, we are all just a bunch of wetbacks, come to America to take jobs away from Americans. They'd be surprised if they knew my ancestors had been in America long before theirs, and they are surprised when they find out my Uncle Manny owns the place and is not just the poor hired help.

I like to think of myself and Manny as entrepreneurs pursuing the American dream. Even though a vocal minority of guests in the complex can be obnoxious, most are decent folks, and I'm happy to be the environmental services manager.

The miniature complex sits between The Oaks, a large garden home development for retirees, and the RV mobile home complex, Pirate Cove Family Campground. Because his motel didn't have a pool, Manny bartered part-time security services to the adjacent properties for swim privileges for his guests. His duties require an early morning and a midnight patrol through each complex. He also responds to random issues if a complex administrator reports a disturbance.

To get to the pools, we have several golf carts the guests can use. I'm not sure which the guests enjoy more, the pools or driving the golf carts around. For some, the beach takes a poor third because after a couple of days, all the sun, sand, and salt can be hard to take.

Manny's cop credentials inspire confidence in his ability to maintain property rules and regulations. Although he's seventy years old and has lost some of his youthful muscular build, he stands well over six foot tall and packs some weight. The extra-large Hawaiian print shirts he favors fit tight around his chest, and his belly bulges like there's a baby in there. His stature is more than enough to quell most inebriated guests in violation of property guidelines and, if needed, his voice can growl out like a bear. But even Manny can't stop crazy, and he's dealt with several break-ins in the Oaks and other shenanigans in the Cove. In Manny's case, once a cop, always a cop.

I hurried through my duties because I needed to get dinner for Ricky. By the time I finished, the cops had left the bar, but thirty-plus new people had crowded into the space along with our guests. Gloria hustled drinks up and down the counter, and guys shouted orders out to her as she swept by. Two part-time servers from the shack crew worked the bar floor. The pretty women ran baskets of hot tacos from the taco truck to the tables and drinks from the bar. A new man I hadn't met before was on the back bar, up to his elbows in drink orders, sweat marking his shirt from the effort. He was cute in a prep way, and worked efficiently amid the madhouse, although I don't usually notice that kind of thing anymore. Somewhere on the drive between L.A. and Florida, I gave up on men in the romantic way. A solo life was just safer.

I joined Manny at a table in the back of the bar. "What are you doing?" I asked him when I saw a glass with ice on the table.

"Don't worry, it's tonic water."

"Who says I'm worried?"

"Moli, don't be like my mother."

"*Abuela* would treat you a lot worse. What are you doing anyway? Don't you have people to interview and stuff?"

"You watch too much TV. Smith got clobbered by someone hiding out, not out and about, available for an interview."

"He could have skipped town already."

"Maybe, maybe not. What would you have done?"

"I would have left Tampa on the first available plane."

****

I stopped at the taco truck and got four orders of steak tacos for our dinner. I don't always get takeout. Like any good Mexican mother, my mother tried to teach me how to cook the three basic Mexican food groups of beans, rice, and tortillas, but I never mastered the skill. Besides, I liked the convenience in getting free takeout. Call me lazy and thrifty.

After our spicy dinner, I put Ricky to bed. Our room in Manny's apartment features a sturdy bunk bed and an old double bed. I sleep in the double while Ricky takes the top bunk and the Dude spreads out nightly on the lower bunk. I kind of like the arrangement. I figure if anyone tried to kidnap my boy, they'd have to go through the Dude to get to him and good luck with that.

I remembered I had switched on the television but fell asleep and forgot to turn it off. When I awoke, the Dude stood over me and slobbered, so I got up to take him for his late-night hike around the complex. In the hallway, the power of Manny's snoring vibrated along the floor.

With sundown four hours previously, the outside temperature had dropped into the high seventies and became bearable. The Dude dragged me through the complex toward the beach. A big moon cast a bright light over the bay, like a spotlight, the reflection of its essence bounced off the nearly flat Gulf of Mexico.

If you sailed from the shore straight west across the Gulf, you'd hit Texas. If you drifted south a little, you'd hit Mexico. Farther south and you'd run into the Yucatan, where my ex and I spent our honeymoon. If I knew at the time what I found out about him later, I would have skipped the whole Yucatan thing.

Our family has several generations born in Los Angeles, but we don't encompass many different heritages, like my Irish ex-husband. My mother warned me not to marry a white guy, even a Catholic one, but at the time, I didn't have many options with a baby in the oven.

My mother and father both grew up in East L.A. but met and fell in love when they served together in the army. She said she fell in love with his smile. We have several photos of them on duty together in Desert Storm, real army buddies. You can see them smile in all the photos, and I can tell they had something special going on between them. Something in the way they regarded each other, with more than love, deeper, like brotherhood. Maybe I should have considered brotherhood when I got married instead of a handsome face and passion.

At the end of their service, they both became cops, but my mom quit when the babies started to come. I'm the youngest of six—three boys, three girls. When everyone else passed on the cop thing, I tried to carry on the law enforcement tradition. In hindsight, I made a big mistake on that.

When the Dude growled out in the night, I observed a shadow of someone in the bar. Normally, I would have ignored the apparition and retreated back to the apartment. The Dude, however, dug in and pulled me in a direct course toward the dark figure. I cinched up on the Dude's leash and hung on.

"You scared me to death," I told Gloria when she stepped out into the light with a wet mop in her hand.

The Dude barked out a greeting and slobbered on one of the lady's legs.

"What are you doing up and about?" she asked and stooped to pet the dog. "Aren't you up past your bedtime?"

"Funny. I couldn't sleep, so I took the Dude for a stroll."

"Who's strolling whom?"

"Do you need help?" I asked her. "I can swing a mop."

"Don't worry about me, Moli, I've mopped bar floors before. My dad used to run a bar, and my brothers, sisters, and I would sleep in a back room. When he closed the place, we'd wake up and help him clean. Besides, I'm done here."

"Well," I said sitting in a stool at the bar, "you keep long hours."

"It only stretches this long on game nights. I'm usually finished by midnight."

When Gloria sat next to me, she lit a cigarette and blew the first smoke stream up and away from my face. "Don't tell Manny." she said, waving the cigarette at me. "I take a drag or two when I'm done here but that's about it. Sometimes he's just like a mother."

"Worse. My mother never expected me to clean toilets."

"Where is the old guy anyway?"

"Sound asleep."

"So, is he going to get involved in this Smith thing?"

"He wants to make sure it's solved as soon as possible so we can open back up to full capacity. Something about not wanting to lose the place."

"Yeah, he's got to watch it," she said, as she flicked her cigarette at an ashtray.

"Is the situation that bad?"

Sighing and shaking her head she said, "There's something in the unique financial package he put together to buy the complex. If he falls behind on the payments, he could lose everything."

"Wow."

"Humm, well, someone needs to remind him that in addition to not being a financial genius, he's not a cop anymore."

"Why don't you tell him?"

"Oh, I told him to let Detective Winters handle the case and to concentrate on the business, but he never listens to me. He's got some notion he can do better and can solve this thing faster."

"Is that why you two broke up, because of the listening part?"

"No, he's just a little too old for me. I'm dating someone younger now."

"That guy running the back bar?"

"No, that's Chad. Did you see him? He's a real stud."

"I can't be bothered by a handsome guy with big

biceps. So, where did you find him?"

"He showed up one day last week and asked if we needed help. I'd been thinking about extra help for the weekends, so I put him on. I don't always need the help, but the extra set of hands comes in handy on the busy nights."

"Say," I asked her before she left, "did you tell Manny everything about Mr. Smith?"

"What do you mean?"

"Come on, Gloria, you must have picked up on more than you told Manny. A guy doesn't sit across from you at a bar for a whole night and not tell you things. Anything would help in solving this thing."

Gloria crushed out her cigarette like she was putting out a forest fire. "I know one thing. Mr. Smith is not a photographer."

"What do you mean?"

"Moli, I used to be a model, and I appreciate the equipment used in the business. When I talked to Smith about the profession, he barely grasped the first thing about the cameras a pro photographer uses." She flashed me a look that said she knew what she was talking about.

"That's one thing he should know, and he didn't."

Chapter Five

Saturday

"Where did you disappear to last night?" Manny asked me the next morning.

I had just woken up. I still had my old housecoat and fuzzy slippers on and stumbled into the kitchen, heading for the coffee I'd smelled brewing from the bedroom.

"I took the Dude for a walk." I poured a mug from the antique drip machine Manny kept warm all day. I stuck my nose up against the cup's rim and breathed deeply of the fresh made brew.

"Thanks," he mumbled. "I can't imagine what we would do without you."

"You did okay before I showed up."

"Yeah, but with you guys here, the Dude is a lot happier. He sleeps with you all now and I don't get slobbered on as much."

"Thanks a lot."

The Dude didn't come along with Manny from L.A., so the partnership didn't rest on love or anything. Before we showed up, Manny found the dog wandering the Pirate Cove Campground, apparently abandoned. The campground had called the local animal control, but they couldn't catch the dog. In fact, Manny said one of the control officers never got out of the county truck.

Manny said when he got there, he stalked over to the

dog and in his drill instructor voice, yelled at the dog to settle down and ordered him into the cab of the truck. Manny figured the dog liked to ride around because the dog jumped in the passenger seat without encouragement.

So, Manny took him in permanently, and the two made kind of an *Odd Couple* situation work, until Ricky and I showed up. Now, we are more of a *Father Knows Best* thing.

"By the way, I ran into Gloria last night as she closed down the bar."

"She's a hard worker, worth every cent I pay her."

"You don't pay her anything."

"That's what I mean."

Just then, the doorbell from reception sounded and Manny plodded out to check who came in. Since we needed to get the breakfast out, I hurried to my room to put some clothes on. I figured the visitor to be an early riser who'd shown up for a cup of coffee and a donut.

Right after he bought the place, Manny had added an eight-foot extension with a glass ceiling at one end of the reception room, so we could get in additional tables and chairs, and built the breakfast bar. We share the shop around town duty for the food and partner on the breakfast set up. He does an excellent job on his part. His talent surprised me because according to my dad, when they grew up together, Manny never did anything in the kitchen except eat.

We provide mostly a continental breakfast menu. Manny shops and gets discounts from all the local bakeries, so you can't complain about the selection of tasty treats. At my suggestion, we put out Greek yogurt, breakfast cereals, just-picked fruit from the local farmer's market, and fresh squeezed orange juice. Manny tops off the set up with a dozen glazed donuts he gets from a local shop, not a franchise.

We understand our vacation guest's needs for caffeine, so we utilize a lineup of five K-cup machines and a selection of coffee choices that would rival any coffee house. Most guests are satisfied, and Manny figures the others wouldn't be coming back anyway, so he doesn't care about them. During our short stay with Manny, I noticed quite a few repeat guests. We book all the cottages during the busy winter season, so I assume most like what they get.

When I got out to the breakfast area, I found Winters in the lobby arguing with Manny.

"Come on, Winters," Manny pleaded. "Gloria wouldn't have anything to do with the assault on that guy."

"What guy?" I asked, confused about the conversation.

"Some guy named Salvatore," Manny said.

"Who?"

"Mr. Smith," Winters said. "We tracked down his rental car and got his real name, Tony Salvatore."

"So, who's Salvatore," I asked, "and why would Gloria want to whack l him?"

"We think Salvatore worked for the Miami syndicate. Gloria lived down there before she split and came up here. When she disappeared, they put out a hit on her."

"Why?"

"Probably because she took fifty thousand dollars in cash with her when she left town."

"What?" I said, thinking maybe I didn't hear him

right.

"Yeah," Winters explained, "she had a thing going with the syndicate's accountant, and when she skipped town, she helped herself to some cash from the company safe."

"Whoa," I said. "No wonder she doesn't complain about not getting paid."

"So, I've got a couple of uniforms down at cottage seventeen right now making sure she doesn't get away, but I wanted to inform you before we take action."

I asked, "Where are you getting all this information?"

"We've got friends down in the Miami PD. They keep a unit that keeps tabs on the syndicate there."

"This is bull, Frank," Manny said, "and you know it."

"She'll get a chance to plead her case. In the meantime, we're taking her in for safekeeping."

"There's got to be other suspects," I said, as the three of us headed out the door.

"There are, and we'll run them down, but when I said safekeeping, I didn't just mean *safe* as in general safety. If they're after her, she's safer with us."

"Oh."

Winters said, "We caught up with the folks who left yesterday, and none have a motive. We'll dig around to see if we find anything else, but right now, she's the best we have."

"I don't know," I said, "if all this is true, I think Gloria can take care of herself."

"Unless the next time they send more than one man."

"Could be a random connection," Manny said.

"Maybe, but Gloria could easily lure the guy into an after-hour rendezvous and when he didn't expect it, whack him in the head. That's means and motive for me, and when you add in a late-night after business hours dark compound, that sets a clean stage of opportunity too."

"Come on, Frank, if Gloria did this, do you think she'd hang around for you cops to figure out?"

"Maybe she believed hiding in plain sight was better than running."

We tramped our way to cottage seventeen and were halfway there when Manny blurted, "What about the weapon used in the assault?"

"We haven't got one yet, but let's see, we might get lucky and find something in her cottage."

When we got to the cottage, Winters nodded to the officers standing guard. One cop yelled out to open the door. When no one in the cottage responded the other cop raised a battering ram-like thing to bust open the door, just like you see on TV.

"Hold on," I said. "I've got a master key." I slid my key in the slot, but the lock wouldn't open.

"Watch out," the cop said, raising the battering ram again.

"Hold on, hold on," Manny said, stepping forward. "I've got a key," and when he unlocked the door, both officers rushed in, guns drawn. We followed close behind but guess what?

"Oh, what the…" one officer said.

"You're kidding me…" Winters said, when he entered.

"Oh no!" Manny said when he entered Gloria's cottage.

"Oh, oh!" I said when I stepped in and didn't see any sign of Gloria, though her stuff seemed to be there, and she had a lot of stuff.

"Soto," one of the officers said, "apparently, your girlfriend has flown the coop."

"Yeah, Soto," the other added, "what happened? Did you warn her we were on our way?"

"You fools only got here a few minutes ago. If you had your sirens going, she probably heard you from a mile away."

"You had enough time to sneak her a message," an officer accused. "Maybe a text."

"I don't text, big mouth," Manny sneered. "Besides, she's innocent in all of this. I wouldn't be recommending she run off. It just…"

"Just what?" Winters finished the sentence when Manny paused. "Running off makes her look guilty, right?"

When no one said anything, I volunteered, "Maybe she didn't come home last night."

Winters and Manny turned to me at the same time. "What do you mean?"

I glanced at Manny to see if he wanted me to continue, and when he nodded, I said, "I saw Gloria last night when she was closing up. She inferred she had a hot date."

"What?" Winters said.

"Yeah, she spent the night with someone," I clarified. "You know, like a sleepover."

"Who's the lucky guy?" Winters asked me but stared at Manny.

"I don't know," I said, which I didn't. "She just skipped out last night like she was heading to the candy store."

"Manny, do you have a name?"

"Do you think I keep up with Gloria's love life?

Winters said, "Okay, we'll talk to your nighttime staff, and I'm sure we'll get a name from someone. The process will take longer, but eventually we'll find out who the lucky guy is. Of course, if you give me a name, we can save a lot of time and trouble."

Manny said, "Frank, I'm not stalling here. I don't keep up with Gloria's after-hours friends. I'll get Moli to give you the names of the bar staff, but I'm telling you, you're wasting your time because Gloria didn't do this."

"Maybe, maybe," the detective said as he meandered about the messy cottage, "but I've got time."

When Manny and I padded back to the office he asked me, "What do you think?"

"I'm with you. I don't think Gloria had anything to do with Salvatore."

"Then where did she go?"

"I wouldn't worry, Manny, she'll show up."

"How do you know?"

"Did you see her closet? She left behind everything she owned. Gloria wouldn't go far without her high heels."

Chapter Six

As we walked back to the office, we heard the Dude's angry bark boom over the complex. "Sounds like the Dude is mad at someone," I said, getting a bad feeling in my stomach.

Manny said, "Better get down there and see if Ricky is okay."

At the mention of my son, I panicked. The case had completely occupied my morning, and I had forgotten all about Ricky. I hadn't even checked the CCTV. What kind of a mother was I?

I ran down the walkway like I was doing the hundred at the Olympics and blasted through the reception door. I found the Dude snarling at someone he'd cornered in the breakfast room, between the coffee maker and the counter where the donuts are usually served.

"What's going on here?" I shouted out above the Dude's growling.

"I just wanted a cup of coffee," a guy in Bermuda shorts said as he cowered behind a chair.

"Doesn't the K-cup machine in your cottage work?"

"You've got Danish in here," he said. "Or at least you did, every other day this week."

Finally recognizing the guy, I apologized. "Sorry, Mr. Delany. We've been busy with the police, so the Dude is kind of in charge of my son."

Just then, Ricky toddled into the room, blurry eyed from a hard sleep. "I'm hungry, Mommy."

"Okay, honey." After seeing him unhurt, relief spread over me. "Go on back to our room and take the Dude with you. I'll be right there." To Mr. Delany, I said, "You hold on. I'll be right back with the Danish."

I put out the morning breakfast, starting with Mr. Delany's pastry. In between scampering back and forth between our kitchen and the breakfast room, I got Ricky something to eat as well. Once I got him settled, I put out the rest of the morning breakfast, mostly the leftovers from the week's offerings.

I emptied the last cream in the carton into the dispenser. Knowing the rest of the guests would be heading this way, I called out to Ricky that I had to go to the storeroom to get a carton of milk and some napkins. He didn't respond, but the Dude let out a bark of recognition, like he understood. In many ways, since I forget we even have the CCTV system, I trusted the Dude more.

We had a large walk-in refrigerator for cold stuff in the storage room behind the service bar. We stored fresh produce for the taco truck in there and limes and fruit for the fancy drinks we serve in the bar. The room also had space for dry goods. Two wire shelves for toilet paper and paper towels rounded out the storage room. We had a second room for laundry. We had our own heavy-duty washer and dryer. Manny found out if we did our own linen, we could save fifty percent off the cost, so he built wooden shelving to store all the clean linen the motel used and put me in charge. *Surprise.*

Manny had bought several heavy plastic bins where we kept the dirty linen, sheets, pillowcases, hand, face, and bath towels. Manny wanted to add some class to the breakfast bar, so we use cloth napkins in there. He figured since we were washing linen anyway, what did a few more napkins matter.

I had just reached into the back shelf to grab some napkins when Gloria's hand shot out of the darkness and snatched back the bundle she had been using for a pillow.

"Holy…" I blurted out, catching my breath and staggering a step back, "what the heck. What are you doing in there?"

"What do you think?" Gloria said, taking the stack of napkins. Fluffing the bundle up settled into a comfortable sleep position.

"Have you been there all night?"

"No," she said with a big yawn. "I snuck over this morning when I heard the cop cars pull up."

"You heard them?"

"They were trying to be quiet, but I was outside having a morning smoke when I heard them. I didn't go back into my place; I just shut and locked the door and hustled here. I hoped I could squeeze in the stacks, and if they searched in here, they wouldn't see me."

"Well, you don't have to worry about that."

"Why not?"

"They think you were out at a sleep-over last night."

"Where'd they get that idea?"

I paused and didn't say anything.

She said, "You sly little devil. Did you tell them I had a hot date?"

I still didn't say anything, not knowing if Gloria would think I was tattle-telling about her dating habits.

"No, that's great. Actually, last night when a hot shower didn't revive me, I postponed the romance, and I just hit the bed."

"They're going to question the staff about their whereabouts the night someone tried to kill this Salvatore guy."

"Who?"

"That's right. You didn't know about Mr. Smith, AKA, Tony Salvatore."

"No, but like I said, I knew something was up with him."

"So, how did you know the cops were after you this morning?"

"The cops drove in quiet like, no screeching tires and brakes, but parked right in front of my cottage."

"They could have been there for Doc Murphy."

"No, you know the Doc, he stays in shape and goes out for a run every morning, so they wouldn't need to sneak up on him. They could have picked him up any time."

"How about Colombo?"

"He's a straight-arrow guy. He talks to me about his wife and kids in Jersey, every time he sits at the bar. He hates the sun and sand. His job was supposed to be a temporary assignment, just long enough to get the project back on schedule, but the company told him he had to stay longer. He can't wait for the end to the project so he can get home."

"But why would the cops come for you? Did you have a motive for trying to kill Salvatore?"

I gave her a minute to think about it, but when she didn't say anything, I asked her.

"What about the fifty thousand dollars you took when you left Miami?"

"So, they found out about that?"

"They found out you dated an accountant from the syndicate, and when you skipped town, you took them for fifty grand."

"I didn't take money that wasn't mine."

"What do you mean?"

"While I worked down there, I dated a guy they call *the accountant.* He's not a real CPA. That's just something they call him. He's a bookie and handles a territory in Little Havana. Well, I made some football bets and rolled the winnings over with him and got on a roll. Before long, I was up fifty grand in his book. When I decided to invest some of my money elsewhere, I asked Willard for a draw, but he stonewalled me."

"Who's Willard?"

"He's the bookie. Anyway, when I started to make plans for getting away, I asked him for my balance, but he said he didn't have it. He made excuses and all, but he'd lost a wad of the syndicate's money on risky spreads. When the collectors arrived to pick up the winnings, he made up the shortfall using my money."

"Whoa, he took your money?"

"Yeah, what a creep. So, when I left, I made a withdrawal from the company safe."

"Well, Winters is adding up the few facts, and they are coming up equal to you. He figures you found out Willard or someone from the syndicate had hired a hitman and you lured the guy in and whacked him."

"Well, he must think I am a bad ass woman, to be able to do that."

"I know, right? I mean, you are beautiful, but bad? Unless, as they say, looks can kill."

****

By the time I got back to the breakfast area, the

guests had eaten about everything. I had just cleaned the morning mess, when people started a line to check out. I got everyone out of the place and rushed out to clean cottages. Since I didn't have to work the North wing, I finished in half the normal time. Lucky me.

When I got back to the apartment, Manny asked why I wasn't cleaning toilets.

"I only had to do the South wing, remember? What have you been doing?"

"I've been calling around about Gloria, talking to her friends."

"Did you find her?"

"No, no one has seen her."

"You've got a bigger problem than that."

"What?"

"You don't have anyone to bartend tonight."

"I'll handle the bar. I've got experience working in crowded places."

"Okay but be careful when you go in the laundry room to get bar towels."

"Why?"

"You might find more than you want."

"What are you…wait, no way."

"Yes, way."

"I'll be a…"

"Now, now."

"Has she been there all day?"

"Yep, I haven't seen you since this morning to tell you. She's in with the sheets and pillowcases. She heard the cops arrive and made a dash for the laundry room in her underwear. She asked me to find her some clothes."

"Why? Does she think she's going somewhere?"

"That's what I asked her. She said she wanted to be

presentable in case the cops find her. At this point, all she has on is her bra and panties and I'm sure you recall those two things don't cover much."

"I recall. Better get her a pair of plain sweats and a hat. She'll want to be out and about, and I don't want her to stand out in a crowd."

"Wearing a sweatshirt and pants in the middle of a ninety-plus degree day will make you stand out in a crowd."

"Okay then. Don't take her anything. It's best she doesn't go out anyway."

"Manny!"

"What? The cops are watching the place. If she goes out, they will spot her. It's better she stays put until I can find out what's going on."

"So, if Gloria didn't try to kill this Salvatore guy, someone else did, right?"

"Right and that's what we got to find out."

"What do you mean, we?" I asked.

"Moli, I think you might have a head for this kind of thing."

"What kind of thing?"

"Detective work," he said, surprising me. It was funny, I mean, I wasn't even a good mother, so what made him think I'd be any kind of a good detective?

"Who are you kidding?"

"I need you on this," he said. "You've got eyes on the place, and you're friends with these people. You can be a big help."

"I don't know, Manny."

"Come on, help me out. You might surprise yourself."

I thought about it for a while and suitably flattered

that Manny thought I could do something else besides clean a toilet, said, "I'll do what I can, God knows you can use the help."

****

Although I got a chance to make Ricky a PB&J for a late lunch, I still had to rush to get to the office counter to check in the afternoon guests at four o'clock. With only half the normal number to check in, I finished in half the time, and I had a chance to gather a few things and take them over to the bar for Gloria. I know, I know, Manny told me not to, but I didn't want Goria to sweat on all those clean sheets. Since the cops were watching the place, I put some clean clothes under a pile of dirty sheets and wheeled the housekeeper cart to the laundry room.

"It's about time," Gloria said. She had set up a chair and a couple of boxes for a table. She held a pen and a crossword puzzle from a stack of old newspapers we collected for recycling. "I wondered if you forgot about me."

"Not likely. I told Manny, though, and he wanted to make sure you stay put. He says the cops are watching the place."

"I need a smoke," she said, as she stood up in front of me in her almost nothing underwear. Even though we are both women and all, I still stared at her. "Any chance you snuck a pack of cigarettes in with the dirty laundry?"

"Sorry." I passed her the extra PB&J I had made. "This is the best I could do."

"Thanks, I got hungry hours ago, so I snuck next door to the storage room and raided the refrigerator. I ate a bunch of martini olives and fruit. Which reminds me, since I'm supposed to stay out of sight, who's in the bar tonight?"

"Manny said he can handle it."

"On my God," she said between bites of the sandwich.

"He says he's worked behind a bar before."

"He's poured beer before," Gloria said, "but not mixed drinks and the high-end stuff. He might have a problem with those."

"Is Chad going to be here?"

"He should be, but I don't think he has much experience with the fancy stuff either."

"Well, let's hope he can catch on quickly. Say, what if we put one of the ladies behind the bar to help."

"Good idea. When Barbara comes in, tell her I can't work tonight, so we have to station her behind the bar. She won't mind. She has experience in the day bar, and she knows the tips are better back there, although she might have to fight Manny over the tip split." She polished off the rest of the sandwich, and said, "Then call Karen Bellows and tell her we need her tonight. Her name and number are on the wall by the landline. She doesn't live far away."

I handed her the change of clothes. I had been deliberate when I picked out an outfit. I didn't want something that would make her stand out in a crowd like Manny said, but with Gloria, the clothes didn't matter. She stood out in a crowd regardless of what she wore.

"Gloria," I asked as she slipped into the pair of shorts and tee shirt, "if you didn't try to kill this Salvatore…"

"What do you mean *if*?"

"I mean, since you didn't try to kill Salvatore, who do you think did?"

"I have no idea," she said, emphasis on the *no*, and a snapping wave of her hand.

"Someone from the Miami syndicate?"

She paused a long time before responding. "I don't know, Moli," she said, massaging her temples like she was getting a headache. "From my experience, they wouldn't worry over this."

"Why not?"

"That particular house takes in millions in a month. They don't need to go out on a limb for fifty thousand dollars that wasn't even theirs to begin with."

"Manny is sure it's someone local."

"Could be," she said nodding her head in agreement, "and if you want to help Manny hold on to this place, you'd better find out soon."

Oh man, I just hate when people put pressure on me.

Chapter Seven

Sunday

Saturday night, after Manny finished bar duty, he told me the crowd had come hungry, but he, Barbara, and Chad managed to keep up. He said the taco truck shut down at nine o'clock when they ran out of fish. We track our inventory and try to buy just enough fish and other perishables to meet expected sales. If we don't sell out, we have left-over product and lose money.

Manny usually says, "It's okay to run out. If the customers don't get their *carne asada* tacos this time, they'll just be hungrier for them the next time they come in."

After the place cleared, Manny closed the register and slogged back to the apartment to count the cash box, and I dragged myself to the bar to help clean up. Barbara finished sweeping out the seating area and left.

I had just swept the bar floor when Chad came over. "So…I'm Chad Jones," he said. He held one hand out for me to shake and gripped a mop in the other. "No one introduced us."

"I'm Moli Soto," I said, raising the broom and dustpan. "Manny's niece."

"Is that Moli like, Moli Maid?" he said with a nod at my full hands.

"Hey, come on. It's really Molina, but everyone

calls me Moli."

"Okay, Moli, not the maid."

When he smiled at me, I noticed my heart beat a bit faster. "So, how did Gloria talk you into taking this gig?"

"She didn't have to try hard. I sat down at the end of the bar one night, and we got to talking. I told her I had tended bar at a local college hangout. She told me she could use some help on the weekends. I was interested so I asked all about it."

"Is that all the interested you had in her?"

"Just like with every guy that comes in here, I think Gloria has a lot of qualities of interest, but so do a lot of girls," he added with a smile at me.

While I'm sure my face blushed, to break the awkward silence between us I asked, "What college did you attend?"

"I went to Minnesota and graduated in May, but I'm taking a year off before med school."

"Medical school?" I asked like I lived on another planet.

"Yeah, I was accepted at the University of Wisconsin, but I'm chilling out for a year before I start again. When I graduated, I didn't want to face another winter of snow and cold, so I ventured south to get some sunshine. I need some extra money; this part-time work is perfect."

"Where do you live?" I asked, even though I told myself I didn't have any interest in men or where they lived.

"That's the best part. I stay at my parents place over in the Oaks."

"The Oaks?" *Oh...like right next door.*

"Yeah, they bought a retirement place over there

about ten years ago. They don't like the cold anymore and wanted a warm weather place to get away to."

"What does your dad do?"

"He used to be a country doctor."

I should have known. I mean, don't doctors run in a family, like cops?

****

The next morning, even though few guests check in or out on Sunday mornings, I couldn't sleep in late because dreams of Chad Jones and his biceps made me toss and turn all night. When I got up, Ricky and the Dude were watching the cartoon channel, so I fixed both of them a bowl of cereal and rushed to put out the morning breakfast offerings. I like to make the Sunday breakfast bar the best because guests would see the spread for the first time, and that expression about first impressions is very true in the hospitality business.

When Manny showed, he said, "I got two dozen fresh donuts and put them out with the other stuff. The donuts are a little much, but I don't think anyone will complain."

I couldn't believe Manny. He'd worked the night before, up to his neck in bar orders, being hassled by distraught servers, then spent a couple mandatory hours on security patrol. Although short in distance, his two security routes in the properties on either side of us still took some time. I don't know where he finds the strength to work the routes and still has the energy to make a morning donut run,

"I can make a grocery trip later for the rest of the week's breakfast bar."

"Don't worry about it, Moli. I have something else for you to do, something of great importance."

"What?"

"I need you to go to Miami."

"Why?"

"I've been thinking."

"Oh, oh."

"No, really, I need you to go down there and talk to my DEA buddy and see about this Gloria story that Winters is pushing."

"But she admitted she took the money."

"Yes, but did the syndicate send a hitman up here to retrieve the money? My buddy, Marco, will have the scoop if that's true or just a scare tactic. They like to scare people down there."

"Who is Marco?"

"Marco Valente."

"Why not just call him?"

"I can't."

"Do I want to know why?" I asked, getting a bad feeling in my tummy. A different feeling than the feeling I got the previous night when talking to Chad.

When he didn't say anything, I said, "Okay, don't tell me." When Manny still didn't say anything, I said, "Wait, yes, tell me."

"He's undercover."

"Great," I said, but not great in, *I liked*, but a great in, *I didn't like*. I didn't need the complication. "An under-cover guy, under cover with a mob?"

"Don't worry, he's working the Little Havana area of town, so I can leave him a text message on his burner phone, and he'll watch out for you. That's how he communicates with the outside world."

"Didn't you say you didn't know how to text?"

"I said I didn't text. I didn't say I didn't know how

to text."

"Why are you communicating with him anyway?"

"He's the one who sent Gloria up here. He and Father Torrez are good friends and they're the ones who got me to hire her."

"Wait, why is he using a burner phone?"

"He's embedded with the bad guys, so he has to watch it. I think they monitor all outgoing calls and communications, but he can receive a random message."

I was beginning to regret I'd agreed to help out on the whole thing.

"Moli, you said you would help out, so I need you on this. For Gloria's sake. Once you're down there and we find out the syndicate is not involved, we'll have less to factor into this case. We need to understand the syndicate's role in all this because right now there are too many possible suspects."

"What about Ricky?" I asked, although I hated to use the boy as an excuse not to go.

"He's too short to be a suspect."

"Funny."

"The Dude and I are here. What more do you need?" Manny knew all about the Dude and his guard duty skills. I wondered if the dog thinks he's the boy's father. "Listen," he continued, "this will be easy. All you have to do is get a ticket, fly down there, take an Uber out to this address," he said, handing me a slip of paper and the business credit card, "and meet with Marco. When you come back, use the same procedure and you'll be home for dinner."

"If it's so easy, why don't you go?"

"Winters has a tail on me. He knows I haven't told him everything about Gloria, so he's got a cruiser at the end of the lot to watch me. I don't think he's worried about you. When you're ready, we'll head out together, like we are on our weekly grocery errands. We'll hit five or six places, lose the tail, and you can grab an Uber out to the airport. By the time they realize I'm alone I'll be back with the weekly goods. They'll never figure out what happened to you."

Unfortunately, I concluded his plan could work. In a bit of bravado I didn't think I had, I said, "Okay, text your buddy and tell him I'm on my way."

What was I thinking? I wanted to help Gloria as much as I could, and I always liked Miami. I might even get a chance to do some shopping. From what I'd been told, there were some glamorous shops down there.

Not that I cared about how I dress.

****

We ditched the cop tail between the party store and Geno's bakery. I slipped out the back entrance of the bakery where the Uber I ordered was parked. On the way to the airport, I connected to the apartment's CCTV on my phone to check on Ricky and the Dude and could see them watching television together.

I bought a round-trip flight out of Tampa, caught a favorable tailwind, and we landed in Miami an hour later, just like Manny said. I took another Uber to the restaurant in Little Havana where Manny had arranged the meeting. I sat at one of their outside tables, ordered a house special cappuccino, and under the Miami heat, waited as instructed.

The coffee house stood on a corner of a neighborhood business district. From where I sat, I could see three restaurants, two bakeries, a *Pharmacia*, two *bodegas*, a *mercado*, and right across the street, a Latino dress shop displaying a collection of fancy *quinceanera* dresses and wedding outfits. I considered shopping, but I'd celebrated my fifteenth birthday eight years ago, and I'd already had my wedding, so why bother?

I had worried I'd be conspicuous meeting a cop in the open, but realized I fit in the neighborhood. I'm a shade lighter than full Mexican, but in little Havana it didn't matter. The whole neighborhood was *Cubano,* and the Cubans take pride in being a lighter skin Latino race. Although we share many similarities, I feel most Florida Cubans are snobbish about their heritage, like they were better than the other Latinos in Florida. I guess the left-over Cuban refugees and their heirs wanted to hold on to an ancestry that didn't have a home anymore. Not since the Castros took over Cuba and the rich fled. I couldn't blame them. I'd probably feel the same way.

So that I wouldn't attract attention, I dressed down for my clandestine meeting with an undercover cop. Unfortunately, after a stream of guys passed me and not a single one looked my way, I regretted not wearing a more attractive outfit, one that accentuated my best qualities. Not that I care about how I look out in public. Still…

While I waited, I took out my phone and checked the security app. Manny had joined the Dude and my boy; the three of them were watching something on television.

I sat for a while, but when the delicious aroma of cooking wafted toward me and my stomach started to complain about sustenance, I asked the waiter for a menu.

"Try the loaded fries and eggs." A sharp dressed Latino guy joined me at the table, bent down, and spoke into my ear. "You'll love it, it's the house special."

"I'm trying to watch my weight," I said and leaned away. "I'm staying away from carbs."

He just smiled and when the waiter came, ordered something in rapid Spanish. Even though I'm a Latino mix, born and raised in East Los Angeles, my Spanish sucks. I did catch the word *huevos*, for eggs, so I figured the guy ordered food and hadn't made a reference to my attire.

"You don't want to stand out," the guy told me. "Do what the locals do, eat what they eat, and blend in."

"I assume you're Marco," I asked the man with deep brown eyes.

"At your service."

"I wouldn't think you'd want to meet in such a public place."

"What's more natural than a young couple having brunch on a beautiful Sunday morning? People will assume we are lovers, out for something to eat after a night of passionate sex."

"Humm," I said, non-committal, as unwanted flashes of dark bodies on white sheets crowded in my head.

"Besides, I'm starving," he said.

I wondered if he craved food—or something else— all of a sudden, I wanted to be a quesadilla or a taco.

"You should eat," he said. "This place has a great menu."

"So," I asked, clearing my throat so I didn't sound like a frog, "did Manny text you?"

"I got something about his niece coming down to ask me about Gloria Cruz, and you're not Gloria, so you must be the niece. He didn't tell me how attractive you were."

"I'm Moli Soto," I said, feeling my cheeks warm.

As I went to extend my hand, he bent down again and offered his cheek for a kiss. When I puckered up and angled my mouth to kiss his cheek, he twirled his face to me and kissed me on the lips, a quick maneuver that caught me by surprise. A pleasant surprise.

"Remember, we are lovers," he said and, taking a seat to my right, added, "Lovers would never shake hands."

It took me a moment to settled back, but I recovered and smiled at the guy.

Our eggs came, and when I wasn't stuffing spicy potatoes into my mouth, I filled Marco in on the reason for my visit.

"No, the family didn't send anyone to Tampa," he said. "They are pissed about Willard and his scam, but they didn't catch on to anything until the cops started asking around. By the time they reviewed the books and found the discrepancy in Willard's records, Salvatore was already in the hospital."

"Could Willard have arranged the hit?"

"No, he doesn't have that kind of muscle. He's strictly bookie material."

"What about Gloria?"

"Gloria's winnings were recorded in the book, and everything balanced out. The family keeps good records, so they determined she only took what she was due. Everyone in the family likes Gloria. When she finished modeling, they gave her a job in the system."

"Then she's in the clear?" I asked, a bit surprised, but relieved.

"As far as the family goes."

"Was Salvatore working for the family?"

"No. As far as the family goes, he doesn't exist."

"Well, someone tried to kill him."

"Maybe," Marco said, nodding his nicely shaped head, "but Miami had nothing to do with it."

"I guess that's good news."

****

After lunch with Marco, we strolled along the main drag, and he showed me the sights. I glowed under the experience of being escorted by an attractive man and treated like a lady. Usually, I'm running behind a curly haired kid and cleaning toilets. I remembered how eyes and smiles can be misleading, so I tried not to drool all over the guy.

He called an Uber for my ride to the airport, and when he wished me luck on the case, he took me in his arms and gave me a big kiss goodbye. After, he said he'd be seeing me again. I smiled back, out of breath, and although I'm not supposed to be interested in men anymore, hoped I *would* see him again.

While I waited to board the plane for the trip to Tampa, I sent Manny a text summarizing what I learned from his pal.

Once on the ground, I got another Uber down the coast to Cabana Bay, getting in right at sunset. When the red ball in the low sky dipped below the horizon, a cheer came out of the bar.

I found Ricky and the Dude sprawled out in front of the television watching an old movie of some brave dog saving his dumb owner from catastrophe.

"Where's Uncle Manny?" I asked my boy.

"Tending bar."

I wondered if I should be worried that my son could

reference bar operations so casually.

"How was Miami?" Manny asked me when I took a seat at the bar.

"Hot, real hot."

"And how is Marco?"

"He's hot, too."

My uncle just grinned. "You noticed?"

"Hey, did you send me down there to fix me up?"

"Now, would I do something like that?"

Making sure no one was close enough to hear him, he whispered, "Marco is in a tight spot down there. You didn't do anything to blow his cover did you?"

"No, I behaved myself because I'm not interested in men anymore."

"Oh, that's too bad."

"I've got enough testosterone in my life between you, Ricky, and the Dude. I don't need another man in my life. Besides, he's an hour away by plane."

"I guess he didn't tell you?"

"Tell me what?"

"The DEA is pulling him out. It's getting too hot for him, so they're reassigning him."

"Oh yeah, where?"

"I don't know, but there's a big drug problem in Tampa, so maybe he'll be reassigned this way."

That's all I need: another stud guy I can swear I'm not going to get involved with. "So…what now?"

"That's between you and Marco."

"Not what now, me and Marco, I mean, what now with Gloria?"

"She may be safe from the Miami family, but she's still on Winters's most wanted list. He's even parked an unmarked car across the street from her cottage, so she needs to stay out of sight."

"You need to tell her that."

"I'll handle Gloria. What we need to do now is shift our attention to other possible victims."

"What do you mean?"

"Just think about it. Now that we've confirmed our Salvatore didn't have a contract to kill Gloria, we can concentrate on other potential victims."

"Victims?"

"We don't know what Salvatore was doing here, but it got him almost killed so my guess is someone sent him. I think the intended mark found out about it and hit Salvatore first."

"But who?"

"I'm not sure, but I'd still bet it's someone registered in the Cabana Bay Cottages."

****

Talking to my uncle about the case gave me a headache, so I retreated to the laundry room to see Gloria. When I opened the room's door, a blast of frigid air hit me in the face. I found her reclining in a pool chair, bundled up against the cold, and with a tall glass of something in her hand. She had in earbuds that I assumed were getting reception from a nearby flashing computer screen.

"Well, are you comfy enough?"

"Yeah, Manny fixed me up," she said, taking out the buds. "He said as long as I'm stuck here, I might as well be comfortable. He stocked the fridge and installed a window AC unit. I think he's afraid I'll go out and the cops will catch me."

"He's right about that. There's a cop car parked out front."

"What did you find out in Miami?"

"Willard didn't send Salvatore, and the family doesn't want you dead."

"So, I'm free?" she asked, here eyebrows up in expectation.

"No. You're still on Winters's most wanted list."

"Oh, come on. I feel like I'm locked up in a cell here and my jailer is a Molly Maid. I need a smoke."

"I don't blame you for wanting out of here, Gloria, but you have to stay out of sight a few more days."

"I've got to get out by Wednesday."

"Why?"

"I have an accounting test on Thursday morning. I can't miss it."

Gloria has a way with numbers and is working on her associate's degree in accounting at the local community college. The college is convenient to the cottages and sits next to the Cabana Bay Senior Center where some of our long terms spend time.

Once a month she does the books for Manny and makes sure he makes his estimated tax payments when due. If she didn't, the IRS would be at the doorstep because Manny can barely add two and two.

"I wouldn't hold your breath," I told her. "The way this case is going, you may be here longer than a week."

"Great."

"Say, do you think Chad could handle the bar tomorrow night?"

"What's wrong with Manny?"

"With all that's going on, I think he's going to be too busy to work in the bar."

Chapter Eight

Monday

An irritated Detective Winters showed up at seven on Monday morning. "Where's Manny?"

"Next door, playing cop," I responded while I arranged the morning breakfast bar. I still had to get Ricky out to the bus and didn't have time to chat. "So, why the early visit?"

"Our forensic tech is back, and we'll be up at cottage fourteen this morning."

"Manny will love hearing that."

"What's he doing next door?"

"Some campers drove their RV off one of the paths and got into a fight with the tow truck driver. Manny's over there to bust someone."

"He isn't a real cop anymore, Moli Maid. He can't bust anyone."

"He wasn't talking about that kind of bust."

"Oh, I see."

Winters was stalling, like he had something on his mind. "Can I help you with anything?"

"I did have a question for you."

"Oh, about what?"

"I understand you traveled to Miami yesterday."

Apparently, Winters' reach around the state was a lot longer than Manny thought. I wondered if he found out about all the kissing between Marco and me. "Where did you hear that?"

"Oh, around. I hear things when I least expect it."

I didn't bother lying about Marco but told him a different lie. "I was shopping for a dress." I remembered the coffee shop location, so I added some context. "My L.A. cousin is getting married, and I'm in the wedding party."

"Long way to go for a dress."

"The bride-to-be is picky. She wants something in the Latina fashion, and you can't find the style just anywhere. Little Havana has several shops, so she asked me to check them out."

"Did you find anything?"

"Not yet, but I texted her some pics of a few dresses she might like."

After he stared at me for a few moments he said, "You didn't let anyone in cottage fourteen over the weekend, did you?"

"Come on, Detective, we said we wouldn't disturb the crime scene, and we haven't."

"Okay, tell Manny I want to see him."

After the cop left, I finished putting out the breakfast stuff just as guests started arriving for their morning coffee. I ran to get Ricky and dragged him out to the bus stop. To make sure he got on the bus safely, I left the Dude there with him.

When I got back to the reception area, Gloria stood in front of the Danish setup, plate in one hand and a coffee in the other. She had on a pair of sunglasses, an attempt to be incognito, but the string bikini she wore defeated the attempt. Other guests, men and women alike, gawked at her.

"See anything you like?" I asked in a muffled voice when I approached her from behind.

"Where are those donut holes Manny usually puts out? Those are my favorite."

I took her arm to guide her out of the line and over toward the South side door. I got her outside with the office complex between us and the North wing of suites where the cops were stationed.

Once safely out of sight, I said, "Gloria, what are you doing out in the open? Winters and his bunch are working in cottage fourteen."

"I know; that's why I snuck out. Don't worry. They can't see me from up there."

"You have got to be careful. Winters could accuse Manny and me of harboring a criminal."

Just then, Manny pulled up to the South side of the building and stopped the Pirate Cove truck in the small parking lot we used for our personal vehicles. Manny parks his truck there, I park my old truck there, and Gloria's convertible VW bug is there. Lou Gigliotti parks his big red Buick there as does Señora Martinez with her old Mercedes. The other long termers park their cars there as well. When the shack ladies come to work, they also park in the lot. Because they leave well past midnight, Manny installed a couple of powerful lights to illuminate the area like daylight.

The Cove lets Manny use a campground pick-up truck for his patrols and when he has to respond to emergencies. They fitted the truck with spotlights and emergency roof lights. He has trouble getting his long frame in and out of the vehicle's small cab, but he likes the extras.

"Gloria," Manny barked, using his drill instructor

voice while prying his big body out of the truck, "what are you doing out here?"

After she gave him the same speech she gave me, Manny responded the same way I did.

"Okay, okay," she said, "I'll go back to my little hole, but I can't stay in there forever. I'll go *loco* if I stay there much longer."

"You'll hate the county lock-up even more," Manny said.

Gloria sauntered away and disappeared around the corner of our suite, and I assumed, entered the laundry room.

"She's going to get us all in trouble, Manny. I don't want a felony charge on my record. A black mark like that would keep me from any work requiring security clearance. Even a big box store would think twice before hiring me."

"Don't worry."

"You always say that. Are you any closer to a lead?"

"No, I'm sure whoever tried to kill Salvatore is right here in the complex. We just need to question everyone and see what we find out."

"Where are you going to start?"

"You are going to start with Doc Murphy."

"Why me?"

"I've seen the way he leers at you."

"Even if true, which I doubt, what makes you think he'll talk to me?"

"Use your feminine wiles on him."

"I don't have any wiles."

"Sure, you do. Every woman has wiles. I read about it."

"In what? *Playboy*?"

"No, smartie, they don't put out *Playboy* anymore."

"Why don't you talk to him?"

"I will, eventually. Come on, the motel is full, and no one is due to check out. I don't have time right now because there was a break-in over at the Oaks and I've got to get over there. Now, be a good girl and go and talk to the Doc."

"Why would you even suspect the Doc?"

"Go talk to Gloria about his background; you'll see."

With that, Manny strode over to the little golf cart the senior homes gave him to patrol their grounds and respond to emergencies. The cart didn't have all the bells and whistles like the campground truck, but Manny likes the cart because golf manufacturers make getting in and out easy for big people. Big people who climb in and out of their carts to hit little white balls over yards and yards of manicured lawns, sand traps, and water hazards.

****

After putting on beach attire more attractive than my black and white housekeeping outfit, I found Gloria reading the morning paper. "Where did you get a paper?"

"The delivery guy always leaves one for me."

"He didn't see you, did he?"

"No," she said. Then, when she peeked at me from over her paper, she noticed my outfit. "My, my, aren't we dressed cute this morning? What's the occasion?"

"Manny wants me to go up and ask Doc Murphy some questions."

"What kind of questions?"

"Questions like, where were you the night Salvatore almost got killed?"

"Oh…"

"Yeah, and Manny said you could fill me in the on background of the good doctor."

"Well, that's the thing. The doctor is not a good doctor."

"Why not?"

"The story he told me is one-sided, but I'm sure there's another take. While the Doc was on the faculty of a small university in the mid-west, in addition to his duties at the medical school, he performed the annual physicals for the members of all the sport teams, including the women's teams."

"Oh, oh," I said, imagining the complication to come.

"Yes indeed. Apparently, a woman soccer player complained the Doc took too long to examine her during her physical."

"Are you serious?"

"Yep, and the player's father reported the incident to the university president."

"What happened?"

"They worked out a deal. Instead of pressing charges and going through a public court battle, they let the Doc resign without prejudice. The provisions of the agreement included a clause to prevent him from practicing medicine anywhere in the Midwest. That's why he ended up in Cabana Bay."

"So, why is he not in practice like a regular doctor. Why is he stuck in Cabana Bay?"

"That kind of accusation follows a doctor around, no matter what kind of agreement you have. When he applies for work the stigma pops up, and no one will hire him. I imagine he'll be with us until everything blows over."

"Wow, I thought he retired early on investments or something."

"A retired doctor could afford a little more than a Cabana Bay cottage."

"How did you find out so much?'

"He's told me in bits and dribbles when he's had one too many at the bar, and I pieced the story together after a year or so."

"Wow that's private stuff. Why would he tell you about it?"

"He's been trying to get into my pants for a year. He'd tell me anything."

****

I had just stepped past cottage fourteen when Winters stopped me and barked, "Have you seen Manny?"

"I did," I answered, a bit defensively, "and I told him you wanted to see him."

"Then where is he?"

"He had to go over to the Oaks to check out a break-in."

"I didn't hear about a break-in."

"The Oaks is a private community, Detective. They rely on their own security."

"By that," he said with a sneer, "you mean your uncle?"

"Yeah, they are particular about crime news, and they don't want a bad word to get out and tarnish their reputation as a safe place, so they count on his discretion."

"There must be a law about informing law enforcement in a situation like this."

"If there was, wouldn't you know about it? I think

as long as no one says anything beyond their walls, there's nothing to report."

"Still…"

"Detective," I said, "it's probably a break-in by teens. Nothing serious enough to contact the local police. Besides, the complex has a hefty insurance policy that covers these things, and the residents get back in value for stolen property."

"I don't like it," he said, standing with his hands on his hips, and complaining like a spoiled five-year-old who didn't get his way.

"What's not to like?"

Winters studied me for a short minute, and I could see the tension go out of his shoulders. He relaxed—and almost smiled. "Okay," he said, as he spun around and stepped back into cottage fourteen, probably happy to have one thing less to worry about, "but you tell Manny I still want to talk to him."

****

Since the Doc never made an appearance outside before noon, I hoped to find him in his cottage. He rarely showed for morning breakfast or a coffee. Realistically, you could probably stay in your cottage forever if that's what you wanted, and no one would bother you, but you'd miss out on the best fish tacos in the state.

I knocked on his door and waited. The Doc liked to keep a tight ship. I'd been in his cottage at least once a week for the past two years, and his place was always freshly swept and tidied, with a lemon aroma hanging in the air, leaving me with only light cleaning. He even managed to clean his toilet. Not just the bowl itself, which can get grungy, but also the area that surrounded the toilet, which most mothers with sons would attest, is usually a mess due to their sons never having perfected their aim.

"Moli, ," the tallish man greeted me, "so good to see you."

I never would have thought much of Doc's greeting before, but with Gloria's words fresh in my head, it creeped me out. I imagined a youthful soccer player would have been creeped out by the Doc too, but I couldn't believe he clobbered Salvatore.

"Hello, Doc, how are you?"

"I've been better," he said, inviting me in.

"What's wrong?"

"All this law enforcement activity. Can't they get their investigation over so we can get back to normal?"

"It is *loco* around here."

"Yes, while I'm trying to concentrate on my writing."

Up until then, I never figured Doc for a writer. Even though I'd cleaned around his computer during my housekeeping duties, I never associated the stacks of printed sheets of paper by his keyboard with a manuscript. I needed to work on being more observant. I didn't know why Manny thought I had a head for this kind of thing. For all I knew, the Doc could be an award-winning author.

"What kind of a book are you writing? I love mysteries."

"There's a bit of mystery in the story," he said and gave me a wink.

Creepy.

"Well," I told him, "I just spoke with Detective Winters, and he said they are making progress on the case."

"Thank God!"

"Say, have you spoken with the cops again?"

"Oh yeah," he said wheeling about and going deeper into the cottage, "they have questioned me a couple of times."

"Questioned? Like maybe you are a suspect?"

"Yes, more or less. It's like that detective thinks I'm the beach version of Jack the Ripper. He even asked me if I had a hammer."

"I think that might be a reference to a possible weapon used to clobber Mr. Smith."

"I surmised that."

"Do you…own a hammer?"

"No, a hammer is a maintenance tool, and the complex handles all maintenance. That's one of the reasons I stay here."

"He's just doing his job."

"Well, if he wasn't a cop, I would have punched him out for his attitude."

I didn't have much more to say and was ready to leave. The Doc creeped me out and I was a little surprised. It appeared he had a bit of a latent violent streak. If Manny wanted more, he'd have to question the guy himself.

****

That night, Chad worked behind the bar. It starts to get busy during the first part of the fall season when the snowbirds roll into town. After avoiding the worst of the Florida summer heat, pro football is ramping up its season, and the bar packs with guys stopping in for tacos and beer. To watch the games, Manny had installed a giant television above the call liquor.

Right after I put Ricky and the Dude down for the

night, Manny came in and said, "You need to go out to the bar,"

"Why?"

"Chad's out there by himself."

"He can handle it. Most guys drink beer with their Monday night football. What's wrong? Did the truck run out of tacos?"

"No, the customers are leaving after one drink. They're not even eating."

"Why?"

"Because Gloria's not out there."

"So…wait, wait a minute," I said from the kitchen island where I had been slicing an apple for a snack. "You want me to go out there so the guys will stay and eat and drink more?"

He didn't answer right away, probably searching for an answer I'd accept. "Something like that," he mumbled after a minute.

"Manny," I complained, waving the knife at him, "I'm going to tell Dad about this. It's not enough I'm helping with the investigation, now you want me to let guys gawk at me, so they'll stick around and buy another beer?"

"I'm just suggesting you could brighten up the place, so the men out there will have something else to gawk at besides Chad and his biceps. It's Monday night football, Molina, not Saturday Ladies Night."

"You're kidding."

"No, I'm serious," he said, glancing away, obviously embarrassed to ask me to parade myself in front of a bunch of men. "You're a cute girl. Put on a pretty outfit and get out there."

Even for Manny, this was low. Being his niece, I

couldn't believe what he asked. Then I caught on to what he was doing. "Wait a minute, does this have something to do with Chad?"

He just smiled.

"Oh, I see. You want me to talk to Chad about what all he knows, right?"

"You might have a detective mentality, after all, Moli. That's exactly what I want you to do."

"Because you've already tried, and he wouldn't talk?"

"Clammed up tighter than a vise grip clamp. He's hiding something, and we need to find out what. If you go out there to help with the orders, he might open up to you, especially if you're wearing something nice."

"Maybe he's not the talkative type."

"I'm not sure what type he is, and that's why I want you to talk with him."

"Really?"

"I'm suspicious. The guy showed up a couple of weeks ago out of the blue, just before Salvatore gets whacked. That's enough for me to ask a few questions. Don't you think?"

Manny had a nerve asking me to do this. Still, if I could help to get this case over with. "Okay, I'll put on a clean T-shirt, but I'm not putting on anything sexy."

"That's my girl."

****

When I got out to the bar, guys were two deep yelling out orders in Chad's direction. The near bedlam made me appreciate the way Gloria handled the crowd single-handedly. The guys might be nice to her, but they were giving Chad shit.

"Need some help?" I asked him, in jest. Anyone

could see he was up to his eyeballs in orders. It took an hour, but we finally caught up with the orders, and the last of the tacos were sold. I doubted my presence made a difference in attendance although one cute guy asked me for my phone number. I didn't give it to him. You got to be careful out there. I mean, someone might bash you over the head with a hammer.

"Thanks for jumping in and helping," Chad said after the last of the patrons left. We had to switch off the television at the end of the game to get the bar to clear out, otherwise they would have stayed all night to watch the follow-up commentary on the game.

"It's okay. Manny said you could use the help."

"I can't understand how Gloria does this by herself."

"It's amazing how she handles it."

Before I ran out of questions, Manny appeared from around the corner. "How did he do?"

"He did great," I said, with a little pride, wondering why I cared.

"Moli was a big help." Chad complimented me, and again I didn't know why I cared.

"So, Chad," Manny said, "since you've learned your way around the bar, do you think you could take over for the rest of the week?"

"I could probably handle that. I told Moli I needed some part-time work to earn some spending money."

"Well, this might be perfect for you."

"Yeah, I can see that." He rubbed his hand over a beginning stubble. "Does this mean Gloria is going to be staying in the laundry room a while longer?"

Chapter Nine

Tuesday

As small as the place is, it shouldn't have come as a surprise that Chad knew Gloria was hiding in the laundry room.

When we asked how long he knew Gloria had been there, he said he bumped into her when he went to get towels, and she asked him to make her a tequila sunrise.

I assume she didn't tell him all the details. Why bother him? Manny just told him to plan on coming back to tend the bar through the rest of the week which, for some reason, made me happy.

Which, for another reason, made me mad, since I'm not into men anymore.

The next morning, I got Ricky off to school, and when I shuffled into the breakfast area, I found Winters and a couple of other cops with coffee and plates piled with donuts.

"Where do you get these cinnamon rolls?" Winters asked, waving one of the sugar-glazed delights at me. "They've got to be the best I ever had."

"Manny gets them from the bakery on Venice Avenue." I didn't tell him they were a day old, and that he bought them at a discount. "Are you guys finished with cottage fourteen? Or do you plan to stay through lunch?"

Winters glowered at me as he chewed. I figured he caught my snideness. "Did you tell Manny I wanted to talk to him?"

"I told him."

"We spent the whole day in cottage fourteen, but he never showed."

"He's been busy."

Just then, Manny sauntered into the room.

"Well," Winters said, "the famous Manny Soto makes an appearance, in the flesh."

Manny's eyes got big, and he swiveled his head around. When he realized he couldn't get away he went to plan B—flattery. "I see you and your men are working hard on this case, Frank."

"Cut the crap, *amigo*, where have you been? I told Moli Maid here that I wanted to talk to you. *Yesterday.*"

"So, talk."

The detective surveyed the collection of motel guests scattered about the room at different tables and at various stages of their breakfasts. "Can we go in the back for some privacy?"

"Sure, but the Dude is back there."

"That's okay. I don't think he understands English."

We gathered in the small apartment, making enough noise to rouse the Dude, so he wouldn't wake up in attack mode. Manny chased the dog off the only piece of furniture in the room big enough for the dog, so our guest had a place to sit.

Winters sat on the sofa, even though the Dude snarled at him for taking his favorite morning spot. I had no idea how much English the Dude understood, but he never forgets a scent, and the Dude got a good sniff of Winters' backside. As the dog left the room, he growled at the man.

"Don't worry about the Dude," Manny said, "he's always a little off his game when he wakes up from a nap."

"How about you?"

"I'm always on my game."

"Listen, *amigo*, how many times do I have to tell you to stay out of police work? What's this I hear about a burglary in the Oaks? I didn't see a crime report on the incident."

"I handled it. It's part of my job over there."

"You still should have reported it."

"They like to keep these types of things quiet."

"What about the insurance report?"

"There is no insurance report since the Oaks is self-insured."

"What kind of burglary are we talking about?"

"Just some kids, out for pocket change, and not too smart either to think they'd find much cash just lying around the home of someone in a retirement community."

"Statistics show senior citizens are more likely to get scammed than younger folk."

"Not on my watch."

"Manny, I've told you, you are not a cop anymore."

"Then call me the new sheriff in town."

That's just an expression for Manny since he doesn't resemble a cowboy sheriff. Manny wears Bermuda shorts, a different flowered Hawaiian shirt every day, an L.A. Dodger baseball cap, and flipflops. In fact, he in no way resembles a sheriff. But as a sign he took his work seriously, he had an authentic tin badge made up. If you only glimpsed it in the night light, you might mistake it for real, but if you got within reading distance, you could see the fancy script lettering spells out, *Security*, not S*heriff*.

"Is that the reason you wanted to talk to me, Frank?"

"No, I want you to tell me what you've found out from all these questions you and Moli have been asking all your guests."

"Who says we've been asking questions?"

When Winters didn't say anything but just stared at him, Manny said, "Okay, we've been asking around a little. I figured some of them would be hesitant to talk to you cops."

"Is that why Moli traveled to Miami?"

Manny hesitated before answering. "After you told us about Salvatore's background, I sent her down there to talk with a buddy of mine who is knowledgeable about the Maimi syndicate."

"What did she find out?"

Manny hesitated again. I could only imagine the factors rushing through his head. To help the case go forward, he'd benefit by filling Winters in on everything. But if Winters dismissed his work, what would be the use? He settled on a partial summary of my trip and said, "She found out the Miami family didn't employ Salvatore."

"Is that all?"

"Yep."

I could tell Winters didn't believe him, but he said, "Okay, Manny, if I can't keep you beating around the fringes of this case, you have got to keep me informed of what you find out. Since you want this thing cleared up quickly you better keep me in the loop. Otherwise, this might drag on for a month."

"A month?"

"Maybe longer but that depends on you."

"Okay, we'll keep you informed if we find out anything important, but this works both ways, right?"

"I don't know about that, *amigo*, but in the spirit of fair play, I can tell you we picked up one of the Lopez brothers last night."

"Which one?"

"I don't know. They all look the same to me."

"What's up with you, Frank? Are you going to arrest everyone with a Hispanic name? What do you have against Latinos anyway?"

"I keep my biases out of my work, *amigo*, but on a personal note, I don't like these wetbacks coming over and getting government checks for not working."

"You're *loco,* Frank, and ill informed. The only checks these guys are cashing are from the three jobs they work. I've never seen a harder working bunch."

"Well, Lopez has a rap sheet, and when we talked to Dante Colombo, he said the guy made trouble on the construction project, so we put him in the tank last night for safe keeping. At least until we figure this thing out."

"What kind of a motive do you think he has for trying to kill Salvatore?"

"I'll figure out something, but in the meantime, I need to have someone in jail and if not Gloria Cruz then Bob Lopez will do."

"You better be careful, Frank. You might be accused of targeting Latinos with that record."

"Oh yeah? Well, maybe I'll pinch a Black guy to round out the field."

****

When alone with me, Manny said, "Don't feed any

false information to Winters. Despite his animosity toward anyone not called Smith or Jones, he's an upright cop and will hold you responsible if you give him bad info. If he asks you anything more and you don't know what to say, just send him my way."

"What are we going to do now?"

"I've got to go to court. The guys who got in that fight the other night in the campground are scheduled for a hearing this morning. I need to be there to give testimony. While I'm gone, talk to Colombo in cottage fifteen. See if he'll open up to you."

"Should I wear a bikini?"

"Don't bother. I heard he's a family man."

"Since when does that stop a guy from looking."

****

At mid-morning, I finished cleaning the after-breakfast mess. I boxed up some donut holes, poured a coffee into a cardboard cup, and padded over to see Gloria.

She had earbuds in, and a sunlamp shined on her naked body. Slices of cucumber protected each of her eyes.

"Aren't you afraid of getting wrinkled skin?"

"This is artificial light," she said, sitting up. "Only the outdoor sunlight causes wrinkled skin."

I didn't want to argue with Gloria about skin care. I mean, she had been a model, and even in her mid-thirties her skin was flawless. I did remember reading something about artificial light, but to keep away from a technical discussion, I just dropped the subject. "Here's some breakfast."

"Thanks," she said, "I raided the refrigerator earlier, but I'm tired of oranges."

In deference to me, or maybe because she caught a chill from the AC unit, she pulled a sheet around her body before sitting down to a late breakfast.

Catching her between mouthfuls I said, "Manny wants me to talk to Colombo."

"Didn't he already talk to the guy?"

"He wants me to talk to him again. You know, to verify his story. What *is* his story?"

"I told you, family man, likes his kids and wants to leave this place ASAP. He wouldn't have anything to do with Salvatore."

"You're probably right, but Manny wants me to talk with him."

"Why?"

"Manny still figures one of the guests might have attacked Salvatore."

"Why?"

"A guest would be familiar with the layout and could fly under the radar. Plus, a local wouldn't need to run."

"Suit yourself, but it's a waste of time."

I left Gloria with her box of sweets. I secretly wished she would gain a few pounds while on her sedentary lock-up, so we'd have more in common.

She had a point on Colombo, but Manny always had another angle. He was playing the cop thing, getting two people to question each guest. Kind of the good cop/bad cop, with me the good cop. Later, he'd ask me what I found out on each guest, and he'd compare notes to see if he could catch anyone in an inconsistency.

Dante Colombo managed the construction project across the highway and ate lunch in his cottage, so I planned to catch him at home. The thirty-million-dollar condo project had run into quite a bit of community protest. Even though the City Planning Board approved the project, a demonstrative group of concerned permanent residents in the area started to picket on the public sidewalk in front of the project. They had really gotten into it with several demonstrators showing up with drums which they beat loudly.

So far, their voices had fallen on deaf ears. Like most cities, the planning board had a rubber stamp to approve commercial projects, especially when the new property would increase the commercial tax base. Anything to keep individual homeowner tax rates down. The energetic group of protestors carried a variety of signs on their picket line, and the local paper ran a series of stories about the project, and how the new development would be an eyesore to the locals and visitors alike. The protestors took advantage of any opportunity to slow the project down, including lying down across the access road to delay deliveries.

I knocked on Colombo's door and a few seconds later he opened it and stood before me in his underwear. "Trying to cool off?" I asked the man who filled out his briefs. Very well, in my opinion.

"I just took a shower. I'm going to another planning board meeting this afternoon."

"Are you going to wear more clothes?"

"I planned to—unless you think I'd get better results this way."

"Are you going through another plan review?"

"Yep."

"Then you better put on a suit. Only a bunch of old men sit on that board. What's happening this time?"

"It's something about the perimeter vegetation

screening," he said as he spun away and strode to his bedroom. I followed him, you know, to keep an eye on him. He slipped on a white shirt to cover the six-pack abs and said, "Concerned citizens are protesting that the approved plan for project vegetation planting is not in agreement with the area plan for the lot. They want us to go by the area plan guidelines."

"What's wrong with that?"

"Nothing," he said, putting on a pair of black slacks over long muscular legs, "but the bosses up north don't want to give in because they don't want to set a precedent. The city shouldn't be changing things once a project begins."

"You've got a good point."

"You think so? Maybe you should come down there with me and back me up."

"Not me. I have to live with these people."

"Thanks a lot."

"So, I guess you'll be working on the project a couple of more months?"

"That's right and in addition to these protests, we've run into supply chain issues, so we're way behind schedule, and no offense, until we get back on, I'm stuck in this place."

"You're from New York, right?"

"How can you tell?"

"I think the black speedo underwear was a giveaway."

"Hey."

"Don't get me wrong, I liked the way they fit, but what would your wife say if she found you standing there like that, in conversation with a housekeeper?"

"Wife? Who says I'm married?"

"Didn't I hear that?"

"Not me. No woman would want to marry me."

"Thanks for the warning."

"Now, if you just wanted to mess around…"

"Is everyone from New York like this?"

"I've not met everyone from New York. I'm from New Jersey."

"That's right. What company do you work for?"

After a just perceptible pause, he said, "It's a private development company. This is one of the first projects we've tackled outside of the New York area, and I'm not going to recommend we take on any others."

"That bad?"

"Worse," he said, going down the hall to the bathroom.

Alone for a second, I took a peek at the correspondence on his desk. The only personal piece of furniture in the place was covered in paperwork. The cottages are fairly spartan and besides the desk, Colombo hadn't made any attempt to make the place homey, not like the other long termers.

A variety of invoices and purchase orders covered the desktop. The company of record appeared to be an LLC. RAMCOD, LLC, New York, NY.

"What can be worse?" I called out.

"Lots," he said when he strutted out of the bathroom, rubbing aftershave on his cheeks. I noticed he'd combed back his thick dark hair. "The boss could be so pleased with the way I handled this one, he could keep me in Florida forever."

"Maybe you shouldn't do such a good job?"

"You obviously never worked for the people I work for."

"Say, what about this stuff with Bob Lopez. What did you tell Detective Winters?"

"Lopez is a troublemaker. He's been trying to unionize the workers on the project."

"Sounds like he's doing the right thing."

"Not from our perspective," he said, showing me to the door. "The family has standards, and we pay a fair wage. We don't need a union on the project."

When I left, I still had questions, like which "family" was Colombo talking about?

****

Colombo worried me. I didn't like his inconsistent answer on his marital status. If he lied about the wife thing, what else could he lie about? I'd have to ask Manny about the whole business. Personally, the guy creeped me out, even with the scented aftershave.

Another thing to worry about. We were concentrating on the North wing of the complex, but we had a whole other wing. If a guest hit Salvatore, we should be questioning the guests in the South wing, too.

An hour before Ricky's school bus arrived, I trekked down to the far end of the complex to talk to Professor Daly in cottage three. Since he first published his book of poems, the Professor has traveled the eastern seaboard teaching in unsuspecting colleges, while grinding out material for what he referred to as a genre-bending new book, but never finishing. He's not a real professor, but a poet in residence, if you can believe it.

When I clean cottage four, I can usually hear him banging away on his old manual typewriter. I asked him once why he didn't use a computer and a writing program. He said he liked the feel of the typed marks on paper. He said it was like the ink gave life to his words.

I don't know a lot about writing words. All those rules about commas and independent clauses always confused me. Where I grew up, a few choice words in Spanish were all you needed to communicate.

When I first met him, Professor William Butler Daly told me he was born into a wealthy, educated family, and his mother fancied herself a poet, thus his name. He wanted to follow in his mother's footsteps, but his father sent him to a military school to be an engineer. He told me he escaped to New York and wrote his book while on a continuous drunk between the years of 1971 and 1972. He published his book in 1973, and his mother died in 1974. He said he hadn't written anything publishable since.

The Professor, dressed in heavy tweed, despite the heat, opened the door and smiled at me. "Moli, lass, you are a wonder to see on this dull day."

"Hello, Professor." The smell of Bushmills Irish whiskey filled the air between us like a morning mist. "We missed you at breakfast."

"Oh, my regrets, child," he apologized and let me into his dark cottage, "but I'm in the middle of writing."

"Don't be a stranger," I scolded the man. The only light in the cottage concentrated its glare on a desk stuck in a niche he had created for himself in the corner of the front room.

"Don't fret, dearie, I'll be down tomorrow."

"So," I asked him, "what do you think of the trouble in cottage fourteen?"

"A sad thing."

"Yes, sir, but he wasn't a regular."

"A shame still. The police dropped by yesterday to ask me about it."

"Oh, what did you tell them, if you don't mind my asking."

"I told the detective I have no idea about the assault. I said I spent most of my time writing."

"Did you meet him? Gloria said he was in the bar the night of the attack."

"No, I don't think so, but my memory is not as fresh as before."

"Before what?"

"Before I got old."

For the next thirty minutes, the professor used the opportunity to talk about his forthcoming book. Now, even though I am a fan of poetry, and I'd read the Professor's published book, I couldn't offer much of an opinion on his new work, but I'd buy the book if it ever got published. I'm all about buying new authors' books.

I've been thinking about writing a book, the Housekeepers of Cabana Bay. Get it? Just like the Housewives of Bevely Hills. If I ever learn about those commas and where to put them.

Since Gloria told the cops she had seen all the guests in the bar Thursday night, I had some concern with the professor's memory. I guess Manny's plan to double-check everyone's statements might prove valuable after-all.

With about thirty minutes to go before Ricky stepped off the bus, I hurried down to the laundry room to run some towels. When I got there, I found Gloria folding sheets. "What in the world are you doing?"

"I got bored."

"Don't let me stop you. Have you seen Manny?"

"He made a quick stop with donuts this morning."

"Say," I asked her, while joining in the sheet folding

exercise, "when you said you saw all the guests in the bar Thursday night, did you mean everyone?"

"That's usually what all means, like everyone."

"Okay, just wondered."

"So, any idea when I'm getting out of here?"

"No, but if you are bored, you could call Winters and tell him where you're hiding. I'm sure he could arrange a couple of nights in the county lockup."

"No, that's okay. But remember, I've got a test to take on Thursday. I already texted my instructor about missing class today, but I'm not missing my test, so whatever you and Manny are doing, remember, come Thursday, one way or another, I'm out of here."

I took Gloria's warning seriously. I admired her dedication, but I also wondered who else she'd been texting.

Chapter Ten

As often happens, I lost track of the time while I folded sheets and nearly missed Ricky's bus. Of course, the Dude got there ahead of me, so I needn't have worried. Sometimes I hate the way the dog shows me up as a mother.

When we got to the apartment, I got us situated with a snack of highly sugared cereal but no milk for the Dude. When Manny arrived, he took a seat at the island and poured himself a bowl of something with a few more nutrients.

"Where've you been?" I asked him, between mouthfuls of sweetened crunch.

"Downtown, talking to Winters."

"What's up?"

"He wouldn't tell me anything," he said, adding milk in his bowl. "Salvatore is still in what they're calling a semi-coma, so he hasn't gotten anything out of him either. But I've got a couple of friends in the division, and they say he's on the hot seat to find the would-be murderer. The mayor's worried about the publicity and wants this case closed pronto. He leaned on the local papers to go easy for a few days, but if he doesn't give them something soon, they are going to go statewide on the case and put pressure on the department."

"Is Winters going to keep Bob Lopez locked up?"

"He told me he has to have someone in jail since he can't find Gloria."

"Uh, oh."

"What?"

"Come this Thursday, Gloria is going to be out in plain view."

"What are you talking about?"

"Didn't she tell you about her accounting test?"

"She mentioned something about a minor scheduling problem."

"Maybe for you, but for her it's like a do-or-die thing. Unless you plan to put her under lock and key, come Thursday morning she's going to be in a classroom at Hillsboro Community College, taking an accounting test."

"Shoot, I can't get a break on this case."

"What are you going to do?"

"What can I do? Just keep digging into this. What did you think about Colombo?"

"He fills out his underwear pretty good."

Manny didn't laugh. I didn't know if it was because he didn't appreciate my humor, or he didn't like that his niece gawked at men in their underwear. "Besides his drawers, what do you think?"

"He's hiding something. He told Gloria he was married but told me he wasn't. You can't trust a man who lies about having a wife."

"He's just trying to get in your pants."

"Is that supposed to be a compliment?"

"No, he told me he was married, too. Let's follow up on Colombo."

"Like how?"

"I'll call an acquaintance in New York. They might

be able to help."

"Do you have acquaintances in every town?"

****

I asked Manny about questioning the guests in the South wing, and he said that we needed to cover all our bases so I should follow through with my idea.

Lucky me!

I put the Dude and Ricky in front of the TV with Manny to watch them and jumped into one of the golf carts. I needed to sweep around the complex and check the cabanas for trash. Well past the bar closing, guests will often retire to their open-air cabanas and continue to party until the wee hours.

Manny had attached two trash barrels to the back of a cart in the same place where golfers strap in their clubs. One barrel is for trash, the other for recyclables. The set up made the chore easier. I implemented the recycling program right after I arrived at Cabana Bay. Sorting adds time to the job, but anything for the environment, right?

I swept up the walkway and finished at the Gigliotti's, the last cottage on the South wing. The location isn't the quietest in the complex since the cottage backs up to a service road where the complex's dumpster is stationed and spoils the ambiance. When you factor in seven days of food truck garbage to be picked up, you can imagine the aroma back there can overwhelm the hardiest of taco fans.

Marge must have seen me through their window because she came out of their cottage. "What are you doing out in this heat? Come in and have a cold drink."

The Gigliottis kept the blinds in their cottage shut tight, which made the place spooky. The units are small in comparison to the homes over in the Oaks, and because of stuff crammed into every corner you could barely move around in their place.

Inside the door, they had a fancy antique hall tree that made the trip with them when they migrated from New York. The unit had several hooks for coats and hats, and a small marble slab for keys and coins. A section on both sides of the piece held a couple of umbrellas and a fancy cane I often see Lou using around the complex. The unit had a nice mirror right in the middle so the lady of the home could check her make-up on her way out the door.

A bookcase took up space on the opposite wall. I had examined the contents of the shelves before and along with curios from their long life together, like family photos, keepsakes, and an award retirement certificate, the shelves contained a wide selection of mystery novels.

The couple had two recliners instead of a foldout sofa. They sat in front of a small TV sitting on a hutch in front of the west facing window. Reading lamps hovered over each space. One of Sue Grafton's ABC books sat on an armrest and a rerun of NCIS was on the television.

Before Marge could start a conversation, I said, "Did you hear about poor Salvatore?"

"I did."

"Did you know him?"

"Oh no, not really, I mean we ran into him at breakfast one morning, but he was Mr. Smith then. He seemed to be a nice man, didn't he, Lou?"

"He was a hood," Lou said coming out of the back, limping a little. Mr. Gigliotti stood tall and wide in the shoulders, with heavy arms, like he had worked hard all his life.

"What do you mean?"

Plopping down in front of the TV he said, "He was a *wise guy*."

"How do you know?"

"I worked with plenty in New York when I was with the local union."

"Now don't exaggerate, Louie," Marge said.

"He registered under an assumed name, didn't he?" Lou shot back. "Good guys sign in under their own names."

"That's a good point," I said.

We'd been running around thinking Salvatore was here on a proactive mission, but maybe he was a target from the start. I'd have to run that one by Manny and see what he made of the idea.

After my break, I started cleaning the grounds. I worked slow, and with the sun beating down on me, I quickly worked up a sweat. I was stalling, waiting for Señora Martinez to get home. She stayed late at the senior center every Tuesday and Thursday, doing crafts. She once told me the center offered a variety of classes and shared instructors and equipment with the community college next door.

Finally, with dinner time approaching and all the cabanas on the South wing cleaned, I gave up on Señora Martinez and retreated to the cool apartment. On the way, I stopped at the taco truck.

Manny started the food truck side business when he noticed a taco truck parked across the street at the construction site at lunchtime every day and the consistently long line of customers. The deal works two ways for him by supplying a food option for the guests and bar customers, and the construction workers come over for dinner and spend money. Of course, the pretty ladies in the bar help. Attendance is not all about tacos for the men.

I picked up several tacos for Ricky and the Dude's dinner. Ricky liked them with beef and cheese; the Dude prefers beef and no cheese. I liked them with fish and extra spicy. Since I needed to check on Gloria, I grabbed a couple for her, too. I hoped she hadn't run off in search of dinner, but with her, anything was possible.

When I got to the laundry room, I found her and some of her shack crew crowded around a folding table comparing notes.

"What's going on?" I asked.

Gloria had on a different outfit, white linen slacks and a beige blouse, so she had escaped to her cottage at one point during the day. She also smelled fresh and clean, which meant she took a shower as well. Self-conscious, I sneaked a sniff of my underarm and picked up an aroma close to rotten fish tacos.

Gloria said, "I put a list together of the names of the regulars in the bar Thursday night. The ladies have taken the names of those they know, and we're putting information together, so they can contact them. Among the bunch of us, we've been hit on by about everyone on the list, so we've got most of their numbers. For those we don't have numbers for, we are tracking down where they work, and we should be able to follow up with them that way."

There was a thick book open on the corner of the table. I could only assume when Gloria wasn't planning interrogations, she was studying for her accounting test using her book she retrieved from her cottage.

"What kind of questions will the ladies ask?"

"I made a list of the questions the cops asked me and

Loraine when they interrogated us."

"Gloria, I wouldn't describe the questioning as an interrogation."

"I know," Loraine said, "more like an inquisition."

"So, what's going on with the rest of the investigation?" Gloria asked. "Have you talked to Manny?"

I took a seat opposite her and put down the cardboard boat of tacos. "He talked to Winters, but didn't find out much. Salvatore is still in a coma, and you are still a suspect, so you need to be careful with your whereabouts and who you tell about all this."

Knowing what I was referring to she said, "I got it, and the ladies are fine with it."

"Oh yes," said Georgia Grove, the oldest mom in the group. Not only the oldest, but the prettiest, in a Samantha Jones sort of way. "It is so exciting to be involved. Don't worry. Our lips are sealed," she said, using the fingers across the lips gesture women use to indicate their mouths are zipped tight, although every woman I've ever known will unzip their mouth with little encouragement.

"And I wouldn't worry about those cops out front spotting me," Gloria said. "They are pretty lax in their stake out."

"What do you mean?"

"They've been leaving for lunch and going down the street to the Seaside Grill for a couple of hours."

"How do you know that?" I asked.

"I've got a friend there, and she told me they were eating there. I asked her to treat them nice, so they've been going there every day."

"Why would she help you?"

"We've been friends for a while. Besides, I don't think the cops have their heart in it, keeping an eye on me, so I can slip out when they are stuffing their faces."

"Okay, just be careful."

Then, someone opened the door, and I had a vision of cops rushing in with their guns drawn. I held my breath and waited.

"Oh, Chad," Gloria said, as she recognized him when he stuck his head around the door. She put her hand over her heart, like she was close to a heart attack, and said, "You scared the life out of me."

"Hi, Chad," all the women in the room said in unison after he stepped through the doorway.

"Good afternoon, ladies."

"Do you need something, Chad?" I asked him, annoyed at the room full of pretty women.

"I'm here for bar towels," he said. From where he stood, he filled the doorway, left to right and top to bottom. "It's getting close to opening time."

"Here," I said, handing him a stack of towels. "Make them last through the night."

"What if I need more?"

Gloria smiled up at him and said, "Honey, you can always come back for more."

After Chad left, I asked Gloria about him.

"Who, Chad and me? No, he's cute and all, but too young."

"You mean…?"

"No, we're only friends. He's more your age. I mean, don't get me wrong, he's a hunk, but I've got other things on my mind."

"Like interrogations?"

"Like accounting."

"That's right, your accounting test on Thursday."
****

Ricky had a hundred questions that night when I put him to bed. He was full of questions about his father, the one who cheated on me. Ricky goes through stages when Manny and I, and the Dude, just don't fill that spot in his heart. I can't blame him. Doesn't every boy need a father? And with Manny preoccupied with the Salvatore thing, he hadn't been able to spend any time with Ricky. Manny didn't sign up for the father thing, but I hoped maybe he could play a little of that role. Instead, I only had the Dude, who didn't speak English.

When I got Ricky asleep, I put the leash on the Dude, and we wandered out to the beach. A cooler than normal breeze from cloud cover wafted through my hair. The Dude, in the cooler air, pranced along in a bouncy step, moving his system into poop gear. After I scooped up his business in a doggy bag, we circled back, and I stopped to check on Chad.

"What a crowd," I said, as I tossed the tightly knotted bag in a trash can. "How are you doing tonight?"

"College basketball is back this week," he explained while he cut limes into wedges, "so the place filled up to watch the Miami game."

"Do you need a hand? I could put the Dude up and come back?"

"Sure," he said, as a smile flashed across his face. "I'd like that."

I hurried back to the apartment, and checked on Ricky, who was fast asleep. I gave the Dude a doggie treat and put him in the lower bunk and closed the door on them. I ran into the bathroom and viewed myself in the mirror, and someone I didn't recognize stared back at me. I had worked all day, and the effort left me looking like a janitor in a motel.

Oh, that's right, I am a janitor in a motel. Who was I kidding? Chad, with a career in medicine in his future, and me a Moli Maid in a run-down motel, lugging a kid around. I wasn't exactly a catch to keep. I more resembled someone you kept around to take out the trash and clean your toilet. Wait, oh yeah, those are my specialties.

When I entered the great room, Manny stood at the kitchen counter holding a wet towel up to his face.

"What happened to you?"

He lowered the towel, and he had a cut lip, and a welt had started forming on his left cheek. All of a sudden, I didn't feel so bad.

"A couple of guys over in the Cove didn't want to lower the volume on their music box."

When Manny made his night patrols of the Cove he frequently ran into unruly campers.

"How many?"

"Okay, maybe more like a group."

"What did they say that got you so riled up?"

"Oh, they made a few remarks about our ancestry."

There was always some jerk who deemed their lineage was somehow better than a recent immigrant's. "Like what?"

"You've heard racial stuff before," he said while dabbing at his bloody knuckles with the wet towel. "They called me a beaner and a wetback. I didn't care about the beaner slur, but I pointed out to them that us Mexicans have always been a part of America even before there was an America. Long before their sorry ancestors crossed over the Atlantic which made them just as much a wetback."

"Did they even understand the logic of your comments?"

"No, which made them even madder."

"What else? I'm sure you've heard worse."

"Well, one of them swiped my badge off my shirt and made a snide remark about my playing cop."

"Uh, oh…"

"Yeah, I socked that guy in the nose and put him on his butt."

"And…?"

"They all jumped me then, but they were unorganized, and I decked the next two which made the others more cooperative."

"Impressive."

"No, they were all drunk. Even you could have handled them."

Which wasn't even close to being true.

"So," he said, throwing the towel down into the sink and putting the episode behind him like one might put behind an evening with a bad date. "Who did you talk to about the Salvatore thing?"

I told him about my talk with Lou and Marge Gigliotti.

"Lou might have something."

"Yeah, maybe you should check with your buddy on Salvatore. If he wasn't working for the Miami team, he could be playing for New York."

"Okay, I'll add him to the New York list."

I also told him about Gloria and her shack crew.

"Darn, how many people are going to get involved in this thing?"

"I don't know. Gloria knows a lot of folks."

"Well, I can't sit on her all day. If the cops catch her, I can't help it."

"What about her test on Thursday?"

"Well, I've got an idea about that."

Chapter Eleven

Wednesday

Detective Winters and his boys showed up Wednesday morning. I had just put Ricky on his bus and took the Dude for his morning outing when I found the trio of cops circling the breakfast bar. Of the three, Winters eats the most, with the cinnamon buns an obvious favorite.

"Do you guys need some more coffee?" I asked, with as much politeness as I could muster.

The trio must have been half asleep because they didn't catch my sarcasm.

"No, we're good," Winters said, making a visual three-sixty. "Where's Manny?"

"Probably making his morning run through the Cove."

"Tell him to call me."

"Why don't you call him?"

"I did, twice. Left a message each time."

"Manny's not too good with technology," I told the detective, using the common excuse my uncle likes to use. Although new to the world of smartphones, he is as adept as the next seventy-year-old but acts otherwise. "I'll let him know."

After the cops left, I cleaned up the breakfast mess and took Gloria her donuts and coffee, but she had already brewed herself a cup. She'd found a spare K-Cup maker, thus the aroma of fresh coffee filled the room, mixed with the scent of Tide.

She wore a slinky nightie, and it didn't cover much. I noticed she'd made up a bed on the stacks of sheets, complete with a silk bed cover. "How did you sleep?" I asked her, as I ran my hand over the silk cover.

"I didn't. I stayed up to study most of the night."

I didn't think the beauty needed me hanging around to commiserate, so I left her with her books. I needed to talk to Manny anyway.

****

The Pirate Cove Family Campground next door attracted RV owners from all over the Eastern seaboard. Half of the campground stood in a shaded forest, and the other half edged toward the beach where the sun beat down mercilessly. Depending on a camper's preference, you could reserve a spot with complete hookups in either area. From my short experience, I gathered the oldest campers liked the shade, out of the brutal sun, so they chose the forested area to camp. They'd been coming to the place for years—maybe decades—kept a year-to-year lease on their sites and didn't give them up until they died. The younger campers chose the beachside with the sun, sand, and salt. Of course, they didn't have much choice.

The Pirates Cove is not an actual campground. Little camping goes on in the complex. In fact, if you don't have an RV of some sort, you can't stay there. A few small van-size campers utilize the campground, but most of the RVs you see come in at the one hundred to two hundred-thousand-dollar class, even higher. The cost of some can be as high as a condo in any major city.

At almost any time during the day, a big crowd of kids and teens packed the big campground pool. Situated at the far end of the complex, away from the beach, a constant din of voices, laughter, splashing water, and the springing sound of someone launching themselves off the diving board, rise up out of the pool area. The campground also has a bathhouse, laundry, and concession area. The Pirate Cove General Store, which sells fishing supplies, cold beverages, ice cream, and snacks, sits next to the pool. On most days, more people shop and hang out in the ice-cold air-conditioned store than out in the sun, for which I can't blame them.

When I hoofed it over to the store, I noticed Manny had parked his pickup out front in a *Reserved for Security* parking space.

Lately, he'd been spending a lot of time in the Cove, even during the day, outside of his nighttime patrol hours, so his absences interested me. Once inside, a blast of arctic air hit me in the face. I circled around the front section where management displayed racks of women's swimsuits and pretty cover-ups. Manny was across the room, sitting on a stool at the snack bar, where you could order ice cream from a twenty-four-flavor menu. An attractive lady with purple hair stood opposite him.

Although a popular shade with teenagers, I didn't think much of the color on a middle-aged woman. Even though she appeared fit, and you could say "cute", in the Pirate Cove uniform all the camp employees wore, I didn't think the splash of color added anything to her beauty. Manny has always been attracted to the sparkles though, so the pretty woman must be the reason for his visits at odd hours.

I wanted to meet her, so I slipped over to the counter.

When I got closer, I recognized her. "Aunt Colleen? What are you doing here?"

Finding my aunt there came as a huge surprise. Manny still cared for his ex-wife, but I didn't know they'd stayed in touch, much less worked next door to each other. The former Colleen Moore and Manny shared two adult children, a daughter and son.

Colleen had been a cop too and a good one. When she got promoted to a captain over the Traffic Division, Manny couldn't work under her and had to transfer. When he switched divisions, he faced rude comments from the other officers about a white wife who outranked him which he didn't like, so the two saved themselves years of unhappiness by separating.

Never soft-spoken or reserved, Aunt Colleen greeted me with a big smile and an even bigger, "Arrrgh, matey. Shiver me timbers; you're a sight for sore eyes."

"Can you keep the chatter down, you two?" Manny said.

Manny told me a year ago that Aunt Colleen retired early. Her older sister had come down with ovarian cancer, and Colleen wanted to spend time with her. Her sister always regretted not seeing more of the country, so Colleen took her buyout, bought a fancy RV, and with her sister, hit the road and crossed the country at a leisurely pace.

Manny leaned toward me and murmured under his breath, "A few months ago, I got a message from Colleen that her sister, Helen, had died. She had told Colleen she didn't want a traditional funeral. Since they didn't have any family left, Colleen had her sister cremated and scattered the ashes out on the Atlantic. I called her about three months ago and told her I needed her and had something for her to do."

"The big bear talked me into coming down here," Aunt Colleen said, glancing around the room conspiratorially.

Moving closer to the counter, where no one could hear, I asked, "Help with what?"

"I needed another set of eyes on stuff going on in the Cove. I can't do a lot with the motel on my plate, and Colleen needed a place to land for a while, so I told her about this, and she agreed. She's flying under the radar for now, just keeping an ear open, seeing if there is something going on."

I still didn't get it. "Going on with what?"

"A couple of months back, I started noticing a surge in drug dealing in the camp. The owners of the place, the Hollins family, are straight shooters and don't tolerate much. No guns and no drugs is their motto, and they expect me to police with force if necessary."

"But why do you think there's something going on there?"

"Do you remember that nasty fight I broke up six months ago?"

"Sort of. I guess. Why?"

"One of the guys who was injured had to go to the hospital; later we found out he was a top figure in the Pagans."

"The who? The what?"

"Big-time motorcycle gang, "Colleen explained. "They run up and down the east coast. Up until recently, they were just small stuff as far as drugs go, but a few years ago, they started running drugs up I-95 from Miami all the way to New York."

"How come you know so much about them?"

"Before I left the force, the local DEA guys gave us a briefing, and we started to research the same pattern along the L.A. coastal highway."

"There's a pattern?"

"Usually," Manny said, "and with the uptick in drug activity around the campground, something is driving it."

"So," I asked him, "you think the Cove is involved?"

"Not the owners. Just the Pagan guy in the fight. He wasn't like any other good old boy and didn't fit in with the other campers."

"What do you mean?"

"For one thing, I just didn't see how he and his wife, that's what he called the woman with him, how they could afford an expensive rig like they had. The RV had two bedrooms with slide-outs and a living room set up with a fireplace. Those outfits run three or four hundred thousand easy."

"Some people have money."

"Not those people," Manny said. "I asked around the grounds about the man and he had given everyone a different background story. These RV people are a friendly bunch, and they like to brag about how many unique features their rigs have. His camp neighbors told me that the guy didn't know the first thing about RV's. Someone even had to show him how to hook up the black water tank."

"What?"

"The poop drain line," Colleen explained, holding her nose with two fingers.

"Yuck!"

"That's what I say. Dumping poop out of a hose doesn't appeal to me. I'll use a campground facility before I go in my RV bathroom."

"Is that all you have to go on?" I asked.

"That and what happened later convinced me," Manny said."

"What happened?"

"The next morning, with the guy still in the hospital, the so-called wife left the campground without a goodbye. When Winters heard about it, he tried to track her down, but the RV and the wife had disappeared. No sign of them anywhere between here and New York."

I asked Manny, "And the guy in the hospital?"

"He snuck out without the staff noticing. So, between the missing wife and an AWOL patient a puzzle, Winters ran the guy's prints. That's when they found out he's with the Pagans."

"So, you talked Aunt Colleen into coming and joining you?"

"Well, sure, she's a good cop and I missed her."

"Wait, wait, you two aren't divorced?"

Colleen faced me and asked, "Who told you we were divorced?"

"Mama told me."

"Oh, Catherine never has liked me. She'd say anything."

"You guys aren't divorced?"

"No," she said, "we tried after we got mad at each other one time and had a big fight and said some things. But the church wouldn't let us divorce without cause, and we couldn't think of a good one. So, we had marriage intervention with Father Pete, and he recommended we take some time away from each other. You know, the absence grow fonder thing. I had just gotten a promotion and with Manny feeling low, we decided we'd separate and spend some time apart to see how we liked it.

"I chose Florida," Manny said, "and Colleen agreed. Better to get as far away from each other as we could. With time and distance, we could decide about what we wanted."

"Unfortunately, Helen got sick, and that put a new wrinkle into everything, but I wanted to take that cross-country bucket list trip with her, so we spent some time together. When all that sister togetherness ended, I found I didn't like all the free time. When I told Manny what I was going through he said he might have a job for me down here, so I agreed."

"So, you're not divorced?"

"Nope," Manny said.

"So, are you getting back together?"

"It's not as simple as that, Moli," Colleen said. "Time has passed but we'll certainly consider that possibility. Let's see if we can work together first and we'll see what happens."

"In the meantime," Manny said, "Colleen's incognito, under her birth name. No one knows she's family. Colleen Moore drove into town last week for a job, and they put her to work. They've got a row of sites on the South end of the complex where a lot of the staff park their RVs, so she and her Winnebago fit right in."

"It's right by the South bathhouse," Colleen said, with a nod of her head.

"Manny, what about the Salvatore case?" I asked. "How can you run two investigations with no manpower or assets?"

"That's why I've got you, and now I have Colleen."

Just then a lean man in a Pirate Cove uniform

appeared out of a storage room behind Colleen and approached us.

"Friends of yours, Colleen?" he asked, as he peered at us.

"Harry, this is Manny Soto, from over in the Cottages."

"Oh, sure, everyone knows Manny," the man said, joining us at the counter and offering his hand to Manny, who stood up to greet the man. The two stood eye-to-eye, but Manny had him by eighty pounds.

"And this is his niece; she works in housekeeping over there," Colleen explained. "They stopped by to introduce themselves."

"So, how are you, little *señorita*," the man said to me with a snicker, trying to be funny, holding out his hand for me to take, which I didn't.

I didn't like his condescending comment about my stature or gender, but said, "I'm Moli Soto."

"Moli? Like Moli Maid?"

For that, I shot him a dagger gaze.

"Harry is the assistant manager in the store," Colleen explained. "He's in charge of running a tight ship."

"Arrrgh, maties," he said as he left, "shiver me timbers, little *señorita.*"

After he left, Colleen saw a line of teens forming at the display case. "You guys better get out of here. We don't want to blow my cover. Besides, I've got a job to do. The kids in this place just can't get enough ice cream."

Manny and I rode back over to the motel in the campground truck.

"Why didn't you tell me about Aunt Colleen?"

"She just got here. I didn't want you over there and maybe blow her cover."

"How's this help us?"

"She's going to track the comings and goings of the RVs. She'll see if anything out of the ordinary happens."

"That could take some time."

"Now that she's retired, she's got the time. This is simply good police work."

"You could have told me about this before."

He didn't say anything and avoided eye contact.

"Wait, is this why you broke up with Gloria?"

"That's another thing," he said. "The less we say about Gloria, the better."

"What about the Salvatore thing? How are you going to work that?"

"We are concentrating on Salvatore and Colleen will work the campground case. Colleen won't be running into Gloria."

"Okay, but Gloria is hard to miss. Maybe it's better if Winters goes on and arrests her and locks her away."

"Believe me, I've thought about that."

****

For lunch, I made everyone sandwiches with leftover breakfast croissants and took Gloria a box. She had her book open and looked to be studying debits and credits. Since I viewed accounting like Egyptian hieroglyphics, I smiled and made a quick retreat.

I made my daily sweep of the grounds and the cabanas and finished up at the bar. I found Chad cutting limes before the Wednesday night crowd appeared. Traditionally a night for southern church activities, over the years, the nonreligious crowd made the day much like other days.

I am ambivalent about church. Since my divorce, I had landed on the opposite side of my faith from the norm. My whole family was born and raised Catholic, but like all religions, the church battled a quickly changing populous, not all certain that guilt lined the road to heaven.

Manny fancies himself a chef and spices up the mid-week Wednesday nights by offering a selection of hot grilled craft burgers in addition to the taco menu. He has a huge flat-top propane grill he cooks on and can cook over a hundred burgers in an hour. He offers a single patty burger, a double patty burger, or a triple burger. They come with an assortment of toppings, which included slaw and chili, blue cheese, avocado, bacon, and my favorite...jalapenos and pimento cheese. The standard is a hot grilled triple cheeseburger on an onion roll with fresh tomato slices and iceberg lettuce. The people line up for the big meal, even out in the oppressive sun, their eyes expectant, and drooling like the Dude. As a side, Manny adds fresh pub chips he fries on-site in a deep fry kettle.

Manny likes to support the local craft beer industry and rotates kegs through the bar from various micro-breweries around the greater Tampa area. To accommodate the volume, Manny installed a rack that held ten kegs of beer along the back wall of the cooler. From there he feeds the beer lines right through the wall and to the draft taps in the bar.

****

At seven o'clock, I gave Ricky his bath, put him in bed, read him three *Clifford The Big Red Dog* stories, and he fell asleep. I took the Dude out for a quick dump, careful to scoop it all up in a waste bag, and when back,

I positioned him in his lower bunk place, where he stretched out and started to snore.

I cleaned up and raced out into the dim light. The closer I got to the bar the louder the din got. The taco service and hamburger cookout just finished, and I passed Manny on his way back to the apartment, but Chad was still mixing and pouring drinks, so I stepped in to help him.

My head was spinning by the time we finally finished the long night. I pulled around a trash can on wheels and cleaned off the tables. The on-duty ladies were sweeping up behind me.

When done, the girls split the tips in the tip jar with Chad, put a split aside for the food truck staff who had already left, and offered me a share. I waved them off, and they left happy.

"Thanks," Chad said to me, and although I didn't want to, I smiled.

"For what?"

"For helping me out."

"Sure, we're all in this together, no?"

"I missed you last night," he said as he counted out the cash box.

"What?"

"Last night," he said again, as he stacked a few twenties, tens, and fives. "You said you were coming back to help out."

"Oh, yeah, sorry about that." And since I didn't want to sound like an old fuddy-duddy I said, "I had a hard time getting Ricky to sleep." Which made me sound like an old fuddy-duddy.

"I'd like to meet Ricky."

"Why?"

"I like kids," he said, as he bundled the cash with a rubber band and made a note in the bar ledger. "I have three younger sisters. I always wanted a younger brother, but Mom and Dad stopped at four."

"I don't blame them. I can barely take care of one."

Chad stood there and smiled. I could tell he wanted to say more, but he didn't get a chance.

"Wow," Manny said, when he came into the bar, interrupting the moment, "what a crowd. You got the total yet?"

Manny reviewed the ledger and took the cash bag, and I stood there and smiled at Chad. Finally, Chad smiled back and said, "Well, I'll see you all tomorrow night."

"Thanks, Chad," Manny said. "You've been a lifesaver."

I didn't say anything.

When Chad shuffled off and disappeared into the night, Manny asked, "Why didn't you say something?"

"Like what?"

"What do young attractive young people say to other young attractive young people?"

"It doesn't matter since I have sworn off men and romance."

"You still could have said something."

"Oh, something like, hey, Chad, why don't you come back to my place for a nightcap. We'll have to be careful, though. We don't want to wake my five-year-old son and his one-hundred-pound bodyguard. Something like that?"

"Uh, oh," Manny said. "You've got it bad."

"Shut up!"

Manny and I retired to the laundry room where we

found Gloria reclining and listening to something through her earbuds.

Before we got away, she reminded Manny about her test in the morning.

"What test?"

"Manny!"

"Just kidding," he said. "In fact, I've been working on a plan for that."

And so, he spent a few minutes describing his plan. On a scale of one to ten, with ten being a full-proof plan and one being it's not going to work, I gave Manny's plan a minus two.

Chapter Twelve

Thursday

When Manny said he wanted me to dress up like Gloria, I told him the plan would never work. The fact that Gloria is nine inches taller than me and several pounds lighter means we're not like twins.

"No," he said, "you misunderstand me. I want Gloria to dress up like you."

"How does that help?"

"We just need to get her out of the complex unseen. Once away, she can go to her class and take her test. It's a piece of cake."

"Says who?" she said.

"Come on, Gloria," he coaxed. "All you have you do is put on one of Moli's housekeeper outfits, put on a pair of low flats, and cover your hair with one of those bandanas that she always wears over her head."

"I can't go to class dressed like that. I'm supposed to be a professional. No offense, Moli."

"You can wear anything you want underneath the outfit," Manny said. "The extra stuffing will fill out your appearance, make you look more like Moli."

"Hey!" I complained.

"No, listen, this is the perfect plan. Add a pair of her dark glasses, and no one will recognize you. We'll go out early and drive to a few of the spots where we usually shop and pick up some breakfast stuff. Moli can go ahead of us and meet us there."

"Where?"

"Genos."

"Won't they see me drive away?" I asked him.

"No, you're not going to drive away."

"Well, how am I going to get there?"

"In the morning, when you go out to put Ricky on the bus, you need to get on with him and go for a ride."

"What? I can't do that. The buses just don't pick up wayward strangers."

"You're not a stranger. You're the mom with the boy and the big dog. Just tell the driver that Ricky's been having a rough time in the mornings with separation anxiety, and you are going to ride a ways with him. Then get off at the Beach Mall where Geno's Bakery is. The bus goes right by there. We'll meet you there; you and Gloria will change places. Geno's has a back door; Gloria can get an Uber for the trip to the college."

Gloria's head drooped down so her chin landed between her breasts.

"Manny," I asked, "is this the best you can come up with?"

"Listen, the cops assigned over here are not at the top of the class. You should have seen the guy this morning. I'd say he wasn't in place for no more than a minute before he fell asleep. Trust me, with these guys it will be a piece of cake."

I looked at Manny and looked at Gloria. Manny looked at Gloria and looked at me. Gloria looked at me and looked at Manny. When we just shrugged our shoulders Manny said, "Okay, I've got to make my rounds and you guys need to get some sleep."

"Not me," Gloria said, "I'll be up half the night studying."

****

The next morning, we put Manny's plan in motion. While Gloria disguised herself as me, Manny put out the morning breakfast, and I led Ricky to the bus stop. I told him I wanted to ride with him for a little way so he wouldn't wonder.

As I got on the bus, the driver gawked at me, but I made a face at Ricky, like saying he's a baby and what can I do. She knew me as the mother of the boy and keeper of the one-hundred-pound dog who slobbered on everything, so she didn't make a fuss. We ambled down the aisle, the other kids probably thinking, like *wow, you've got a great mother who rides to school with you.* I wondered what they would think when I abandoned Ricky later in the ride.

The bus made several stops, and a variety of kids got on. Most were young elementary age, but there were fifth graders as well. Once, Ricky told me about some older kids giving him a hard time. The next day, when the bus stopped, I let the Dude get on the bus and he plodded up the aisle and met Ricky. On their way off the bus, they got to the row of fifth graders that were picking on Ricky. As if he knew, the Dude stopped and looked at the boys and slobbered all over them. The other kids were so scared they froze in their seats. Ricky said the older boys stopped picking on him after that.

When the bus stopped at Beach Mall to pick up a couple of kids, I gave Ricky a hug, like I was going to my death, got up, and ran down the aisle to the door. I squeezed between a boarding fourth and fifth grader and jumped off the bus.

I hustled across the nearly empty lot to Genos, the only business in the center open at that hour. Inside, five sleepy people stood in line expectantly waiting for their morning caffeine. The aroma of fresh brewed coffee hovered over the crowd like a warm blanket. I checked out the menu board and joined the others. A minute later, the door to the place opened, and Gloria entered. She nodded at me and made her way down a back hall to the ladies' room.

I had just stepped up one spot when Gloria came out of the hallway. "Your restroom is locked," she said to the kid behind the counter.

The kid said, "It's only for paying customers."

"I'll buy something already."

"You have to buy before you use the restroom. Store policy."

Manny's plan didn't cover this contingency.

"She's with me," I called out to the kid.

"You haven't bought anything either."

"I'm going to get a Frappuccino and a cannoli."

"Great. As soon as you pay, I'll give you the restroom code."

Gloria gave up any chance of subterfuge and joined me in line. We must have been a sight. Like Chris Tucker and Jackie Chan in black and white housekeeping uniforms.

We finally got to the front of the line and ordered for ourselves, plus a plain black coffee for Manny. Having properly ordered and paid, the kid gave Gloria the door code; number one, two, three, four.

I didn't wait to see the transformation of Gloria from housekeeper to corporate accountant, but I'm sure if anyone witnessed the event, they would find the whole thing mystifying.

"What took you so long?" Manny barked when he opened the door for me, and I climbed in the truck with a coffee in each hand and my cannoli in my mouth. I didn't want to go into the details, so after I handed him his coffee and pulled the tasty treat out of my mouth, I just told him about the long line.

"Where's my cannoli?" Manny asked.

I forgot to order him one, so gave him mine. I'm watching my weight anyway, even though I don't care how I fill out a bikini.

After a pause, and he took the pastry, shrugged and said, "Okay, let's get out of here."

As we drove out of the lot, a little economy car pulled in and circled around the back of the bakery. Gloria was going to make her test after all.

Since we were out, Manny figured we'd go ahead and do our weekly shopping, so we drove down Ocean Blvd, stopping at the big supermarket.

Lucky me.

****

When we got back to the motel, Manny helped me unload groceries, then jumped in the Oak's golf cart for his morning run-through. Although anxious to hear about how Gloria made out, I had to clean the remnants of the morning's breakfast. When I got out to the breakfast room, I found Chad with a broom in his hands.

"Hey, that's my job," I said, mad at myself for being happy to see the guy.

"I wanted to help."

"Why?"

"You help me, and I help you."

"This is different," I said.

"I'll say. Here you don't have people screaming at you."

"Oh, it's obvious you've never been with a group of old people before they have their morning coffee."

"That bad?"

"No, not totally. A couple of guests don't even drink coffee. For them, just hot water and a choice of tea calms them."

"Can I have a coffee and a Danish?"

"Try the bagels," I said. "A Jewish couple run a shop in town and makes them fresh every day." And even though I already had a big coffee, I poured another one.

Somehow, we found our way to the lone window table facing theGulf.

"We're lucky."

"I think so."

"No, I mean, we're lucky to get this table. Usually, Lou and Marge Gigliotti grab this table before anyone else. If you did sit here before them, you'd have to eat through their dagger stares, but this late in the morning, they are both off to the senior center.

"How do you know so much about these people?"

"I've gotten to be friends with all the long-term residents, and I understand about why they are here."

"Like?"

"Like Señora Martinez, she's Cuban and from Miami. She only has one daughter who lives in Fort Lauderdale, but she likes the beach here. She hasn't accepted me because I'm Latina, and she thinks because she's Cuban she's better than me. I don't let the slight bother me. I don't blame the Cubans for being mad at everyone because they had to flee the Castro takeover and, in the process, leave all their money behind.

"Then there's Professor Daily, in cottage number two. He arrived last year. He teaches poetry at the community college. He's proud of the one book he authored some years ago.

"Doc Murphy is in cottage sixteen."

"Medical doctor?"

"Yep, but not in practice. He used to teach but retired early."

"Is this the best he could do in retirement?"

"Hey!"

"No, I meant…"

"It's okay, I get what you mean. Every one of the long terms has a different reason for being here. Some love the beach and take long morning strolls on the shore, like Señora Martinez. Some don't like the beach, like Mr. and Mrs. Gigliotti. For some, it's about money. For others, they like the accommodations. Others are here thinking their relocation is temporary, between phases, like Doc Murphy. For others it can morph into a long-term stay, and now they are stuck."

"How about for you?"

"I'm stuck, but happy to be away from my ex. This is about as far away as I could get without crossing over a lot of water."

"From L.A., right?"

"Right. My father is Manny's youngest brother. He leaned on Manny to shelter me for a while. Going on two years now."

"You're an ex-cop, right?"

"No," I said, wondering if I needed to tell the guy about my sordid background. I mean, I wasn't interviewing for a job, was I? "I dropped out of the academy when I got pregnant. I'm not anything close to being a cop."

"Don't be modest. Manny told me about the case you broke over in the Oaks last year."

"The real cops missed a bit of evidence."

"Tell me what happened."

"Manny found a man in a long-time resident's place, but when the cops investigated, no one could say whether or not he had permission to stay there. The man spun a good story about being an old friend of Mr. Cooper, the owner. He told the cops that Cooper let him stay there for the months he was away. Well, Cooper had left town on a cruise, so they were going to let the guy stay since they couldn't confirm the story.

"In the middle of questions, a fat cat sauntered across the porch. I asked the man what the cat's name was. He said their pet cat was Fluffy. The problem was, I didn't see a litter box in the house and anyone with a cat knows a pet cat needs a litter box. So, he lied about Fluffy being their pet cat. As it happened, Fluffy was just a stray, but the guy didn't know. He took the cat as a pet."

"That's observant, Moli. You should have stayed in cop school."

"Nah, just lucky. If you have a pet house cat, then you need a litter box."

"Well, apparently, there are no cat lovers in Winters' unit, and you have a head for detective work."

"Some things run in our family like cops and divorce."

"What about your ex?"

"What about him?"

"Is he a cop?"

Okay, now this is dicey. How much should I tell

him? Like, I wasn't even supposed to be into men, so why bother? "He's an ex-cop now, thank goodness."

"Does he get to see his boy? Being this far must hurt."

"He's not the hurting type."

"What type is he?"

"The cheating type."

"I got it. So, what type do you want? I might be a fit."

I paused a minute, a chunk of blueberry bagel with cream cheese in my mouth. After taking a sip of coffee to clear my throat I said, "Okay, Chad, I mean, this is nice, the attention and all. The small talk and the anticipation, but I'm just not ready to start up with anyone right now. Besides, why would you want to get involved with someone like me?"

"Oh, you mean someone like you, who is kind, thoughtful, a great mother, and has a pretty face? Someone like that?"

"You don't really know me."

"I know you like to clean."

I knew we were doomed because I hated to clean.

****

After we straightened up the breakfast mess, Chad rushed off, and I sat at the reception desk to check messages and the status of reservations. The rule of thumb to cancel or change a reservation is to inform the guest at least forty-eight hours before their arrival. If we weren't going to be able to use all the cottages by Saturday morning, I needed to tell five paying guests today that we'd be refunding their deposit money. I dreaded the task, especially the refund part.

Manny lumbered in while I slumped at my desk with

my head in my hands. "What are we going to do about next week's reservations?" I asked him.

"Don't worry about next week."

"What do you mean? We've got two days. Only two more days to solve this case. Even then, how do we know Winters will let us open the North wing?"

Manny stood there fuming. Was that steam coming out the back of his Hawaiian shirt? Well, he needed to make up his mind.

"Okay, hold off calling anyone until this afternoon. I'm going to talk to Winters and see how this thing ends. They've had more than enough time. If he doesn't have enough to arrest someone by now, I doubt keeping us closed is going to change anything."

"What about Gloria?"

"Frank will have to put up or shut up about Gloria. I think he's using her to get back at me, but I'll call him out on it."

"Better be careful, Manny. Frank's got a temper."

"So does Gloria."

****

With the cancelation calls put on hold, I shifted to other tasks. I usually do my heavy cleaning of the bar and grounds on Thursday afternoon, before the busy weekend starts kicking in. I retrieved my yard cart then peeked in the laundry room to see if Gloria had come back from taking her test.

"How did you do?" I asked her as she rested back on a pool lounge chair.

She had her ear buds in and the tanning light on. A layer of oil covered her silky skin. I wasn't sure what she wore to take the test, but the skimpy bikini she had on probably wasn't the expected business class wardrobe.

"Oh, I'm sure I aced it."

"Wow, that's great. That stuff makes my head swim. Now what?"

"You tell me. I'm sick of this place and I'm ready to get back to work."

"What's the hurry?"

"Don't worry. I'll keep Chad around on the back bar, but I'm moving to first position again."

"Well, you shouldn't have long to wait. Manny stormed out to see Winters."

"Oh, well, he's going to miss him. The good detective and his deputy dog drove up a few minutes ago."

"Where?"

"When I left campus, I got an Uber to the Cove next door and used their bath house to change in before sneaking back. I saw Winters from the beach trail."

I got my grounds clean-up cart and started sweeping the cement patio. A combination of cigarette butts, bottle tops, and broken palm fronds littered the area. The hardest part to clean is the sand area where our plants formed a nice perimeter around the complex. To pick refuse off the sand, I use a long grabber.

We planted a mixture of palms, yellow trinitites, multi-colored crotons, firebush, and Spanish bayonet. They are all hardy, salt and drought-tolerant plants, which thrive in the hot, humid weather. They have to be tough with the heat from the sun and the rough treatment they get from the customers.

I made my way around the complex, working closer and closer to cottage fourteen. Winters spotted me through the window and sticking his head out of the door shouted, "Where's Manny?"

I paused a breath, not sure what I should say. I settled for, "I don't know. Why?"

He squinted at me, like he couldn't see in the bright sun. "Okay, I guess I can tell you."

"Tell me what?"

"You can open this end of the complex but not cottage fourteen."

"That's great news. Does this mean you found out who attacked Salvatore?"

"No, not yet. We've still got some leads to chase down."

"One cop to another, can you tell me anything about the case?"

"Moli, do I have to remind you again that you and your uncle are not cops anymore. Manny driving around in his little truck playing one doesn't count."

"Well, he kind of is."

"No, he's not. He's more like a playground monitor."

Ouch! To counter the harsh assessment of Manny's police skills I said, "He takes his work seriously."

"I can see that, but he and his little golf cart better stay out of my way."

"This doesn't have anything to do with the shooting in the campground last year, does it? Manny responded to that incident like a professional."

"Oh yeah, so professional he let the murderer get away."

The year before, to settle an argument in the Pirate Cove Campground, two men in the middle of parked RVs started shooting at each other. When Manny arrived on the scene he found one guy bleeding out, and he had to decide to chase the shooter or save the bleeding guy's life. Manny chose the bleeding guy. He assumed the shooter owned one of the big RVs, and even if the guy managed to unhook his unit in a hurry to make an escape, he wouldn't get far.

Unfortunately, several campers said the guy ran away in the night, and they heard a bike start and roar out of the complex. The next morning, Manny checked, and the campground confirmed all the RVs on the lot were accounted for, and there was no trace of the shooter.

"Manny made a call on that."

"He let the shooter get away."

"He made a decision to stop and help the wounded man. Tell me you wouldn't have done the same? It's easy to criticize in hindsight, but in the moment, he made the right call."

Winters just stared at me. I hadn't meant to come out so forceful in Manny's defense. Back in L.A., Manny had a good cop reputation, but in administration circles he was known to cut corners to get a job done.

"You tell Manny Soto to stay out of police business. If he mucks up this case or any other case I've got, I'll make sure he never messes up another case again."

"Okay, okay, don't get your underwear in a wad. I got it."

Winters hesitated, like he wanted to say something more, but his Deputy Dog sidekick interrupted our conversation and asked if he needed to do anything else.

He said, "No, lock up and let's get out of here."

I hesitated to ask anything more, but just to be mean I said, "Can I take down the crime scene tape?"

"Keep your hands off that. I don't want to come back and find that tape even an inch out of place."

****

I finished my yard work and met the Dude and Ricky at the bus stop. I took the buddies back to the apartment for a snack of tortilla chips and salsa. For a change in our afternoon routine, I leashed the Dude up and the three of us hiked over to the campground. I had a feeling I'd find Manny next door at the Cove's General Store.

I'm always a little apprehensive about moving about in a crowd with the Dude, but besides the lunge he made at a passing jogger, he stayed under control. I doubted the usefulness of the leash I attached to his collar. If the Dude wanted to take off in another direction, I'd never be able to stop him. I hoped his attachment to little Ricky would keep him under control, but I had no evidence to support my theory. To the contrary, my experience has been that boys are inclined to fits of rage and running off, just like dogs.

At the Pirate Cove General Store, Manny's little pick-up truck was parked out front. I figured he and Aunt Colleen had hooked up again. I didn't know about those two carrying on, but even with everything happening, Manny and Colleen seemed happy. I just hoped I wouldn't have to wait until my seventies to get my second chance at happy love.

A "No Dogs" sign hung from the railing out front of the General Store, but I took the Dude in the shop anyway. With his size and slobber, I didn't think anyone would be brave enough to approach us and complain. As we roamed through the crowded floor, passages magically opened. *Shiver me timbers!*

Besides, the Dude under close watch was far better than if I left him outside leashed up someplace within jaws length of pedestrians.

When Aunt Colleen saw little Ricky, she couldn't help herself, and she rushed from behind the counter and scooped him up in her arms. The Dude must have recognized the maternal instinct because, besides barking out a friendly woof, he let Colleen manhandle my baby boy.

"I wasn't sure he'd recognized you, Aunt Colleen. He was young when we made our escape."

"I know. He sure has grown."

"Ricky," I told my boy. "This is your Aunt Colleen. Do you remember her?"

"No," Ricky said with some concern in his voice. A concern the Dude at once recognized, and he let out a low growl.

"That's okay, Dude," I said, as I took Ricky away from Colleen. "Sorry, Aunt Colleen, the Dude is kind of a protective big brother to Ricky."

To show the Dude things were normal, I put Ricky down and let the dog slobber him.

"Mommy, can I look at the toys?"

"Sure, honey, but take the Dude with you."

The two of them wandered off in search of adventure and I switched my attention to Manny and Colleen.

Aunt Colleen asked, "Aren't you afraid to let him wander around?"

"With the Dude by his side, anyone who tried to touch Ricky would come up short a hand."

"So," I said to Manny, "you're spending a lot of time here."

"Now, don't you start. I check in with Colleen every day, to see if she's seen anything suspicious."

"Uh huh."

"That's right, strictly business, like I said, and she's figured something out."

"What?"

"Well," Colleen said, as she checked the crowd, to make sure no one could listen in to the conversation, "if Manny's right about this drug thing, they might be using the campground as a transfer station."

"What do you mean?"

"It's risky to use the same vehicles for the whole trip north. I figure they run the stuff out of Miami in one RV and transfer the stuff over to a second one when they arrive here. A clean RV with no Florida connection to make the final leg North."

"But why use an RV?" I asked her, surveying the room for potential spies listening in on our discussion. "Aren't they expensive?"

"The big units have a dozen places to hide the stuff if they ever get stopped. And they never get stopped because most of the time they are driven by families or old people, not your typical drug runners."

"I don't see it," Manny said, making his voice quieter when a group of ten-year-olds went by. "For an operation like that, to transfer from one RV to another, that would draw a crowd."

"Right," Colleen said, "that's why they would need two campsites, side by side. Some sites are only separated by a few steps. I'm not sure how much they ship, but you wouldn't want to run all over the camp carrying big bags of drugs back and forth, but a step or two would be doable and not attract attention."

Manny said, "But, since this campground is full most of the year, you'd have to be lucky to find two adjacent vacant sites at random dates. That would be virtually impossible."

"So," I said, "the bikers must have rented two sites in advance."

"That's right," Colleen said.

"That must be expensive," I said.

"What do they care?" Manny said. "They probably run a million of dollars' worth through here every month."

"I don't know," I said.

"What?"

"Think about it. Two prime, expensive camp sites, side by side, and vacant for most of the year. That would be suspicious."

"Yeah," Colleen said, "that would be obvious. They couldn't take that chance."

"That's right," I said, scanning the room for the Dude and my boy. "So, how do they do it?"

Colleen said, "I figure they own the sites and rent them out. Management has a multi-year registration calendar. You can reserve a site up to two years in advance. You can roll your reservation over year to year, and you can always come back to the same site every year. There're some people who have been coming back to the same site for ten, even twenty seasons."

"Wait," I asked, "can you sub rent your site? Wouldn't the campground object to that?"

"They started with sub leases back when Air B&B became popular," Colleen answered. "They don't mind. They charge a hefty sub-lease fee, so they make a large premium off those rentals."

"Can you get a hold of the reservation calendar?"

"No, not from the snack bar register system. Reservation info is over in the administration building."

"So," I asked when a minute passed and no one said anything, "what are you going to do?"

Colleen said, "We need to get into the admin building and see the reservation calendar. If we had it, we might be able to figure out which campsites they're using."

"Can I have an ice cream cone?" Ricky asked when he and the Dude returned.

"Sure," Colleen said, going to the display case. "What flavor?"

"Chocolate."

As Colleen scooped ice cream, I asked, "Just how do you think you'll get into the admin building?"

After a minute, Manny said, "I think the early mornings are best for this kind of thing."

"Yeah," Colleen agreed, handing Ricky his cone. "People sleep their deepest at four in the morning. No one is awake around that time for this kind of thing."

"What kind of thing?" I asked.

"Breaking and entering," they both said at the same time.

Chapter Thirteen

After our clandestine meeting and Ricky finished his cone, I rescued a bunch of teenagers from the Dude before he drooled on them and led him and Ricky out of the shop. We rode back to the motel with Manny, but with limited capacity in the cab, the Dude made the trip in the truck bed.

Back in our apartment, once I situated Ricky and the Dude in front of the television, I turned to Manny. "Are you two crazy? You can't break into the campground admin building. Who do you all think you are, Mulder and Scully?"

"Who?"

"The guys from the X Files."

"They were FBI. We're more like Holmes and Watson. Wasn't there a retelling of the Sherlock character with a female Watson?"

"This isn't a joke, Manny." I was a little surprised by his cavalier take on the job. "You could get in trouble for something like this." That's why I got Colleen to come and help."

"Manny, this can't sit well with you; you guys were cops."

"We're just trying to catch the bad guys, Moli, any way we can."

"Isn't there a right way and a wrong way to do that?"

"There's only the way that works."

When I didn't say anything for a long minute, he said, "Moli, this could be a big bust. There's a lot on the line here. Cops follow rules and such, but now, we don't have to toe that line. If we get the bad guys everyone's happy."

"Speaking of busts, I spoke with Winters. He said we can open up the North wing."

"That's great. Did they find the attacker?"

"No, not yet."

"I told you. Those guys couldn't arrest a shoplifter."

"He told me to tell you something."

"What?"

"He said for you to remember you are not a cop anymore and to stay out of police business."

"Yeah, yeah."

"Which reminds me, what about this early morning caper."

"Right now, it's the only lead we have on the Pagan thing, so it's a good call."

"What if we get caught? And arrested?"

Who would take care of Ricky? The Dude was a good guard dog, but could the Dude be counted on long term? Dogs get old seven times faster than us people. He wouldn't be around for Ricky's teenage years when a kid really needs a parent.

"Moli, we're picking a lock and copying a calendar. We're not robbing a bank."

My uncle may have had a simplistic view of this after-dark caper, but the plan worried me. On a scale of one to ten, I gave the plan a minus one.

****

The size of the Thursday night crowd in the bar depended on which Florida pro football team the national networks carried on any given night. With the Tampa Bay Bucs on, we expected to be slammed.

When Manny agreed to stand watch over Ricky, I got my boy and the Dude settled in for the night. Excited as a teenager going to a middle school dance, I rushed to the bar to give Chad a hand. I didn't like that. For some reason, the more I was around him, the more my vow to *not* get involved with a man got weaker and weaker.

Men and women packed the bar shoulder-to-shoulder. The men came in all sizes, shapes, and in all manner of dress, from flip flops and shorts to business suits. The women wore mostly skimpy beach wear.

"Am I glad to see you!" Chad shouted at me above the din, as he passed a tray of drinks to a server.

"Are you just glad to see me or happy I have two hands to help out?"

"More the latter, but still great to see you."

Up to the last minute, the Bucs were headed for a loss, but their veteran quarterback took over the game. He completed several tough passes and got them into position for a short field goal to win the game. When the kicker missed the goalposts by three yards, a collective moan rose from the crowd in the bar and almost immediately the grumbling crowd started to file out of the bar. When the last of the disappointed fans left, Manny and Colleen strolled around the corner together.

"Who's the lady with Manny?" Chad asked.

"Ah, that's his wife."

"They're not divorced?"

"Nope. Separated."

"Wow."

"I know."

"What about Gloria?" he asked.

"What about her?"

Chad glanced at Manny for a second. A bit embarrassed, he started to count out the register. When Manny and Colleen joined us at the bar, I made the introductions all around. Colleen asked Chad what he was doing in Florida.

"I graduated but I took a year off before medical school. I needed a break."

Colleen said, "I took an online night course a couple of years ago, and about died. Don't wait too long. When you get older studying is harder."

After Chad finished the paperwork, he glanced at me. "Hey, do you want to grab breakfast in town? The pancake house has an all-night pancake special."

"Sorry, I've got to get back to Ricky."

"No, you don't," Manny said. "Colleen's coming over; we're working on something, so we'll be up for a while."

"Yeah," Colleen said, "you kids go on and have fun. We'll watch over the little one."

"No, I couldn't," I said.

"Go on," Manny said, "take a break. You work too hard around this place."

I wanted to continue my objections, but I had lost the argument, and my vow to be celibate was fast becoming a long-lost whisper.

****

The pancake special was okay, if you like pancakes. I enjoyed the company more. Later, Chad dropped me off at the motel, and I checked in on Ricky and the Dude. I had forgotten all about Manny and Colleen's little job, but they sat at the kitchen island with a campground map spread out before them.

"How was your date?" Colleen asked.

"It wasn't a date," I said.

"What's with her?" Colleen asked Manny.

"She thinks she's still a mother."

"I am a mother," I said, pouring myself a glass of chardonnay. "Maybe not a good one but still a mother."

"No," Colleen said, "you're a single mom. There's a significant difference."

"What's the difference?"

Manny said, "The difference is you are one babysitter away from being a single lady again."

"You guys should talk."

"We were discussing you, not Manny and me. So, what's the fuss anyway? He seems like a nice boy."

"He is."

"Then what's the problem?"

"He's kind of young."

"Oh, I see, like a year younger than you? What is he, twenty-two?"

"He's twenty-three, but it's not the years I'm worried about. It's the maturity."

"Maturity," she laughed, "do you think Manny's more mature now than when we got married?"

"Hey!"

"Don't fuss, Manny, it's your most endearing quality, your little boy view of life."

"Okay, you two, enough about me. Now, what about this job tonight?"

"Are you in?" Manny asked me.

"What about Ricky?"

"The Dude's back there."

"Well, okay. I can't let you two old people have all the fun."

****

"It's a piece of cake," Manny said about the job, as far as breaking and entering, but I hesitated since I'd have to leave Ricky. I worried how the little guy always seemed to be the last thing on my mind. Did all mothers do it? Was I like the parent who loses kids at the mall or the parent that forgets about their kid in the back seat of their car and locks them in a one-hundred-fifty-degree oven while she has her hair and nails done?

I checked on Ricky and made sure the Dude was firmly camped out under my boy's bed. I realized, even if I had someone to call to babysit, no one would protect Ricky like the Dude. As much as I hated to admit, in some ways, the Dude was a better parent than me. I doubled checked the security app before going out to the kitchen feeling guilty.

Colleen had studied the administration building and its security system. She said the campground itself had an entire array of cameras that covered most of the grounds, but there were a few blind spots. She said the biggest hole in the network existed right around the admin building. She had drawn the camera locations on the campground map, and Manny had traced a route with a black marker ending at the admin building. He marked the spot with a big "X," just like a pirate treasure map.

"Are you sure no one is there overnight?" I asked her.

"Yes," Colleen said, "I stayed up a couple of different nights to confirm. They lock the building around nine at night and the next shift doesn't start until five the next morning. They only run two shifts. Trying to save money, I'm sure."

Manny said, "I figure we'll take twenty minutes to

navigate through all the blind spots and approach the admin building from behind. The lone camera on the building is on the North front of the building. I've got a black tarp I'll carry. Once we sneak up on the blind side of the camera, I can throw the tarp over the camera. If anyone goes back and reviews the recording, the system will be blacked out during the time we are in the building. They'll just think the system had a glitch. We'll be in and out of there fast enough no one will suspect."

"All set?" Colleen asked.

"Well," I said, standing there in my white bar server shirt, alongside the variety of flowered shorts and T-shirts Manny and Colleen were wearing. "Shouldn't we all be in black clothing or something not as colorful?"

Manny paused and eyed his shirt. He said, "Moli, this is one time watching too much television is useful. We'd better change into something less noticeable."

"I don't have anything to change into," Colleen said.

"Come on," Manny said, "I've got something you can wear."

When they started back to Manny's bedroom, Collen said, "I'm not wearing that old black Oakland Raiders jersey of yours. Since they switched to Las Vegas, I disowned them."

****

Manny was off by several minutes. We took longer than we planned to navigate around the complex. It slowed us down to dodge the high-placed flood light covering the campground. In fact, if you camped under a flood light, the brightness made you feel like it was daylight all night. Mainly aimed at the roads and paths around the paved part of the complex, the system didn't cover all the dirt and wood trails shrouded in darkness.

Long past our target time of four o'clock, we finally stumbled out of the trees behind the camp's admin building.

Manny carried along a broom handle and used it to drape a black tarp over the building's lone CCTV camera. Safe from the camera recording, we crawled to the single entrance door.

A standard deadbolt secured the office. Manny peered at the lock in the glare of a floodlight stationed right over the building and whispered at us, "I've got this. Piece of cake."

Manny worked with the burglary unit from time to time and picked up a few tricks along the way. "It's an old lock," he whispered and took a small leather pick kit from a pocket and used a couple of thin prods to work the lock's tumblers. A minute later he used a set of plyers to twist the prods over, and the lock clicked open.

Once inside, Aunt Colleen used her phone flashlight to find her way to a computer terminal. A black screen greeted her, but when she wiggled a mouse, the system lit up, and the password box opened. Colleen typed in a series of words and on the fifth try she got the hit.

"How did you know the password?" I whispered to her.

"All the passwords are a version of pirate or something to do with pirates. This one was *crossbones*."

"Like, Skull and Crossbones?"

"That's it. The one in the ice cream shop is Skull."

"Cute."

Since I couldn't offer any other useful assistance, I volunteered to stay at the door and make sure no one surprised us. While there, I pulled my cell phone and checked in on Ricky and the Dude. The bedroom camera showed them sleeping soundly. The Dude's loud snore was a dead giveaway.

Colleen opened the system's calendar and started making copies. Manny stood over the printer and gathered the sheets as they printed off. When the printer paused, he added paper to the print tray, so no one could tell we used the printer.

The operation had the earmarks of good police action. And why not? Manny and Colleen had been good cops. Everything would have worked out perfectly, except the printer ran out of ink, and the warning signal sounded, filling the room with a loud beeping.

"What's that?" Colleen asked.

"It's from the printer," Manny said. "It says it's out of ink."

"Do something," she said.

"Like what?"

"Turn it off and find some more ink."

"Even if I found ink, it wouldn't help. I can't even replace the ink in my own machine."

Colleen glanced quickly at me, and I nodded my head. Manny couldn't replace ink cartridges, even if his life depended on it.

"Aren't you done?" Manny asked, powering off the printer. "I've got a stack of paper here."

"I've gone through November, but I still have December."

"Is the screen on?" I asked her.

"Yes, right here."

"Okay, let me see."

I used my phone to take a photo of each December reservation page we pulled up on the screen.

"That's the last one," Colleen said. "Manny, gather

what you have, and let's get out of here."

Before we made three steps to the door, Colleen held up her hand for us to wait. "I hear someone coming," She hissed, "hide."

Since I had left my post to help with the printing, I had neglected my night watch duties. Colleen locked the door and switched off the monitor which left the room in darkness. The room held several desks randomly situated around the room. There were a couple of doors along the back wall, but I didn't have a clue what was behind them.

I headed for one of the doors. I calculated that even if I found myself in a restroom, I would be safe. I didn't figure someone would leave the comfort of their own home and bathroom facilities first thing in the morning, to go to a dirty staff restroom. Another possibility for the door could be a storage room. Based on our own storage room usage, there would be no telling what I'd find in there. Most likely shelves of office supplies, including ink cartridges, but you never know.

A key in the lock clicked and the door to the administration office started to open. The overhead lights clicked on right after, about the time I closed the door of my chosen hiding spot. In the dark room I didn't smell the telltale odor of urine or disinfectant, so I figured I entered a supply room.

To avoid the loud click of a door just shutting, I only closed the door to the jamb. I heard footsteps in the outer room, but they stopped. I waited and hoped no one on the other side of the door could hear my heart beating hard enough to escape my chest.

After a long minute, I heard someone type on a computer keyboard, then the loud beep of the printer, which still signaled the machine needed ink. Like the ink that was probably on a shelf somewhere in the room I shared with office supplies.

Great.

After a few chosen words, I identified the typist as a man. Then heavy footsteps approached and the door to the supply room opened. Luckily, from where I stood, I slipped farther back behind the inward swinging door, just as the overhead light flicked on. Unless my visitor got on the floor to peek under the one-inch gap under the door, he wouldn't see me.

The sound of the man rummaging around, and a few more choice words, filled the space. *"Got you!"* the voice said.

Not got me, like in someone found me, but a *got you*, like he found the ink cartridge.

Before my heart calmed down, the light blinked out, and the door slammed. Left alone in a comfortable darkness, I breathed easier.

The typing started again, then the printer engaged and started printing. More footsteps and more choice words filled the room. Finally, the room light switched off, and I heard the outer door open and shut.

I relaxed, the tension in my muscles eased, and I opened my door to peak out into the empty room. Colleen stepped from her hiding place first. She had ducked in one of the closets. Manny rolled out from underneath one of the tables.

"That was close," I said.

"That was the assistant manager, Harry," Colleen said. "I saw him through the closet slats. He printed something off the computer, probably today's staff schedule. He gets to the general store early to open and needs the day's shift schedule, so he knows who to yell at."

We all retraced our steps and got out on the landing in front of the building. The campground still stood quiet. Manny couldn't relock the dead bolt, so we left the door unlocked. We just had to hope whoever arrived next would figure the last person out just forgot to set it.

On the way around the building, Manny pulled the tarp off the camera, and we worked our way back to the motel in the last of the darkness. By the time we got back, the morning sun started to brighten the sky in the East. The exhaustion from the ordeal, and the stress of participating in my first-ever break-in, set in on me.

"Now what?" I asked him when we had settled on various pieces of furniture in the small apartment, trying to catch our breath.

"Now, we need to check these reservations and see if we can find any adjoining lots reserved at the same time and are owned by the same people. I wouldn't expect too many people could afford to own two sites."

"And just how are we going to do all that?"

"I've got it covered," Colleen said. "The general store oversees all the delinquent site maintenance payments. If a site owner doesn't pay the monthly maintenance fee, we send them a bill."

"What if they're not delinquent?" I asked.

"Doesn't matter. I've got their contact info. The campground recently increased the monthly dump fee, and we sent a letter to every owner last week."

"This reservation list must have had six hundred campsites," I told them as I reviewed the stack of paper. "Manny, it's going to take a while to go through this list. There must be thousands of combinations, and it's not like we have an AI computer program we can run this through. I don't have time to work this. I've got work to do around this place, and the weekend check out starts this morning."

Manny stared at Colleen.

"Not me, Manny, you already got me a job, remember?"

"Well, I can't either. I'm late for my patrols now."

I said, "We need someone with time on their hands who is good with numbers."

Manny didn't respond to my suggestion.

"Manny?"

"What's she going on about?" Colleen asked.

"Tell her, Manny."

"Tell me what?"

I said, "We know someone who could help us."

"Okay, that's good, no?"

"Manny?" I said again.

"Okay," Manny finally said, "there's a guest who could help us. She's good with numbers. She usually runs the bar."

"Usually?" Colleen said.

"Yeah, usually, when she's not under suspicion of assault with a deadly weapon."

Manny explained to Aunt Colleen about Gloria and Salvatore.

"So," Colleen asked Manny, "is this Gloria pretty?"

"What's that got to do with anything?"

"Manny?"

"Okay, okay, she's fairly attractive."

"Did you go out with her?"

When Manny didn't say anything, Colleen asked him again.

"Okay, okay, a couple of times."

"Manny?"

"No more than a couple. You see," Manny said to me, "this is why I didn't want you to say anything about Gloria."

"You talked to Moli about keeping this from me? Wow, you must feel guilty about it. Good. You do remember, we are not divorced."

"I know, but when we split, we said all rules were suspended."

"Yeah, but I didn't know you were going to jump in the sack with the first young woman you met."

"It wasn't like that. I met plenty of women before Gloria. Besides, she's not that young and we never did anything."

"How old?"

"That doesn't matter. Thirty…almost forty. But what matters is, after the first date, I realized how much I missed you, and that's when I got in touch with you and asked you to come."

My Aunt Colleen paused a few seconds. Maybe the confession from Manny got her right in the heart. Then she burst out laughing.

"What's so funny?" I asked.

"Same old Manny," she said to me, laughing out again. "I would expect nothing less from the old fart."

"Come on, Colleen," Manny said, "that part about how much I missed you got to you, didn't it?"

"Almost, Manny. That was some good stuff from you, especially on the fly. Is that why you and, what's her name, aren't a couple anymore? She finally caught on to your bull?"

"That and the age thing. What can I say?"

Still laughing, Colleen faced me and said, "It's okay,

Moli, Manny and I have been going like this since we got married."

"You're not mad?"

"No, when we split, I figured he'd jump in the sack with the first young thing he met. He never strayed when we were together, but he had those wandering eyes. I half expected to find him shacked up with a harem of bikini-clad women when I got here."

"Now, come on, Colleen, I'm too old for that kind of stuff."

After Colleen fell into a laughing binge again, she calmed down enough to say, "Yeah, I guess you are slowing down in your old age."

"Colleen."

"Don't worry, you big lug, I'm not keeping score, and in the spirit of full disclosure, I've not kept to the narrow lane during this separation either."

"I didn't expect you to. Lovely thing like you must have had them lined up."

"Okay, Manny, enough with the sweet talk, and unlike you, I'm not telling."

"Okay, okay," I finally said, "no one is mad. So, can we agree to use Gloria on the campground case?"

"From what you say, you better hurry and sign her up, before the cops lock her up. Where did you say you kept her?"

"She's in the laundry room around back."

"Oh, oh, that reminds me."

"What?"

"Friday is staff laundry day. If we put our uniforms out on Friday morning, they get them back to us the next day. Clean and ready for the next week."

"So?"

"So, I missed the laundry pick up, and they'll know I didn't come back last night."

"How will they know."

"If anyone reviews the camera footage, they'll see me leaving the campground but not coming back. At least not coming back through the regular routes."

"Don't worry about it," Manny said. "I'll drive you back over, and they'll see you come back. They'll just suspect we're dating each other."

"Won't that blow your cover?" I asked.

"No," Colleen said, "Manny's on to something. People will think we started a new relationship. This way, we've got an excuse for seeing each other so often."

"Okay, then," Manny said to me, "get this stuff around to Gloria so she can start working on it."

"Manny, it's still early in the morning. She's not up yet."

"Take her a coffee."

"Coffee," I said. "Oh, oh, we've got to get out the breakfast."

Chapter Fourteen

Friday

I ran around like a mad woman for three hours. I had to get Ricky and the Dude up, put out breakfast for the guests, get Ricky to the bus, and stop in to see Gloria.

When I explained what we wanted, she gave the stack of papers an eye, like they were a personal challenge.

I did the checkout routine with the couple in cottage six and a single in cottage seven, who were leaving a day early trying to beat the traffic north. I settled their accounts and got them on their way. Then, I ran back to the laundry room, grabbed my housekeeping cart, and rushed to clean the recently vacated rooms.

Apparently, the departed guests were type-A personalities who left their cottages in tip-top shape. I still tore them apart and mopped the floors. Even meticulous people will leave hair or a nail clipping somewhere, and the next guests are always sure to find them.

I had just finished with the last cottage when Chad appeared.

"Hello," he said, standing in the doorway of the cottage.

"What are you doing here?"

"I'm hungry. Do you want to get some lunch?"

"Lunch?" I repeated, like he spoke in a foreign language. "Sure, I could eat, but I have to be back by three o'clock to meet Ricky's bus."

"No problem."

"Let me clean up and get out of this uniform."

I couldn't remember the last time I had a lunch date. *Like maybe never.* I didn't expect much, but a window seat with a view of the marina in Venice couldn't have been nicer. Not to mention the company. In addition to being handsome, Chad actually spoke in sentences. Conversation took the place of the grunts and nods I usually got from Manny, Ricky, and the Dude, my regular lunch partners.

"So, why did you drop out of the police academy?"

"I had an affair with my training instructor."

Chad raised a thick eyebrow, a prompt that said, *tell me more.*

"William is older than me, but handsome. Plus, he made me feel desirable. A few months after we started dating, I realized he didn't want a long-term relationship. But when I told him I was pregnant, he agreed to marry me. That's when I dropped out of cop school. I found out later he only agreed to the marriage to save his job. It's okay if your cop husband knocks you up, but getting pregnant by your training instructor can get a training instructor fired, and that means they can lose their pension."

I sometimes feel like I copped out a little on the whole marriage thing. My ex was a jerk when we got married, but my starry-eyed insistence that he would change and settle down proved incorrect. We were doomed by the end of the first year. Even though he semi fought the divorce, I just had to get free of him for my own well-being. Of course, if I knew I was going to end up as a maid in a run-down Florida motel, I might have acted differently. Actually, no, I would have done the same thing.

"I wanted to make things work," I confessed to Chad, "but old dogs and new tricks apply to men as well."

"Like…?"

"Like in performing tricks with recruits."

"Oh. *Those* kinds of tricks."

"That's right. So, Ricky and I joined Manny in his entrepreneurial pursuit."

"Well, I, for one, am glad of that."

"Yeah, we've talked about this."

"What?"

"About us starting a relationship. I'm a little old for a summer romance."

"You're never too old for love. Manny and Colleen are great examples."

"They've been together for forty years."

"Give me a chance."

"I don't know. The last time I agreed with a guy to do that, I ended up where I am today."

"I'm not like other guys."

"No, you're certainly not."

****

I got back to the complex just in time to greet Ricky at the bus stop. As usual, the Dude beat me there. His internal clock appears to work better than mine. When Ricky got off the bus he had a school flyer in his hand, and he tried to show the Dude the sheet of paper. When the dog didn't react, the boy realized the Dude didn't read, so he had to show the flyer to me.

"What's this?"

"It's about the school's fall play."

"Oh, I see, for Thanksgiving?"

"Yeah, the first Thanksgiving. When the Indians shared their food with the Pilgrims."

"Oh sure, when everyone ate turkey and cranberry sauce."

"Yeah."

"You understand, Ricky, that the first Thanksgiving was a little more complicated than everyone remembers."

My son gazed at me with innocence written all over his face. "What do you mean?"

I hesitated. Who really cared if Ricky grew up thinking of the Pilgrims as benevolent partners to the Native Americans? Then again, maybe I should tell him that the visitors to the new world arrived to steal the Indians' land and kill them with smallpox. What would a good mother do?

When I got back to the apartment Manny and Colleen were there, saving me from the Native American genocide conversation.

"What's up?" I asked the two love birds, as I got Ricky and the Dude a snack and put them in front of the television.

"We've been comparing notes, "Manny said. "Did you ever talk with Señora Martinez?"

"No, I've been trying to catch her, but haven't been successful. Why?"

"Because she's the last guest on the list of folks we haven't spoken to about their knowledge of Salvatore."

"You think she whacked Salvatore? Like between making pottery at the senior center and having her hair done at the beauty college?"

"Don't be smart. We're just trying to make sure we've talked to everybody to cross reference their answers."

"Come on, Manny, she must be eighty years old. What could she have against Salvatore?"

Before answering, he glanced at Colleen and nodded, like he was telling her to continue. "It's bit of a stretch, Moli," she said, "but a few years ago the department worked on a case where a family grandmother ran this drug-running operation. A seventy-five-year-old grandmother. She had her kids and grandkids all over the L.A. basin dealing meth. Now, her boys supplied the muscle and handled distribution, but she provided the brains."

"Yeah," Manny said, "you should have seen her play the granny card in court. She had everyone crying about the injustice of arresting a grandmother. Even the judge fell for her routine and wanted to let her go. But after the prosecution played a tape of her giving the order to whack a competitor, she got twenty years."

"Okay, okay," I relented. "I'll have a talk with Señora Martinez."

"So, tell us, what did you think of Colombo?"

"He looks good in his underwear."

"Funny, Moli, but what about his background story."

"I don't know. He's a little seamy, but isn't that standard for most men in general?"

"Don't lump them all together," Colleen told me. "If you do, you'll always be disappointed."

"Well, like I said, if a man is going to lie about his wife, he'll lie about anything."

"Yeah," Manny agreed, "he's at the top of my list."

"I don't know, Manny," Colleen said.

"He told Gloria he had a wife and told Moli he didn't."

"I've been thinking about that, Manny," I said, working a scenario over in my head. "Maybe he told Gloria that because she was coming on to him, and he didn't want that complication."

"Who wouldn't want to get complicated with Gloria?"

"Manny!" Colleen yelped.

"I'm just saying."

"No, listen," I said. "Maybe he had an important job to do."

"Like what?" Manny asked.

"Think about this," I explained, "before Salvatore is almost killed, Colombo tells Gloria he's married, but after Salvatore is attacked, he tells me he's not married. Why?"

Manny said, "Because he thought Salvatore was out of the way and not a threat. So, he's free to continue like any good bachelor/husband and try to get into your pants."

"That works for me."

"Maybe," Colleen said.

"Then again," I said, "maybe that's giving him more credit than he deserves. The man could just be a sleazeball who looks good in his underwear."

Before we could carry the conversation further, the office buzzer sounded, and I hustled out front to see who had come in.

"Detective Winters," I greeted the man from the opposite side of the reception desk.

He said, "Doesn't anyone work at this place? You guys do your best to do the lazy Mexican imitation."

"I'm sorry, Detective," I said, ignoring his incessant racism, "I was in the back room, working. What can I do for you?"

"You can get Manny out here, and before you say he's not here, I heard the guy's voice a second ago, so don't deny it."

Realizing I had no choice, I called for Manny.

"What's up?" he said when he came out front.

"Listen, *amigo*," Winters said. "I've got some news, but I'm hesitant to fill you in since you're not a cop anymore."

"Come on, Frank. What have you got?"

"I've got some news on Tony Salvatore."

"He didn't die?" I asked.

"No, he's still hanging on. In fact, the doctors say he may come out of it."

"That's great," Manny said. "So, what more can you say about him?"

"A lot more, and that's what I mean about you playing cop. You don't have the resources or experience, so whatever you do, you only get half the facts, so you only do half a job."

"Oh yeah, so what fact am I missing?"

"Well, you were right about Salvatore not being connected to the Miami syndicate."

"We told you that."

"But, like I said, that's only half the story."

"Oh yeah, so, what's the other half?"

"Salvatore is a P.I. from New York."

"You don't say?"

"A Private Investigator?" I asked. "What was he

doing down here?"

"Well, he wasn't working on his tan."

"So, he was on a case? What case?"

"That, *amigo*, is, as they say, is the big question. But at the least, this takes the case out of the random assault sphere and lands the investigation right into the attempted murder queue."

After Winters broke the news on Salvatore and left, I said to Manny, "This deal with Salvatore being a P.I. helps us out."

"How, so?" he asked.

"Salvatore was hired," I said, "to investigate someone, but whoever he was trailing got wind of him and tried to kill him before he could find out anything."

"Or, before Salvatore could report his findings, whatever they were," Manny said, "to whomever hired him."

"At this point, anything he found out, or was on to, doesn't matter. Once we find out who whacked him, we'll find out why."

"You think?"

"Oh, yeah," I said. "Why else would someone stay here? A big shot New York P.I. could stay anywhere, but he chose the Cottages because his mark is here."

"So, now what?"

"Now we can concentrate on potential victims."

"What do you mean?" Colleen asked.

"Someone here has something to hide and is lying to us, and the secret is big enough to almost get someone killed."

And for my money, there was no bigger secret than lying about being married.

****

Between vacationers just ending a week in the sun, sand, and salt—or locals, finishing a week of hard work in the sun, sand, and salt, the bar packed them in on Friday nights. Usually, all four Lopez brothers worked the taco truck on the busy night. But on this Friday night, since Bob was locked up, they asked me to help out with the food.

In addition to attesting I was never a great housekeeper, my mother would also swear I couldn't boil water. Although an exaggeration, since I regularly make instant oatmeal for Ricky, she'd be right.

"So, what do you want me to do?" I asked Raul Lopez, the eldest of the four brothers, hoping he wasn't going to make me fix guacamole, or fry the cod for the fish tacos.

"All you have to do is stand at the window and take orders. Write them down on the order pad. We've got everything priced in whole dollars; five and ten dollars, so there is no change to make. If someone uses a credit card, we've got one of those charge things and you can run the card through it. You know how to run a credit card, right?"

"I'm a woman, aren't I?"

"Make sure the customer pays first," he said, ignoring, or not understanding gender humor. "After they pay, pass the order sheet to Ray, and we'll start to put the basket together. Once completed, we'll hand the basket to you, and you call out what the order is and pass the basket out through the window."

"So, I don't need to make anything?" I asked, a little disappointed.

"Just make change—fives and tens."

"Oh," Ray said, when he handed me a big plastic tip

jar with 'TIP' printed in black block letters on it, "put this on the counter."

"We get tips?"

"If you smile at the men."

Why does everyone assume if a woman smiles at a man, she will get a tip?

I don't know how many baskets of tacos they made, but they ran out of ingredients before eight and closed the truck down for the evening.

Lucky me.

With Gloria still in hiding, Manny and Chad worked the bar. So, when I left the taco truck, I ran back to the apartment to check on Ricky. After I opened the bedroom door, the Dude growled out at me, so I knew my boy was still safe. Just in case, and to settle my misgivings about leaving him alone, I confirmed the phone app for the security cameras still worked and I left the apartment.

Satisfied that armed men couldn't sneak up on my boy, and if they did, couldn't get pass the Dude, I jogged to the bar and made sure Manny and Chad didn't run out of supplies.

When the night finally ended, I collapsed on a bar stool. With my biggest day of the week set to start early the next morning, I wormed my way out of clean-up duties and snuck off.

"How about some breakfast?" Chad asked when he caught me at the laundry room door where I was going to throw my apron and a wad of bar towels in the dirty laundry hamper.

"Chad, I'm not hungry, and I've got a big day tomorrow, so I'm going to bed."

"Oh, you don't want to go out? What's wrong?"

"Nothing's wrong. Can't I be tired? I work hard in this place and have Ricky to worry about. I'm not on summer vacation down here. I've got responsibilities, and one of them is not worrying about making some guy's night."

Oh, wow, where did all that come from? I was tired. I'd been up for a good twenty-four hours, and my feet throbbed. Luckily, Chad just smiled, like he knew where I was coming from, which made me madder.

"Look, I'm sorry. You didn't deserve that, but I'm tired, so how about we do lunch tomorrow instead?"

"Lunch would be great. What time?"

"Geeze, Chad, I don't have a crystal ball. I can't tell what will pop up tomorrow, but let's shoot for one o'clock."

He smiled at me again and said he'd come over at one unless something *popped up.*

After he left, I opened the laundry door and tossed my apron and wet bar towels across the room in the general direction of the dirty laundry bin. The wet mess smacked Gloria in the back.

"Whoa, girl, watch where you're aiming."

"What are you doing in here?"

"Ah," she said, as she stooped to pick up my laundry, "hiding out?"

"Oh shit, I'm sorry. It's been a long day."

"Yeah, I heard."

"You heard all that?"

"Yeah," she said, as she gathered up my dirty stuff and tossed the wad into the bin, basketball style. "If it's any consolation, he's a bit assertive. You know, the rich kid who always gets his way. If he hasn't laid you by now, he'll think he's lost his touch."

"Did you?"

"Me? No way. I've had young and anxious, but young and anxious never lasts long, so what's the point?"

"I haven't had anything in a while. Young and anxious might be all I can get."

"Don't say that. You're a pretty girl, and any guy would be happy to be in a relationship with you. But you'll have to get out of that housekeeper uniform and get out more. It's like you use the way you dress as a shield. Besides, he asks about you all the time."

"What?"

"Before his shift starts, he comes in here and asks me all about you and what you like and what you do. He's all about you and who you are."

For some reason instead of being creeped out by this, I found myself pleased.

"Don't overthink it," Gloria said. "You're better off keeping things light with him. He's like a kid at a beach summer camp. He gets room and board with his grandmother, hangs out at the bar and makes pocket change, and picks up broads. Next spring, he'll be gone and out of your hair."

He was a big kid, and even though you could say the same about me, I did have responsibilities.

I was beginning to like the guy, so I needed to check with Manny on Chad's story. If he told Manny he stayed in his grandmother's house like he told Gloria and told me he stayed at his mother and father's retirement home, then depending on how he answered, we might have another potential suspect on our hands.

That's just great!

Chapter Fifteen

Saturday

Thank God, Ricky doesn't have school on weekends. Worrying about him on a Saturday morning would be the final peg in my coffin. I can barely get him a bowl of cereal before I have to get busy.

Once I settled the boys down in front of the kids channel on TV, I rushed to put out the free breakfast. We build the cost of the breakfasts into a guest's daily charges, so the meal really isn't free. Luckily, most guests who check out on Saturday morning don't have time to sit down and eat a lot. More than likely, they get a large coffee and a donut and make a run for the road home before the traffic starts to back up on Interstate 95.

Although Manny is supposed to help with the breakfast set up, he has a full schedule with his patrols around the Cove and the Oaks. Those responsibilities, and the newer interest in hanging out at the Cove General Store, have cut back on the time he devotes to the motel. I had to have a long talk with him about my workload.

Fortunately, most guests used the motel's app to make final payments and check out, but they still have to drop their keys off at the desk. Yes, we still did things the old-fashioned way and didn't employ a card system with magnetic strips. Manny says he likes the feel of metal. Something traditional about a metal key. He says the guests like it too. He says they feel like they are staying in a real home, instead of a temporary one. Something he calculated would make for repeat business. We've had a lot of repeaters in my two years of employment, so who am I to contradict tradition. Of course, for Manny, there was always the cost of installing a card swipe system to consider, but he wouldn't admit that.

Manny seems a bit of a bumble dumb on the outside, but his mind works a mile a minute, and if he can figure a way to make or save a nickel, he will.

Only three guests required my assistance to check out and pay. By ten-thirty, all guests, except the six permanent ones, had checked out. I had a moment to check on Ricky and the Dude before I started my cleaning routine.

The yellow crime scene tape that still draped cottage fourteen made the unit loom a bit forlorn, but since I couldn't get in, I worked through the others faster. I finished well before one o'clock and lunch with Chad. Even though I treated him poorly the night before, I hoped he still wanted to meet.

Chad came, and I talked him into eating with me, Ricky, and the Dude. I mean, he said he wanted to meet my boy, and if you meet him you have to meet the Dude.

Of course, when I said I talked him into lunch with us, what I meant was, I talked him into running over to the condo construction site where the taco lunch truck parked. The truck fed over a hundred Latino men who worked there every day, weekends included. I wished the general American citizen would recognize where the construction industry would be without the Latino men who work construction. I am especially in wonder of the people who complain about lax immigration but live in homes and work in buildings built by those same immigrants, and eat food produced by American food service companies who employ Latinos in their low wage production jobs.

The challenge with the Dude is he could eat a couple of dozen tacos all by himself, so for him, I empty the fillings from a half dozen steak tacos in a bowl and mix with several cups of his dry dog food meal. He likes the concoction, especially when I mix in the hot salsa we get from the food truck. He likes the red chili kind—the one that burns the roof of your mouth off.

When Chad got back, the aroma of grilled *carne asada* tacos filled the room and temporarily distracted the Dude so he didn't react to a stranger in the room. However, when Ricky raced off in his direction, things changed quickly and he squinted at the man, and it grew tense in the space. At the sight of a stranger, the hackles raised on the dog's shoulders and along the top of his back. When his ears flattened down, his eyes hardened, and his tail shot high, we were in trouble. When the dog bared his teeth and growled, I figured I had about two seconds to get the guy out of there.

Ricky sensed the change in the air and spun to the dog and hugged him but showing him love only temporarily eased the pressure building in the room. When the Dude took a step toward Chad, he had to stop because Ricky still held on to his neck. The brief pause in the action gave me a couple of seconds to pull the guy out of the room and into the outer office area.

"Wow," I said, as I slammed the door between rooms, "sorry about that. The Dude's a little protective of Ricky."

"I can see that."

"Yeah, they are kind of like brothers, only closer, and they don't pick on each other. It's been good for Ricky."

"I bet he doesn't have many friends over."

"No, we haven't worked up to play dates."

"I'd be careful."

I smiled at him and said, "Let me go and fix a plate of tacos for Ricky and the Dude and I'll come back with a plate for us."

"The dog likes tacos?"

"Yeah, especially with hot sauce."

"Figures."

We ended up at the window table with the view of the Gulf. I ate four tacos, but Chad had lost his appetite.

****

We had just finished our lunch when the first guests of the week showed up. I saw them park their big SUV at the temporary check-in and check-out zone and a large man worked his way out of the driver seat and slowly lumbered to the door.

"Howdy," he bellowed out like we were standing on the other side of a football field and not ten feet away. I figured he was hyped on coffee, an attempt to keep awake on the long drive down the interstate from someplace up north.

In a game I play with myself, I guessed where they were coming from. By his appearance and his car, I guessed Pennsylvania.

"I'm sorry, Mr. ..."

"Shields, John Shields. From Pittsburg. We've got a reservation."

"Yes, sir, Mr. Shields," I said. "We were expecting

you, but as we noted on your reservation confirmation, check-in isn't until four o'clock."

"Oh, yeah, but we've been on the road since yesterday, and we hoped to check in early. I'm all worn out from the drive."

"Well, Mr. Shields, let me see if your bungalow is clean. You wouldn't want to rush in before housekeeping is finished since someone just left this morning."

"Oh, you bet. We want a clean place."

After I rolled my eyes at Chad, I stepped over to the reception desk and found their reservation on the computer system. I stared at the reservation line for a long time, and wondered how in the world I forgot we couldn't use bungalow fourteen. I stared at the screen for so long, Mr. Shields coughed.

"Sorry, Mr. Shields, your cottage hasn't been cleaned. If you don't mind waiting, housekeeping shouldn't be too much longer. Why don't you go out to the bar. Chad here can show you the way. There's a nice lady out there and I'm sure she could fix you up with a tall and cold drink and a snack."

"Chad?"

"Yes, sir, Mr. Shields. You can see the Gulf from the bar. Why don't you and Mrs. Shields come on out, and we'll fix you up with whatever you need. I'm sure there's a college game on the television."

Mr. Shields stood there a moment. I could see his eyes narrow, and his lips puckered like he was struggling what to say next. I was beginning to think he didn't understand what I offered.

"It's not Mrs. Shields with me," he said. "It's an associate."

Chad picked up on the meaning quickly and

countered, "Well, you and your associate can take the path around the side, right out to the bar, and pick out a private spot. I'll meet you out there."

The man was hesitant, but he finally left. I surmised he was going to fetch his associate.

"What's wrong with their bungalow?" Chad asked. "I thought you cleaned them all already."

"I overbooked."

"How?"

"The cops still have bungalow fourteen locked up, and guess who is supposed to spend the week in bungalow fourteen?"

"Mr. Shields and associate?"

"That's right. So, you need to go out there and keep them busy until I can figure out something."

When Chad left, I put my head down in my arms. Overbooking or mistakes happened but I usually had time to notify people about the problem and switch them someplace else before they arrive on our doorstep. In this case, I was so involved in other things, I didn't keep track of the reservations, and with all the potential guests already on the road here, it would be hard to contact everyone. Someone would arrive unnotified and would stand across the counter from me, disappointed to find out they didn't have a room. But who? More than likely the last party to arrive, and suddenly, I wished we had a wider counter.

I didn't have to wait long. Between four and four-thirty, nine guests arrived, and I booked them in as quickly as possible. With a full house, I hoped the last family liked camping.

At five o'clock sharp, I got a ding on my phone. Our reservation app included a red flag function if someone makes, alters, or cancels a reservation. The motel gods were with me when a guest with a reservation texted to cancel. Normally, I'd be mad but not this time.

It took another hour to get everyone that checked in, settled in. A couple of guests requested more towels in their cottage, and as a precaution, I reminded them about their agreement to not take the bungalow bath towels to the beach. I told them if they didn't have beach towels, they could rent supplies at the beach shack.

The couple in cottage seven had trouble with the air conditioning, but I showed them how to adjust it, and the family in cottage nine wanted directions to the pool. I reminded them of the pool arrangement we had with the campground and showed them where the golf carts were. After I made sure the dad could drive the cart, I gave him a key and they happily drove over to the pool. I wasn't sure if they were happy to be going to the pool or happy to be driving around in the golf cart.

When done, I circled around to the bar to see Chad and found him deep in prep for the big Saturday crowd starting to filter in for the evening. "Did you get Mr. Shields and his associate a place to stay?"

"Yes, we had a cancelation, so he and his *associate* are settled in cozy like." Seeing he was busy, I asked, "Are you ready for tonight?"

"Getting there. Are you going to help out?"

"Well, I've got Barbara back here with you at six, but if you think you're going to need me, I'll come back about seven. The bar doesn't get busy until then and I have to get Ricky and the Dude settled for the night. Can you manage until then? I'm not sure what Manny has planned, but I imagine he'll be by as well."

"I would hope so. It's his place, isn't it?"

That last comment was open to debate, but I waved at Chad and made my escape while I could.

****

Only a solitary insect reflecting yellow bulb cast a dim light in the corridor between the apartment and the storeroom and laundry room. Since it was off limits to customers, we didn't need more. I paused at the laundry room door, thinking maybe I'd confirm that Gloria was there, and if the shack crew's inquiries had found out anything, like a possible killer. But I figured if they had discovered anything, I would have heard by then.

I had just stepped past the door of her hideout when someone opened the adjacent storeroom door, grabbed hold of my arm, and yanked me into the dark space.

I found myself face down on the concrete floor. Before I hit the ground, I managed to put my arm in front of me, shielding my face from immediate damage. I could tell by the weight on top of me that my assailant was a man. I hadn't forgotten the last time I had been under as much weight, especially face down, and I could still tell the difference between the weight of a man and a woman.

"Uh," I said, trying to squirm my head around to see who my new friend was, "you're on top of me."

No response. Maybe he enjoyed the position on top of me.

Even in the dark, I could see the guy wore a ski mask. The ones with eye holes but I had to question the guy's choice considering the sweltering Florida heat.

"Now, little *señorita*," the man said, "you need to stop your little investigation.

"But everyone is having so much fun."

The guy didn't appreciate my humor because he put

his hand on the back of my head and shoved. Luckily, my arm provided a cushion, or the guy would have ground my face into burger.

Now, I know what you're thinking. What happened to all my police training, but I had already dropped out of the academy before I got into the hand-to-hand fight training, and the confined space limited my options, and he did surprise me. I mean, who knew I'd be accosted in the passage between the apartment and the laundry room?

Trying something to get away, I started kicking. I was about to start shouting when the door to the walk-in refrigerator opened. Barbara Wallace stepped out with her arms full of limes, the limes we cut into wedges and use to juice the glass rims of the margarita glasses we dip in coarse salt.

Startled, she dropped the limes, and they rolled everywhere. Before Barabara could even think to scream, my man jumped to his feet, slipped on a lime and fell, but got to his feet and disappeared through the outer door.

"Uh, tell me I interrupted a sex thing."

"Ah, no," I said, as I sat up and checked myself for damage, "not even rough sex."

"What was it?"

"That was an assault," I said, standing up, and to make her feel good I added, "you probably saved my life."

"Great, I just love to work on Saturday nights. Anything can happen."

"Don't worry. I'm okay."

"Are you sure?" she asked, picking up limes. "That guy could have hurt you. What happened?"

"I don't know, maybe he doesn't like our accommodations."

"Stop kidding. Does this have anything to do with what happened in cottage fourteen?"

"I wouldn't be surprised, but if so, remember, don't talk to anyone about this incident. Everything on this case is confidential, right?"

"Shouldn't we tell Manny? He's like security around here."

"Let me tell Manny. You just go out to the bar and start serving customers."

When I got back to the apartment, I found Manny and Colleen huddled at the kitchen island. They had some legal pads out and were making notes. "What's up?" Manny said when I stumbled into the room.

"Ah, I think we're close to something on this case."

"How do you know?" Colleen asked.

"Because some guy just jumped me out back and told me to stop our investigation."

With that, they both got up and rushed to my side, and escorted me to a stool.

"I'm fine," I told them and explained what happened and how Barbara saved me.

"Well," Manny summarized for everyone, "you're right. We must be getting close to something, close enough to spark some real interest from the guilty party."

"Yep," I agreed, "someone is getting nervous." I just wondered who.

****

Not feeling up to a long night shift in the bar, I begged out of the duty and settled on the sofa with the Dude and Ricky. To relax, we watched The Call of the Wild movie, featuring a hero big dog in the snow of the

Northwest. To cover for me, Manny and Colleen took my job in the bar.

At the end of the movie, I sent Ricky to bed and took the Dude out for his night-time stump out on the shore. The sound from the bar area filled the night air, so we wandered south, away from the cottage complex. We skirted the beach in front of the campground and had just stopped at the edge of the tide line when two guys stumbled out of the Cove and lurched our way, obviously drunk. They worked their way toward me, giggling like a pair of teenagers, but before they could say anything, the Dude stepped in front of me and let out a loud growl.

"Holy cow," one of the guys said, and they stumbled away fast.

I bent down and gave the Dude a thank you hug, and he slobbered my face. We started back to the complex, the dog pulling me quickly along. Even a dog knows you shouldn't be out in dark places.

Chapter Sixteen

Sunday

"I'm glad you're here," Colleen said the next morning when she came in. She was dressed in a light blue one-piece dress, cinched at the waist, and fresh as a daisy for a Sunday morning. "I've been going over our notes on the case."

"Which case?" I noticed her hair wasn't purple anymore, but now a shade of pink.

"Gloria's case."

"You mean Doc Murphy and the soccer player case? What about it?"

"Well, Gloria said Murphy was from Kansas, right?"

"I'm not sure about Kansas, but somewhere in the Midwest."

"Well, I did a search online last night, but I didn't dig up a single reference to a Doctor William R. Murphy and any impropriety. But guess what I did find?"

"What?

"I found an old reference for an adjunct professor of health with the University of Kansas."

"So?"

"So, there's nothing else. No Facebook, no Instagram, no Twitter, no nothing."

"So what? I'm sure there's nothing on Manny out

there either."

"That's where you'd be wrong. The year before he left the force, Manny investigated a hit-and-run. The runner, in this case an old Hollywood film star, claimed innocence and when the police wouldn't listen to her, she proceeded straight to the mayor who quickly shut down the investigation and put an eyes-only tag on the case files. But even with all the effort, cyberspace ran with the banner headline, and the story hung around for months with Manny's face all over social media platforms. In fact, if you go online now and cross-reference the star's name with Manny's, the case will come up. It's actually spawned several conspiracy theories."

"What happened to the star?"

"She lucked out when the person she hit recovered. They eventually settled out of court. But even though the incident happened years ago, the whole story is still out there, in a variety of renditions."

"What does that have to do with our Salvatore case."

"The Doc's case should have been just as big, since it happened right on the heels of the scandal with the U.S.A. women gymnasts and the team doctor. That alone would have started comparisons and spawned multiple conspiracy theories, but I didn't read anything about the episode."

"Because?"

"Because the university squashed the story. They obviously didn't want a whisper to get out. That's why they made the deal with the soccer player and her family."

"But why?"

"I don't have all the answers, but we'll have a better handle on this if we can find out what Doc Murphy has written."

"What's your guess?"

"Moli, as cops we shouldn't guess on cases. Someone's life may be at stake."

"Then, what does your intuition say about this?"

"My intuition says the university covered this up and hustled the good doctor out of there, so the story wouldn't come out."

"And now?"

"I think the Doc told them about the book and threatened them."

"Like blackmail?"

"Yeah, and I think they got nervous. So nervous they hired a private investigator to track him down and to see what's in his book. I figure Salvatore is the one the university hired, and he was in the process of discovery when the Doc caught on to him. I figure he whacked Salvatore to keep him quiet while he finished his book."

"I don't know, Colleen. What did Manny say?"

"I talked to him last night, but he says I'm off base."

"Maybe he's right."

"That man never could add two and two."

"Speaking of adding things up, did Manny tell you about the motel financial package he put together when he bought this place?"

"No, what about it?"

I told her what Gloria had explained to me.

"That bad? He's never said a word to me."

"I think he wants to work the problem himself, which means solving this case."

"Then you've got work to do."

"Me? How?"

"Don't you clean the long-term cottages once a

week?"

"Once a week."

"What day?"

"Mostly on the weekend, if I can find the time."

"And what's today?"

"Sunday."

"So, go clean Doc's cottage today, and while you're there, sneak a peek at his manuscript."

"I can't do that. That's like his personal stuff."

"Moli, I know you like the Doc and all but finding out what's in the manuscript could clear him."

"No, I meant Doc Murphy will be in all day. How can I read his manuscript if he's there?"

"Won't he be in church? Irish name like that, I figure he's a churchgoer. At least that's what Manny says. He says the guys goes to Our Lady of Perpetual Help at least three out of four Sundays."

"I don't know. I'd feel kind of creepy sneaking around the guy's place. I don't know if I can do that."

"What's to lose? I figure if he's guilty, he'll be in church seeking forgiveness. If he's not, he'll be there giving thanks. Either way, you should have an hour to read that manuscript. If we're going to solve this case we need to look into every lead, no matter how creepy it gets."

"No, I won't have an hour. I take a good half hour to clean a cottage, sometimes longer."

"Then clean fast. Manny might be running out of time."

****

I changed into my uniform and retrieved my housekeeping cart from the laundry room. Gloria sat under her sunlamp, in her bikini, reading her accounting book. She'd fixed herself a tall fruit smoothie. I assumed she had added a hefty amount of tequila because she gave me a dopey smile when I came in and waved when I left.

I didn't have to worry about reading time with Doc Murphy's manuscript, since I found less than the usual trash and clutter in his cottage. Over the year I found him to be a bit of a neat freak, so he kept the unit clean and organized, except for the three-week span when Notre Dame lost three football games in a row.

I didn't want him to find me in his room without a purpose other than spying, so I opened the windows and the door to air out the place and started cleaning. I surprised myself with this whole detective thing. Maybe I did have a head for this investigative stuff.

I finished cleaning in record time and at the door, I glanced along the walkway to see if anyone was coming. With the coast clear, I sat down at the Doc's desk where I found several stacks of printed pages. The title page of one of the stacks read, *"The Secrets of Red Valley"*. Another title read, *"The Western Trail"*. The third stack read, *"University",* so I pulled that one to me and started reading.

As far as I could tell, the rough pages read as an expose, but not yet in book form, more just a series of narrative notes. He was developing a story that implicated the university's chancellor and the family of the player who accused him of inappropriate behavior, which led to his early retirement. I also read several implied references to collusion and a cover-up of something big, but the unfinished manuscript didn't provide any evidence or corroboration.

I couldn't tell what the Doc had in mind since he hadn't finished the thing. He might still be gathering information. He did spend a lot of time writing and had taken several trips out of town. A couple of times, he had been gone for a week or more because when I returned for my weekly cleaning, I could tell he hadn't been in the cottage.

After a few minutes of reading, I got a headache thinking about possible motives leading to Salvatore's near-death experience. I was so confused, the theory that I had a head for this kind of thing evaporated like water on hot sand. So, even though I didn't have any answers, I decided to leave. Before going, I took out my phone and took a few photos of the manuscript, then I poked through Doc's desk drawers. I found random correspondence, invoices and receipts, and bank statements, all arranged by date and held together by paperclips. I didn't have time to examine each item, so I flipped through the pages and snapped off photos of random pages, not knowing the important from the not important.

After the last page, I put everything back and got up from the desk. I hustled to the back to retrieve my housekeeper cart, and when I came out to the front room, Doc Murphy stood in the doorway.

"Moli," he said, "cleaning on a Sunday? The Lord's day of rest?"

I had no idea how long he'd had been standing there. He could have just arrived, or he could have come while I was snooping through his stuff, and I hadn't noticed him. "I've been so busy I haven't had time to keep up, but I'm done now, so I'll be on my way."

"What's the hurry, ?" he said, not moving from the doorway. "Why don't you stay and visit? We could talk about my book. I need to bounce a few ideas around."

I wasn't interested in bouncing anything around with the man. "Sorry, I've got cleaning to do, so I better get going."

There was a long pause, as he stood in the doorway. Until then, I never realized how big the Doc was, both tall and wide. From my perspective he filled out the doorway. Several scenarios flashed through my head. One was to take the housekeeping cart and ram the man and hustle out of there. Of course, there was no guarantee I had enough strength to actually force him out of the way, but I was willing to give it a shot if he didn't move.

Fortunately, he smiled at me and stepping aside said, "Another time, then, .."

I hurriedly pushed the cart out the door and had just swung down the path when he called to me. "Oh, Moli?"

I held my breath. Caught red-handed, and visions of me being carted off in handcuffs by Detective Winters, and Ricky being hauled off to foster care flashed through my mind. I mean, what kind of mother was I?

"Aren't you forgetting something?"

I tried to appear perplexed, "What?"

"You haven't closed the windows."

****

I closed the windows in the cottage, grabbed the housekeeping cart, and legged it out of there, my heart racing in my chest.

Instead of clearing up matters, the little escapade only confused me more. I hoped Manny and Colleen were better detectives than I was showing. At least for Gloria's sake.

Since I had the cart out and cleaning to catch up with, I kept working. The next cottage in line belonged to Dante Colombo, but I didn't have the energy to fence with the guy if I happened to find him there. I made a mental note to come back and clean his place during the workday when he'd be gone.

At the South wing, I stopped at Señora Martinez's cottage. I still hadn't seen the lady in over a week. She'd even missed breakfast. With all the hectic activity around the complex, I could have missed her, but I started cleaning her cottage anyway.

Señora Martinez kept her cottage dark and cool. In fact, it is too cool. Manny had come out several times to fix her frozen air conditioning system. Since she insisted on setting the unit at fifty degrees in the Florida heat, her unit had broken down several times over the summer.

Señora Matinez told me she joined the local church when she first arrived, but she didn't like the priest, so she stopped going. Instead, she goes to a prayer group that meets at the senior center every Sunday morning, and after, they eat lunch together at a local restaurant.

The local senior center offers a variety of activities to the retired citizens of the community, including a book club, handicrafts, and game nights. They even offer free transportation. Unfortunately, being located on a beachfront property, the church van doesn't come down this way. I figured the church isn't giving free rides to anyone who can afford to live at the beach.

So short-sighted.

I found Señora Martinez's cottage in neat order, although her trash can was stuffed with takeout bags from the Towne Drug Store. The older lady must have been ordering breakfast biscuits from their grill by delivery in recent mornings, so I understood why I hadn't seen her at our free donut breakfasts.

I cleaned the cottage bathroom and kitchen and

remade the bed with clean linen. I dusted off the shelves, which held several pieces of pottery that I assumed Señora Martinez had made in seniors craft class. I swept out the floor of the whole cottage including clay dust. Apparently, Mrs. Martinez had been working on a little clay project, and the remnants from her pottery efforts had gathered under the kitchen island. Thankfully we didn't have a kiln in the complex, and to fire her clay, she had to take her work back to the senior center.

I mopped out the cottage from front to back and I finished with Señora Martinez's cottage. When I stepped outside, I saw that the Professor had arrived.

"Have you been to church, Mr. Daly?"

"No, lass. I'm afraid the church and I don't completely agree on a number of matters. And you?"

"No, the church and I have had a bit of a falling out."

"Yes, but you are young, my dear, and there are many paths to heaven."

"I hope so. Well, I'd like to finish with my housekeeping, can I clean your cottage today?"

"Not today, I'm in the middle of writing. Early next week would be better."

"Okay, but you'll have to sleep on week-old linen until then."

"Do not worry, I hardly sleep most nights."

****

When I got back to the apartment, Manny and Ricky were watching football. "Where's the Dude?" I asked.

"Colleen took him for a stroll."

"Colleen? Do you think that's a good idea?"

"What's not good about it? She loves dogs. Did I ever tell you about…"

Manny never got a chance to finish his story because

of Colleen's scream. We couldn't understand her shout, but I could tell she didn't yell out in happiness. When the three of us got outside, Colleen was running down the beach road, waving in the air, but no Dude in sight.

"Get in the golf cart!" Manny yelled at me and Ricky. We had barely sat down when Manny floored the pedal, and the electric golf cart took off. Manny took a shortcut around the front of the cottages and drove through the Oaks complex, zig zagging around garden homes, at an intercept angle to the Dude and Colleen, before they got too far.

The Oaks had a wide shoreside wooden boardwalk the retirement community members exercised on regularly. The evening made for a great after-dinner stroll, to aid old people digestion, but the morning hours were the busiest as members paced from one end to the other to fight the age thing, and to beat the heat.

As expected at midday, only a few couples were on the boardwalk, but Colleen and the Dude chased a man running for his life. The man barely stayed a step ahead of the big dog. In the pursuit, the dog ran dangerously close to an older couple dressed in matching white Bermuda shorts and pale blue polos. Fifty feet beyond that encounter, he dodged a cigar smoking man with a cane and nearly wrecked a lady in a wheelchair.

Born to sprint, the Dude had some endurance when the sun wasn't too hot, and for a moderate distance, he could maintain a vigorous pace. By my calculation, the man out front had only seconds before the brute caught him and bit into his behind. Also, by my calculation, Colleen stood no chance of catching either of them, so when Manny drove on the boardwalk, he slowed down just enough to allow her to jump in the rear-facing seat.

Once aboard, Manny sped off again and the pursuit continued.

Manny flew by another couple with canes. As he drove by them, they both waved angrily at us.

"What happened?" I yelled back to Colleen as we drove, trying to close the gap with the underpowered golf cart, especially with her weight added to the equation.

"The Dude saw a guy creeping around the end of the complex and ran toward him. I tried to hold him back, but he tugged the leash out of my hand."

I had to admire the man trying to keep some distance from the jaws of death, but I could see he only had a matter of seconds until the dog caught him,

When the man got to the end of the boardwalk, he surprised me. Instead of swinging off in a different direction, or maybe confronting the Dude, he dove off the wooden ramp without hesitation, cleared the jetty, and went into the small cove separating the Oaks from the next-door community.

"I was afraid of that," Manny said when we caught up. The Dude was prowling along the jetty, growling, so Manny grabbed the dog's leash before he jumped in to follow the guy.

"He doesn't like to swim," Manny said, "that's why he didn't jump right in."

"Why?"

"I don't know. I think he's so heavy, he might be afraid of sinking."

"Not the Dude?" I said, giving the dog a back rub for the effort.

As we stood there watching, the guy used big powerful strokes against the incoming tide and quickly crossed the cove. Once on the breakwater he climbed up onto the other side. On dry ground, the guy waved to us, then took off at another dead run.

"Let's drive around and catch him," I said, mad that the guy escaped.

"No, my jurisdiction ends at the cove. Even if we caught the guy, I couldn't provide cause for stopping him. Did you get a good look at the guy?" Manny asked Colleen.

"No, just his backside."

"Well, he's going to get away, but the Dude sure gave him a scare, didn't he."

With the chase over, we piled on the golf cart and drove back to the motel complex. As we made our way, the golf cart steadily lost power and finally died a couple of hundred yards short of the cottages, its electric batteries drained. We had to traipse the rest of the way on foot, feeling foolish.

****

After our midday adventure, Ricky and the Dude settled in for an afternoon of football. Though only five, Ricky liked to watch the games. I think all the action kept him interested and the bright green field and all the uniform colors added to the effect. Now, why Manny could sit mesmerized with the action on the eighty-four-inch screen was a puzzle.

"So," Colleen asked me when we sat down at the island with cold drinks, directly under the air conditioning vent blowing cool air on us, "what did you think about Doc Murphy's manuscript?"

"As far as I could tell, it's an expose, but it's not anywhere near finished. Just a bunch of notes and a start on a narrative. I'd say the first thirty pages of a first draft. There's some interesting stuff in there but hard to see the final product."

"Do you think it's bad enough to hire a private investigator to snoop into, like I said?" Colleen asked.

"Bad enough for someone to pay to keep the story quiet?" Manny asked.

I let a minute go by while I gathered my thoughts. I was the amateur in our little unit. I mean Colleen had twenty-five years in the LAPD and Manny had more years on the streets than I had on the earth. When taken together, what could I come up with that they hadn't already considered.

"Well," Manny said, "do you think the Doc is involved?"

"Colleen, I think you might be on to something.

"I figured it!"

"Yeah, if Salvatore reviewed the Doc's manuscript, like I did, he might have decided the university has nothing to worry about. I mean, the man's been working on that thing for a while and doesn't have much to show for the effort. Maybe Salvatore decided the expose is nothing and planned to tell the university to ignore the threats."

"Then," Colleen said, "the Doc won't get the big payday he wants."

"That's right. No book, no blackmail, no money."

"So," Manny concluded for us, "the Doc whacks Salvatore. That way the PI won't report back to the university. With the school in the dark, they might think they need to keep the man quiet, so they would agree to pay him."

"Works for me," Aunt Colleen said. "Money is always a good motive."

"Me, too," I said. "Now, I only have one question,

how do we prove it?"

****

After Colleen hiked to the campground where she had the afternoon shift in the camp store, I ran to the office to catch up on new reservations.

As I feared, the app had booked cottage fourteen for the rest of the season. Since I had no idea how long the cottage would be unavailable, I had hesitated to block the cottage out of the system. Now, I'd have to send an email to everyone with a reservation for cottage fourteen. I couldn't complain though, since my hesitancy caused the overbooking. Luckily, there were other cottages still available for most weeks, and once I corrected the availability mistake, the system would go back and send a text to the guests informing them of the change. For my own piece of mind, the system didn't say anything about how my careless administration of the reservation system caused the problem in the first place. Which was a good thing.

I had just reset the system when Chad strutted into the reception area.

He wore swim trunks, flip flops, and a beach towel draped around his neck.

Nothing else.

I had often wondered about the double standard for men and women. When a man parades around near naked, we are supposed to think nothing of it. But if a women dresses skimpily, people consider it risqué. What is that all about?

After I took a moment to gawk at him, I said, "Don't you have anything else to do besides hang around here?"

"What? I like the scenery here."

"Dude," I said, "you need to get a life."

"Come on, let's go to the beach. I think there are some actual waves out there."

"The weather radar noted a hurricane off Yucatan. When theGulf gets tossed around by a system, it can stir up a few swells, but they don't last long."

"Well, let's go down there before they disappear."

"I don't do the beach."

"Lady, you literally live on the beach."

"I know, weird, right?"

"What's wrong with the beach?"

"Let's see, in no particular order, it's hot, it's sandy, and it's salty. I'm more of a lake person, or maybe a river. Somewhere you can relax without horse flies trying to eat you."

"So, it's not the water? Just where the water is located?"

"Now you got it. Back in L.A. I never visited the beach."

"Aren't all you California girls, surfer girls?"

"You listened to the Beach Boys too much. It's not all sun, sand, and salt in L.A."

"Come on," he said. "It will be fun, and we can take Ricky with us."

"Ricky?"

"Yeah, Ricky, the little five-year-old hobbit who lives here, protected by a dragon called the Dude."

"Oh yeah? Well, Ricky loves the beach."

"He does?"

"Yeah, go figure."

"He's not afraid of the water?"

"Oh, no, he's been swimming since he before he could walk. We lived in a big apartment complex with several pools when we had him, and they arranged for free swimming lessons for toddlers. I think their liability insurance required the precaution. Anyway, he swims like a fish, all arms and legs. You should see him."

"Then let's go."

Now, don't think that Chad standing there, half-naked with muscles bulging everywhere, influenced my decision. Not at all. I mean, Ricky hadn't been out of the apartment all weekend. Not counting the time when we chased the bad guy down the boardwalk, which you couldn't call exercise since the kid never left the golf cart.

"Okay, I'll see if Manny will watch the Dude."

"Why?"

"The dog gets anxious when Ricky is out of sight."

"Okay, good idea, go and check, but I'm staying out here."

Before I left the desk, the door opened, and a man stepped into the lobby.

"Can I help you sir?" I greeted the man, knowing what he probably wanted. Although not tall, the man's stature filled the room, and even Chad paled a bit in the man's presence.

"Yes, young lady," the man responded in a neutral accent," My name is Johnson, and I need a room for a day or two. Do you have a cottage available?"

"I'm sorry, sir," I apologized, realizing I had neglected another duty when I didn't switch on the *No Vacancy* sign. "But we are all booked."

"Oh, I didn't see the sign lit up."

"Yes, sorry, I haven't had the chance. I just now checked our system and discovered we were booked solid."

"I see."

"But we have an agreement with the campground next door, The Pirate Cove RV Campground. They have a few cottages similar to ours, and we can recommend them and guarantee the same rate as we have here. Just tell them Moli Soto sent you."

"You say, right next door? Near the beach?"

"Yes, sir," I said, though I wondered at his excitement of the proximity of the campground to the beach. Dressed in a long-sleeved white shirt, black pants, and shiny black wing tips, he wasn't exactly channeling a surfer dude that liked sun, sand, and salt.

****

After I checked with Manny, I got Ricky into a pair of swim trunks, and we spent the rest of the hot, sandy, and salty afternoon at the beach. To combat the sun, I sent Chad to the beach supply shack for a tube of sunscreen so I could lather up my boy. During the afternoon I sent him back several times for, in order of need, a Margarita with no salt, a root beer, an umbrella, a big bag of Doritos, another root beer, a beach ball, another Margarita with no salt, and later, when we were about to leave, another Margarita.

When we were packing and cleaning up our mess, I noticed Mr. Johnson watching us from the beach in front of the Cove. The campground put out a line of picnic tables and umbrellas for their guests, and Johnson had taken up residence in the shade of the one closest to the motel complex. He was still dressed in the long pants and shirt he wore when I talked to him in the lobby. For someone spending a day or two at the beach, he hadn't dressed for the sun, sand, and salt.

Chapter Seventeen

Monday

I had a feeling Detective Winters would make an appearance Monday morning, and he did not disappoint. It's not always great to have any type of feelings about Frank Winters, but sometimes feelings come in handy.

The evening before, after we spent our long afternoon in the sun, sand, and salt, we ordered pizza and watched football. Actually, Manny, the Dude, and Ricky watched football. Chad and I sat out in the breakfast room and ate and debated the benefits of delaying major life decisions until you are old enough to make logical choices. We also discussed at what age that might actually happen.

Our conversation didn't result in any breakthroughs in the art of decision-making, but the goodnight kiss made the conversation worthwhile.

"Do you need another coffee?" I asked the detective the next morning as he stood there, cup of coffee in one hand and a cinnamon roll in the other. Showing up alone, he appeared out of his element without a uniform or two for company.

Our guests filled every seat in the breakfast room, so he had to stand. We actually had the capacity to seat sixty-four. With sixteen cottages we have sixteen beds and sixteen-fold outs for a capacity of sixty-four guests.

With eight tables and thirty-two chairs, we can seat everyone in two stages. Even when we have a single in a cottage, we usually balance out when we'd get a couple with an extra kid or the odd mother-in-law tagging along, making an uneven five at a table. I never ask about the sleeping arrangements in those cases.

"No, I'm good," he mumbled. "These are the best cinnamon rolls."

"Yeah, Manny gets them from Geno's Bakery. You should go by there."

"Where is our Manny boy?"

"Over in the campground, doing his morning check."

"They have a lot of crime over in the Cove?"

"I wouldn't say that, why?"

"He spends a lot of time at that place."

"Maybe that's why there's not a lot of crime over there."

"Moli, I know what Manny is doing."

"What?" I asked him, afraid he'd discovered Colleen.

"He's playing cop again."

"Don't they say, *once a cop, always a cop.*"

"No one says that. Once a cop retires, they usually never pick up a gun again. Manny is the only retired cop I know who can't leave the job behind. Why did he retire if he loves working so much? Why doesn't he take up golf or something?"

"Geez, Frank, what's up with you?"

Winters stood there, studying me. Then, he tilted his cup up and finished the last of his coffee and stared at me some more. I briefly wondered if I was supposed to offer him another cup.

"Okay, Moli, since Manny's not here, I'm going to tell you, again. You and your uncle have got to stop playing cop. The mayor's mother lives over in the Oaks, and she witnessed the little escapade on the boardwalk yesterday. She asked the mayor, her son, all about it. The mayor didn't say anything because that was the first time he had heard about it. He hadn't heard anything because the chief hadn't told him anything, and the chief hadn't told him anything because I didn't tell him anything because you two didn't report it!"

"There was nothing to report."

"I told you to report anything unusual," he said, his facing reddening and his voice rising, "and I think a golf cart full of crazy people flying down the boardwalk, scaring a bunch of ninety-year-olds to death, is plenty unusual. Add in a big dog and a man running for his life, and I think that might fit the definition of *unusual*."

"What's unusual?" Manny asked as he entered the room and caught the last bit of Winters' comment.

After scanning the room, Winters likely decided the thirty guests didn't need to hear what he had to say, because he directed Manny and me outside for some privacy.

"So, *amigo*," he said when we got outside and he took a breath to calm down, "what the heck happened over at the Oaks yesterday?"

Manny shrugged like it was no big deal. "We saw some guy snooping around one of our cottages, like he was casing the place. I thought he might be a druggy, but no, someone in good shape."

"How do you know? Did you get a good look at him?"

"Not really, but he ran like the wind. The Dude got

on his tail, but the guy outran him to the end of the boardwalk, where he dove into the water. He swam across the cove like a Tarzan to the other side. So, he had to be young. A run and swim like that would have killed me."

"Who chased the guy?"

"Me, Moli, and Ricky," Manny said, leaving Colleen out of the conversation for the moment, "and the Dude."

"Word has it you nearly ran down ten people in your pursuit. I'm surprised you haven't heard from the management over there. I'm sure they got a boat load of complaints from the seniors."

"What's to complain about? They probably haven't had that much excitement in years."

"Manny, this might be just a joke to you, but I used to work in the investigation unit down in Sarasota. I took this job because I wanted less stress and trouble. And here I am, in trouble with the mayor half the time, and all the time it's because of you. Now, I have ten years more until my retirement, and I had planned to coast to the big day, but if you keep burning me, I might go down for all this, and I might take you down with me."

"I'll talk to the mayor."

"You will not. I don't need you to cover my behind. What I need you to do is stay out of my jurisdiction."

"The Oaks hired me for security on their property."

"The boardwalk is not on the Oaks property. The city built and maintains the walkway, from one end to the other. And when you stepped on it, you were out of your jurisdiction."

"I didn't know that" Manny said.

"That's right. That's what I've been telling you,

amigo. You're only half aware of everything you do around here. Now, this is my last warning, and as much as I would hate to, the next time I find out you are interfering with town police business, I'm going to charge you with obstruction. You probably wouldn't get more than a mild reprimand, but I don't see the Oaks or the campground keeping you on if you are charged, even with a misdemeanor."

"Frank, have a heart."

"No, Manny, you had your chance, and this has to stop. Stay out of town police business." When Manny had no response, he said, "Listen, *amigo*, I need to hear you say it."

"Frank, I hear you about doing your job, so I'll stay out of town business, but on my property, I'll do what I have to. At the Oaks next door and over on the Cove, I'm working for them and it's their property, so I'm going to take my direction from them."

"Okay*, amigo*, but don't expect any more favors from me." Shifting to me he said, "That includes Moli Maid here, too."

It was kind of a sign of respect to be included with Manny in police-like business even though I hated the Moli Maid reference.

"Now, I've got to go talk to the mayor's mother about this and smooth things over. She's an old biddy, but she's the mayor's old biddy, so we must mind her." And with that, Winters marched off in the direction of the Oaks.

"Don't worry about Frank," Manny said. "The Oaks would probably fire me, but the campground would keep me. They'd think I earned an honor if the town cops arrested me for something."

****

I got Ricky to the bus stop late but the driver held the door open for my boy. When she saw me, she gave me the *is it so difficult to get your five-year-old here on time? What kind of a mother are you?* frown.

I stepped away from the curb and the big yellow bus whisked my son away. While I stood there, Colleen raced across the parking lot, waving at me.

"What's up?" I asked her.

"Where's Manny? We've got to talk."

We found him in the bar, doing inventory. Usually, the weekend bar business depleted our inventory of everything, and Manny took Monday to order the re-supply. "Why the grumpy faces?" Manny said when we approached. "What's going on?"

"I've got some news on Gloria's case."

"Oh yeah," he said, stopping his count.

"It had only been a hunch, but when Moli told me Colombo managed that condo project for a group up North, I checked with a friend in the NYPD Major Crimes Division."

"Do you two know cops in every city in this country?" I asked her.

"No, but L.A. and New York share information on major crimes, so I had met this guy last year, before I left the force. He told me if I ever needed something, to let him know. So, I did. I told him about our Colombo and the condo project, and the group backing it, and he did some background work. He texted me this morning and guess what?"

"What?" Manny and I said at the same time.

"That RAMCOD, LLC, is a new shell corporation that the Jersey syndicate set up for its real estate ventures. Apparently, they are expanding their real estate holdings down the eastern seaboard."

"What does that have to do with Salvatore?" I asked.

"I don't know," Colleen said, "but I have my guy following up on the connection. We'll just have to wait and see how Colombo fits into this."

****

Mondays are usually the slowest day of the week for me. All our cottage guests are just settling in and still enjoying the excitement of their vacations. The thrill of sun, sand, and salt hasn't worn off yet. That usually happens around Wednesday when the three S's start to exert their negative effects, and guests start to get ornery. That's when I am usually inundated with requests for more towels and linen, and complaints about the HVAC systems not working properly.

On most Mondays, with a little extra time, I get my own housework done around the apartment, and do several loads of laundry for Ricky, Manny, and me. Thankfully, the Dude wears the same fur coat every day.

When I got to the laundry room, I found Gloria folding sheets. "I know, I know," she said. "Pitiful, right, me resorting to folding sheets to escape the boredom."

"Hey, thanks, I need the help."

"I figured you'd need it. Is that your stuff?" she asked about the laundry bag I carried.

"Yeah, the weekly household laundry, Manny's and Ricky's stuff.

"Where's your things?"

"I wear the housekeeping uniform during the day and a tee and running shorts at night."

"How about when you go out on the town?" she asked. When I didn't respond to that, she said, "Oh, right.

You don't go out much."

"Also pitiful, right?"

"Well, today is your lucky day. I'm doing the laundry today."

"Why?"

"Because of this," she said, handing me a page of yellow legal pad paper.

"What's this?"

"It's the list of items we need in the beach shack. We missed restocking last Monday so, it's a lengthy list."

With Gloria still hiding out, she couldn't follow through with one of her responsibilities, managing the inventory in the beach shack. The shack team wasn't part of management and not empowered to spend motel money for replacement goods. They were, however, empowered to compile a list of what they needed to keep the shack stocked.

Glancing down at the items on the list, I said, "Why don't we just order online and have things delivered?"

"Manny had me figure out the costs, and he said the local shops have competitive pricing. Plus, he said he wants to keep the dollars in town instead of an online resource with an out-of-town bank account.

"Here," she said, taking back the list, "I'll write in the shops and stores where we get the different things. If you organize the stuff by location, you won't be running around in circles."

****

With my supply list in hand, I told Manny about my upcoming shopping spree.

"Since you're going out, how about stopping to pick up the liquor order?"

"What about the beer?"

"All the distributors are coming by today. I'll handle them when they come."

"You know, Manny, not having Gloria available for all this is keeping us busy."

"What can we do?"

"Talk to Winters and fill him in on all we got on the case. He can see Gloria is the least involved of anyone and call off the search for her."

"Do you think we have enough for him to stop looking for her?"

"Well, how about we tell him about my mugging? Gloria certainly didn't mug me."

"Yeah, but Gloria could have gotten someone to do it. She knows a lot of people, and Winters knows it. We'd better hold off a while longer until we get some tangible evidence that she's not involved."

For my trip to town, I grabbed my fanny pack and the keys to my pickup truck. When I escaped from L.A. I drove my old pickup. I packed the truck bed with all the belongings I wanted from the apartment that my ex and I had shared. I covered everything with a tarp and tied the mess down with rope. I worried a little about the trip, not about the truck itself which was usually reliable, and I didn't doubt it could make the journey, but I worried about the tires. A set of four truck tires could set you back a thousand dollars easily, and at the time, I didn't have much money.

When everything was ready, with a full tank of gas, and Ricky snug in the second row in a car seat, we drove out of L.A. in the middle of the night. I didn't slow down until the next morning when I crossed the Arizona border and stopped for gas.

Several months after I got here, I replaced the tires

with some retreads I bought at a local tire shop run by a bunch of Latino guys. Although you might have questioned the retreads durability for a cross-country trip, they were good enough for around town. Besides, I didn't have any plans to drive back to L.A. and when several of the Latino guys whistled at me, I decided to buy a set from them. How pitiful is that when a whistle from a couple of teenagers makes you feel like Salma Hayek.

When needed around the complex, I drive one of the golf carts, but if I'm not tagging along with Manny in his campground truck, I use mine. The truck is showing age with rust and dents everywhere, but the engine always fires up when I need to drive into town.

When I switched the truck ignition on, the old thing spurted like a two pack a day smoker but after a few seconds, roared to life. I gave the beast a minute to warm before I engaged the gear, and I headed to town for the shopping spree.

Around noon I got hungry. Even when young, I could go a while without thinking of food, but then, unexpectedly, I would get hungry. Just like that, and if I'm not fed fairly quickly, I get irritable.

The first hunger pangs hit me at the Old Towne Drug Store while I wheeled a shopping cart full of sunscreen and other items on the list. The aroma coming from their lunchtime grill may have had something to do with it.

For the last hundred years, the O'Malley family-owned business provided for community pharmacy needs and also ran an old-fashioned lunch counter for breakfast and lunch. The food serving area used to be a whites only counter, and Blacks and Mexicans alike had to get a bag lunch if they wanted to eat. But when lunch counters across the South were desegregated, the head of the O'Malley family decided not to fight the law and welcomed everyone with a dime for the blue plate special. The town's sundown laws were a little tougher to overcome, but eventually even those faded away. I guess as far as making money goes, the only color you need to worry about is the color green.

The counter's menu offered year-round staples and seasonal favorites. Most times I order the grill's signature BLT, since it's the best I've ever had. Unlike other states where tomato growing follows the sun, in Florida, the prime growing season starts in October, with the Cherokee Purple Heirloom tomato topping the favorites list.

The food counter had a roll of red top vinyl upholstered stools that spun when you twisted in them. Unprepared for the action customers could find themselves on the floor if they weren't careful.

I had just settled in at the counter when Chad appeared, smiled wide, and called out to me. "Are you stalking me?" I asked him.

"No, this is a regular stop for me when I get the chance. Their BLT is a killer."

****

My long lunch and shopping took longer than I expected, a result of the hour I spent with Chad. The lost hour caused me to get back to the complex with just enough time to unload the truck before Ricky's bus drove in. Mrs. Hall, the mother of three teenagers, staffed the beach shack that day. She had long blonde hair and eyes the color of the Florida sky on a bright day.

Although she wore a one-piece swimsuit, the thing

had so many holes and openings you could see plenty, and what little you couldn't see, you could imagine. When I came in with the bags of inventory supplies, she broke into a big smile, since she had just sold her last tube of sunscreen.

"Ah, Moli," Mrs. Hall asked me as we restocked the shelves, "the ladies and I had a question about the list."

"Oh, is there something else you needed from town?"

"No, not the shopping list. The list of potential suspects Gloria asked us to put together."

"Oh," I said, only then remembering that Gloria had asked the shack crew to help us on the case, "what about it?"

"We all developed our list of customers, careful to include anyone we remembered. It's kind of exciting and all, and we worked carefully, but when the other ladies and I compared our lists, we noticed something."

"What?"

"Well, I'm not sure how to put this, but there's a name missing from the list."

"Whose name?"

"Well, that's it, we're not sure."

"Then how can you tell his name is missing?"

"Well, it's kind of embarrassing, but we all have a nickname for him. We call him Mr. Big. You know, like from that old TV show—Mr. Big?"

"Oh, I get it, like a big shot."

"No, not like that."

"What do you mean?"

"Well, he wears these tight Speedo-like swim trunks, and that's how he got the nickname from us. But we've never known his real name, but Gloria does."

"What do you mean?"

"He's good friends with Gloria. He always talks to her, and they've gone out some. And anyway, his name wasn't on any of our lists, so we were just wondering. I mean, he could be a suspect like anyone else, right?"

"At this point, Mrs. Hall, everyone is still a suspect."

****

With Mrs. Hall situated with the replacement stock, I rushed to the front of the office to greet Ricky's bus. As usual, the Dude arrived ahead of me and waited patiently as my boy climbed down the steps.

After slobbering all the way around, we retreated to the apartment, where I fixed Ricky and the Dude a snack. Feeling guilty about using the television and the cartoon channel as an after-school babysitter, I got out the art supplies and sat Ricky at the kitchen island with watercolors and paper.

"I want you to paint something for your grandma's birthday next week. We can go to the post office and send her a nice card. I think she'll love getting something from you that you made."

"I'm making you something, too," Ricky said.

"You are? What is it?"

"It's supposed to be a surprise."

I wanted to pry a little more into this surprise, but the office door opened.

"So, you are stalking me," I said to Chad, finding him standing in the lobby.

"No, I just needed to grab a stack of bar towels, ahead of opening. We should have a big crowd for Monday night football."

"Well, they are always in the same place."

"Ah, that's the thing."

"What?"

"When I ran to the laundry room to grab a stack, I didn't see Gloria."

"What do you mean?"

"She wasn't there."

"Did you check her cottage?"

"I did. No one there either."

"I wonder where she is. Maybe she's on the beach?"

"I glanced out there, but no sign of her."

"No sign of who?" Manny asked when he showed up in the lobby.

I glanced at Chad, and he nodded at me.

"Who didn't you see?" Manny asked again.

"Gloria's missing," I told him.

"Since when?"

"Just in the last couple of hours."

Manny didn't say more but headed out the side door and around to the laundry room. We didn't see Gloria. Her makeup kit, some clothes, and her accounting book were on the table, but no Gloria.

Manny said, "Since the place isn't tossed, I don't think anyone kidnapped her."

"No, but why run off now?" I asked. "She could have taken off anytime. Why now?"

Manny asked Chad, "Something must have spooked her. Did you see anyone when you got here?"

"Mrs. Hall was closing up the beach shack. That's the only person I saw."

"Uh oh," I said.

"What? Manny asked.

"Mrs. Hall and I talked while we unloaded supplies. Gloria may have heard us."

"Talking about what?"

I summarized the conversation for Manny.

"Any idea who this mysterious character is?"

"No, that's what started the whole thing. None of the shack ladies know his name."

"So," Manny said, "Gloria hears you, and the subject of the conversation is someone she knows, and she disappears. What does that infer?"

"Probably that she took off to warn the guy he might be a suspect. But a suspect in what? The Salvatore thing? I'm lost."

"Wait, did Mrs. Hall say what the guy looks like?"

I said, "Yeah, she said he is tall, young, and athletic."

"Hey, that could be the guy we chased down the boardwalk the other day."

"Could be," I said, "I think athletic is a good description of him. So, what now?"

"We need to find Gloria and ask her."

Chapter Eighteen

Tuesday

The Monday night crowd didn't disappoint. With Manny in his usual spot in front of the tube, I put Ricky and the Dude to bed, then ran over to the bar to help out. I put on an apron and started serving customers. The taco truck had already closed, but the football fans still crowded the space in front of the TV.

When the last seconds of the game ticked down to zero, we switched off the television, closed the bar service, and people started to leave. As I glanced across the emptying bar, the *not dressed* for the beach man got up from his table. He had taken off his long-sleeved shirt, down to his undershirt, but still wore his black pants and wing tips, which were scuffed and not as shiny after a couple of days in the sun, sand, and salt.

"Chad," I said, putting my head down, "did you talk to that guy out there?"

"What guy?"

"The one out there," I said, keeping my head down, "in slacks and regular shoes."

When Chad glanced up. "What guy?"

When I raised my head, I didn't see him. Marjorie and Brenda were busy cleaning the last of the tables but no man in wing tips. "He sat at one of the high tops along the back wall."

"I don't see anyone now, and I didn't pay much attention to anyone except the thirty guys yelling at me from right in front of the bar. Why?"

Just then, Marjorie and Brenda, who always worked the Monday Night Football shift together, approached the counter to tip out. They split with Chad and the truck crew, and they started to gather their stuff from behind the bar.

"Say," I asked them, before they got away "which of you waited on that guy in the back?"

"Which guy," they asked at the same time.

"Balding guy in wing tips. Not dressed for the beach."

"I had him," Marjorie said. "Kind of weird, but he tipped big."

"Did you talk to him any?"

"Did you see the place, Moli? I could barely stop for a breath out there, much less find time to stand around and chit-chat with anyone. Why?"

"I just wondered. He wanted a cottage here, but we were full, so I sent him over to the Cove. I wondered if he was satisfied."

"He was happy enough. He ate a basket of fish tacos. Now, guys, we are out of here. Okay?"

Thirty minutes later Chad finished closing out and Manny sauntered around the corner of the bar to lock up the place. "How did we do tonight?"

"The Steelers lost by eight," Chad told him.

"Uh, oh, someone lost money tonight."

Chad walked me back to the apartment and talked about going out to eat, but when I hesitated, and frowned at spending another three hours awake, he kissed me goodnight and we took a rain check. Honestly, how young people can party all night is a mystery to me. Oh, wait, that's right, they don't have five-year-old sons who have to go to school in the morning.

****

My phone alarm jarred me awake the next morning with a boom from some rock band playing a poor, but loud, Stones' cover song.

I noticed the Dude and Ricky had already left the room. When I got out to the kitchen, my three housemates were halfway through their bowls of cereal.

"I set out the breakfast bar and coffee," Manny said.

"Wow, you must have gotten up early."

"A security alarm tripped in the Oaks about four a.m., so after I checked on that, I worked on the breakfast counter."

"What happened at the Oaks?"

"Old man Hollister forgot to disarm his security system before he opened his front door. The loud noise confused him and scared the you-know-what out of him. In all the excitement, he forgot his security code."

"Poor guy."

"Yeah, I felt sorry for him, so I took some time to get him settled before I left. Well, we're all going to be old one day."

"Not you, Manny. You're never growing up."

After I got Ricky dressed for school, the Dude and I escorted him to the bus stop. I gave him two dollars for his lunch. On Tuesdays, they always serve chicken tenders, one of his favorites. The lunches are big, so big that he always has a big piece of leftover chicken, which he sticks down in his book bag. Later, when he gets home from school, he gives the Dude the chicken piece. I have a suspicion that's one of the reasons the dog is so happy to see Ricky get off the bus on Tuesdays, but how the dog knows it's Tuesday is a mystery.

The big yellow bus had just driven away from the curb, when two patrol cars and Winters' unmarked sedan, pulled to the front of the building.

"Where's Manny?" Winters called out even before he stepped completely out of the car. The show of force scared me enough for me to clam up.

"Did you hear me?" the detective repeated as he strutted up to where the Dude and I stood.

Now, anyone could see the Dude loves Ricky, and he would fight off a gang of cutthroat pirates to protect the boy. Until that moment, I wasn't confident about how the dog felt about me. I'm sure in his eyes he identified me as Ricky's mother, but I wasn't sure how much protection that entitled me.

When Winters got within a couple of steps of us, the Dude stepped around me and stood between us. The hackles along his back stood on edge; he bared his teeth and growled. When he let out a loud bark and followed up with an even louder howl, Winters stopped and retreated a few steps.

"Hang on to your dog," the man said, as he and the two cops with him reevaluated their approach. "I've got to talk to Manny."

Having gotten a few seconds to assess the situation, I lied. "He's at the Cove. They called him over for a break-in. What do you want to talk to him about?"

The other cops shifted, like getting into position.

The Dude caught their movements, lunged at the closest guy and snapped at him. It was only a warning lunge and snap, because the Dude quickly stepped back to me, and the guy quickly retreated to Winters, as if he could protect him.

"Hold your positions, guys. She's not who we want to talk to."

"Are you going to tell me why you're here?"

"I've got to see Manny, I've got a search warrant, and I need to talk to him."

"A search warrant for what?"

"To search the premises."

"Why?

Detective Winters paused. By the pucker of his lips, I could tell he was struggling with how much to tell me. He didn't need my permission to search the place. If a judge issued the warrant, Winters had provided a compelling reason. Still, I guess he wanted to be fair with Manny.

"Can you call him?"

"Sure."

"Get him then. Tell him to meet us."

"Where?"

"At his workshop."

****

As expected, Manny didn't answer when I called him. He had probably left his phone on his nightstand, plugged into a port to recharge overnight. With the cops on their way to the workshop, I dragged the Dude back into the apartment.

I found the place empty, no Manny and no phone. I stopped to wonder just how he left without me seeing him. There were only two ways out and if he had left by either, we would have seen him.

Leaving the Dude locked inside, and still mystified by how Manny disappeared, I ran to catch up to Winters. They were at the workshop door where one of the cops held a battering ram, ready to bust down the door.

"Hold on," I called to them when I got within shouting distance. "I've got a key."

"Didn't you say Manny had the only key to the shop?"

"I said, Manny doesn't let anyone into his shop. He and I both have a master key and a set of duplicates for all the doors in the complex."

I got out my master key, but it didn't work.

"What's wrong?" Winters asked, as I struggled with the key.

"Nothing," I said, giving up on that one and flipping through my ring for the shop duplicate, "wrong key."

"Did you find Manny?"

"No, he didn't answer his phone. So, what are you searching for?" I asked, unlocking the door and letting them in.

"Evidence," Winters said.

"What kind of evidence?"

"We got the forensics back from the lab, and they identified the kind weapon used to whack Salvatore."

"What kind?"

"A blunt instrument, most likely a hammer."

"So, you think because Manny might have a hammer in his shop, he's the perpetrator."

"No, I didn't say that. I said the weapon might be in the shop, not that he used it. That's why we have to get in and why we need to talk to him."

Manny had laid out his shop like a real carpenter. Against one wall, he built a ten-foot-long workbench. On the opposite wall, he had built a series of cabinets and counters. In the middle of the room, he had built a heavy table where a table saw blade protruded from the center.

On the wall to the left of the corridor shop door, he had double farm doors that could be opened right onto our private parking lot to load or unload longer pieces of lumber or bulky plywood. He had every machine and work surface in the room connected to a central vacuum that efficiently sucked sawdust away from the work areas. The system kept the room nearly dust free, but if you ran a finger along the top of a shelf, you could still pick up a fine layer.

When Winters got into the room, he drifted over to the counter that lined one wall. Above the counter, from right to left, a peg board held all of Manny's woodworking hand tools, which included his assortment of hammers. "Manny has a nice shop laid out in here."

"He likes to work with his hands."

"Tell, me, Moli, would you say Manny is a good carpenter?"

"Sure."

"I can see he values his equipment, the way he has his tools all arranged in here."

Then with a nod of his head, he sent the two cops off on a scavenger hunt.

With the two men tearing the place apart, Winters said, "I like the way Manny has all his hand tools arranged on the wall. Everything within an arm's length and everything organized."

"Manny might not fit the image of an organized businessman at first glance, but he likes to be orderly."

"I can see that. Which is why I can also see there is something missing from this wall of tools."

"What's missing? I see a bunch of hammers up there."

"Yes, but the most familiar is the claw hammer, and

it's not here. I couldn't tell you what these other ones are used for, but every carpenter has at least one if not two, claw hammers."

"He could have put the hammer in his truck."

"Maybe, but we just agreed how organized the man is, so I wouldn't think he'd have a tool just thrown randomly about somewhere."

"Manny's got a toolbox in his truck, a big one."

"Yes, I'm sure he does, and he probably has a number of tools in it, even a claw hammer, but they would be his second set of tools. Maybe even older tools. Maybe different tools, just for auto repairs. But his woodworking tools, his primary working tools, no, they are all right in front of us. All except the claw hammer. And the lab report says Anthony Salvatore was hit in the head with a hammer, probably a claw hammer."

"That doesn't prove anything. I mean, I'm not a detective or anything, but I suspect that if you didn't find an assault weapon it is not like you actually found an assault weapon."

"No, but I'm still in the dark about why Salvatore ended up whacked in the head. Any ideas?"

"Why ask me?"

"Don't play dumb, Moli. You and Manny have talked to your guests about this. Are you going to update me on what you've discovered?"

I paused. Winters stood there, leaning on Manny's saw table, waiting for my answer.

"We've not done much on the case," I lied again. I also noted that my continued license with the truth might warrant a trip to church confession to clear my soul. I hadn't been in years, but the ever-growing weight of lies might tip the scales into the confessional booth range.

"But when we get something, you'll be the first to know."

I know Winters didn't believe me, but without talking to Manny, I just didn't see how I could tell him anything.

"Okay, guys," Winters said to his team, who came up empty-handed in their search of the shop, "we're done here."

"Are you going to tape the shop off?" I asked, hoping he would, so Manny wouldn't see the mess the cops made.

"No, if guilty, I don't suppose Manny would be dumb enough to put the assault weapon back in its place."

"So, what are you going to do about Manny?"

"I don't know. I'll make that decision if and when I ever see him."

****

I didn't bother straightening things in the shop. I figured Manny should get a firsthand view of the damage the cops did. As I passed through the alcove between buildings, I opened the laundry room door, hoping maybe Gloria came back.

"Oh, heck, Manny," I said to the man I saw reclining on a pool chair when I opened the door. "What are you doing here?"

"Hiding out. Are they gone?"

"They just left. Are you comfortable enough?"

"I figured what was good for Gloria is good enough for me."

"Did you hear any of what Winters said?"

"I heard enough."

"Are you worried?"

"No, he's trying to scare me into cooperating. They don't have anything."

"I don't know about that. He sounded serious."

"His boss is probably on him to get something done on the case, so he's trying to pressure me to work with him."

"Okay, why don't you?"

"Frank is part of the system. We have more leeway working independently. When we get something concrete, we'll let him know."

"What do we do now?"

"Now, we have to find out who took my favorite hammer, and why."

Chapter Nineteen

Worried that, in case Manny showed up, Winters would put another stakeout on the place, I ran to the South wing of the building to see if they left a patrol car there. I didn't see a new unit, but the patrol car assigned to Gloria's cottage had repositioned itself to the center of the complex, right in front of the office. I guess Winters figured one sleeping cop in one cop car could watch two suspects, as well as two sleeping cops in two cars.

Maybe some budget considerations played a role. The local paper ran at least one town budget story each week about the mayor announcing some money saving measures in the next fiscal year. In fact, the mayor talked about belt tightening so many times in the last couple of years, I would have expected every member of the City Council to be prancing around with the smallest waists in the state, especially the mayor. Of course, the last time Mayor Aldridge came to our Wednesday night cheeseburger cookout, he wasn't watching his waist. I guess all those budget cutting measures only involved the services for the working citizens of town.

After I checked out Winters' dragnet preparations, I carted over to the Cove to talk to Colleen and found her in the food court. Apparently, she had received a promotion from the kid's ice cream line in the camp store to assistant manager over the food court. Along with the new position came a new hair color, red. At the rate she was going, she would probably be in upper administration by Christmas and get back to her natural hair color, whatever that was.

Because the property owners had prominently located the food court in the middle of the complex, the scent of fried food drifted over the whole campground. No matter what corner of the facility you camped in, you were only a few steps from French fries and cold drinks.

The communal area was set beneath a huge wooden pillared shelter with a tall roof covered in fiberglass. The area caught enough ocean breeze to keep the air temperature under the shelter in a tolerable range, especially when compared to being out in the sun, sand, and salt. Campers scattered about on picnic tables eating and seemed to enjoy the respite.

"You're kidding?" she said and smiled wide when I explained about the cops. "Don't worry, Moli, "she said as she cleaned off a table, "Winters is just trying to scare us."

"Well, he's doing an excellent job because I'm scared. If I get charged with anything, I can kiss goodbye any plans I had for most any career in public safety. In addition to lying to a cop, I could get charged with harboring a suspect and obstructing an investigation."

"Only if Manny and Gloria are guilty of something," she pointed out while stocking the condiment counter with packets of condiments. "So far, Winters is only guessing. That's why he hasn't put out an arrest warrant on anyone. He's still trying to investigate but his hands are tied by the law, and he has to toe a fine line between following the law and breaking it. Believe me, I know all about that line.

"Speaking of breaking the law," Colleen said, "I've

been meaning to ask you. Did you make copies of Doc Murphy's manuscript the other day when you broke into his place?"

"I didn't break into his place. I had a key."

"Whatever. Did you get a copy of anything?"

"No, but I took some photos with my camera."

"Did you?" she asked, scanning the food court, making sure no one could hear. "Sit down and show me."

I took a seat next to her and cozied up, shoulder to shoulder. I opened my phone's photo files and displayed my pictures. I tried to scroll past a bunch of photos of Ricky when we were at the beach, but Colleen stopped me.

"Hey, when did you take those? You must have had fun at the beach. Are you and Chad becoming a couple?"

"It was just a day at the beach."

"Don't you hate the beach?"

"Shut up."

I scrolled down and found the shots I took of Doc's manuscript and showed her.

"Here's the first few pages of the book." I pointed, glad to be on another subject. "You can see it's rough, just a lot of notes."

"Like he hasn't even started."

"I know. That's what I said."

I scrolled through the remaining manuscript photos showing her what I had of Doc's other records.

"What are those?" Colleen asked me.

"I took some shots of a stack of documents from his desk."

"Why?"

"I don't know. Isn't that what detectives do? Snoop around taking photos?"

"Well, if I'm reading these bank statements right, the Doc isn't short of money, so a blackmail motive might be off the table."

"Wait," I said, now with a chance to closely examine the bank statements, "you see these entries here, for each month?"

"Yeah."

"Around the same date each month, five thousand dollars is recorded as deposited, every month."

"How far back do these go?" she asked, snatching the phone from my hands.

"Several months, and I guess I have ten or twelve of these."

"Eleven," she said, "you've got eleven stretching between two years. All with the same deposit amount, on or close to a specific date. But so, what? A lot of people have direct deposit."

"These are not direct deposits," I said. "They started a couple of months after the university incident but are not on the same day every month."

"So, what do you think?"

"I think that's why the good doctor hasn't finished his book. He's already getting paid. Going back at least two years. The boy's family must have settled personally with him, and they are paying him off. They probably didn't want the publicity, so they jumped ahead and just settled."

"What publicity?" Colleen asked. "If the Doc was in the wrong, they've got nothing to hide. I don't see the family paying off anyone. No, ma'am."

"Then, maybe it's the university," I said. "They have the most to lose. If they pay off the Doc, then they get what they want, no publicity. What's your guess?"

"Doesn't matter," Colleen said, "remember, no guessing in police work, just the facts."

"So," I said, "with the money coming in, the Doc doesn't need to finish his book."

"That's probably part of the deal," she said. "No book for the money."

"So, Salvatore wasn't investigating the Doc."

"No, he wasn't."

"Just wait until I tell Manny. He won't believe it."

"I don't believe it," Colleen said, "and I've seen the evidence."

Just then, the man in wingtips, Mr. Johnson, trudged by carrying a large coffee. He marched by so fast I almost didn't see him.

"Do you recognize that guy?" I asked Colleen, as I pointed to him walking away.

"I first saw him a couple of days ago, so he's new."

"Yeah, he tried to check in with us, but since we were full, I sent him over here."

"Makes sense."

"Have you noticed anything funny about the man?"

"You mean besides his wing tips and black slacks."

"I know, right? I don't think he's a regular beachgoer."

"He's probably from New York."

"That would make sense."

"Say, I've got to run. One of the lunch cooks called in sick, so I have to juggle some assignments."

"Hey," I said, "don't tell Manny about the Doc; let me. I want to see his face when I tell him us gals broke a big piece of the case."

"You figured it out, Moli. You've got a head for this kind of thing."

"Maybe I do."

****

I left the food court and stepped out into the warming sun. Even though I'd not been much for the sun, sand, and salt of the beach before coming to Cabana Bay, over the last couple of years of living in close proximity to the Gulf, I had grown a little more flexible to its beauty.

Standing there in the warm sun, I was thinking I should have been happy about dropping Doc from our suspect list, but for some reason I wasn't.

Then, Mr. Johnson tramped by again.

I don't think he saw me because he had his head down, working his phone. For whatever reason, I followed him.

The campground had two nice rows of cabins for rent, twenty in all, and they lined the fence at the far end of the complex. In addition to being isolated, the cabins stood beneath the complex's thickest forested area and managed to stay out of the sun, sand, and salt for most of the day.

Mr. Johnson, the wingtip man, slog over the sandy walkway steadily, but paused briefly to take a call. I couldn't hear the conversation, but all his gesturing in the air, with his free hand, indicated some importance. He ended his call and started off and working his phone again, and I continued to follow him.

When we entered the cabin area, he detoured down the dirt path between rows and disappeared.

That area of the camp loomed spookily making the hair on my neck stand up. All the cabins stood on stilts, surrounded by a thick forest of trees and hidden beneath long strands of Spanish moss and eerie shadow. I mean, even in the middle of the day, just walking through the area gave me the jitters. I had my doubts about following him in there, but I walked up to the first cabins, hoping I'd see the man.

"You're Manny Soto's niece, aren't you?" he said, from behind me, making me jump, my heart skipping several beats. Wondering how he got behind me. The man spoke in a New York accent.

"Why do you ask?" I said, my voice a croak. "And what are you doing sneaking up on me?"

"What are you doing following me?"

"Who said I was following you?"

"The Cabana Bay Cottage complex is way over on the other side of the campground. If you're not following me, you have a terrible sense of direction."

"Who are you, anyway? I don't think Johnson is your real name."

The man glared at me. Since he didn't say anything at once, I imagined he was debating with himself whether to respond.

"Okay, you seem like a good kid, so let me tell you. You and your uncle and his wife are getting into something you don't know anything about."

"What do you mean?"

"Now, don't play dumb. I've found out all about ex-cops Manny Soto and his wife Colleen, and all about you too, cop drop out, and now a Moli Maid."

Boy, do I hate that reference.

"I know about your ex-husband too and your boy Ricky and even your dog with the stupid name."

"How?"

"Because it's my job, and I am telling you to be careful where you stick your pretty little head, or you might get your nose bitten off, and not by the Dude."

"So, who are you, a cop? Or maybe you're with the FBI?"

"No, I'm a private investigator."

What, another P.I. in town? "Are you here because of the campground case?"

"No, I'm here because of the Salvatore case."

"Why are you interested in Tony Salvatore?"

"I'm interested because Tony's my brother!"

****

The realization that Tony Salvatore had a brother put a different light on the matter.

"When did you hear about your brother?"

"We work together, and Tony is fairly deliberate about sending in daily reports, but he stopped. I didn't worry right away. He often goes off the grid when a pretty girl comes his way. But a few days ago, a group we've done some business with told me the local cops were inquiring around about a guy in their hospital. These people have a wide presence along the Eastern seaboard, and they told me about Tony. That's when I came. Once I visited him in the ICU, I wanted to stay around a couple of days to make sure he recovers and to check on the investigation. To tell you the truth, I'm not too impressed by the local police."

"What was your brother doing down here?"

"Working a case."

"Obviously, but which one?"

The man paused again, staring at me. "That's the thing," he said, "it's a private matter. Unlike the cops I don't have to reveal my clients or their motives."

"Well, I'm sorry about your brother…ah, what's your name?"

"Mike Salvatore."

"Well, Mike, I'm sorry about your brother, but we're just working the case because our friend Gloria is implicated."

"Yeah, I saw your pretty friend in the laundry room."

"You found out about her?"

"It wasn't hard."

"The cops think she's a suspect."

"Who thinks? That short detective with the plaid pants?"

"Yeah, Detective Winters."

"Well, he's way off on this. I mean, Tony may have hit on your friend, Gloria, and that's his MO, and yeah, she's definitely Tony's style, but she wouldn't have gotten the drop on Tony. No, Tony's too sharp for that. The person who got the drop on Tony had some experience, or he got lucky and surprised him."

"That's what I thought."

"So, what else have you and Manny found out?"

I debated with myself about what to tell him. When I waited a while before saying anything he said, "Come on, Moli, I've been square with you. What do you have?"

Since his brother was in ICU, I filled him in on what Manny and I had come up with.

"So, let me get this straight, you got a possible with Colombo and the construction project, some mysterious character lurking around the grounds, and a doctor with an incomplete book. And what, you've been working on this for two weeks?"

"Hey, we've all got other jobs to do and other things on our plates as well."

"Sure, Manny and his little security business."

"We've got the cottages too."

"What do you want, a trophy? Now, I'm heading over to the hospital, we've got family coming down to see Tony, and I'll be escorting them around for a couple of days. So, I hope something breaks on this soon, either from the city clowns or you ex-cops."

"What are you going to do if nothing breaks?"

"I'll take a more personal approach. Maybe that will get results. And another thing."

"What?"

"There's more going on here than local law enforcement."

"What do you mean?"

"You asked me earlier if I was FBI? Well, I'm not, but someone in your little circle is connected there."

"Who?"

"That's up to you to find out."

Chapter Twenty

Taco Tuesday

Just as I got back to the complex, Winters pulled up out front. I ducked my head and tried to skip past him, but before I could, he waved at me to stop.

"Wow," I said, when he got out of his vehicle. "Two visits from Cabana Bay's finest on the same day. Why am I not expecting this to be a friendly visit?"

"Listen up, Moli," he said, approaching close enough I could smell bad cologne, "I have some news for you. I'd ask you to go and get Manny, but you wouldn't be able to find the guy, so I'm skipping that part of the chat."

"So," I said, bracing for bad news, "what do you have?"

"We just got a hit on our canvass of the pawn shops in the area on the Salvatore camera equipment."

"Oh yeah? How did you even know what was stolen?"

"We got a list from Salvatore's office and sent a description out to all the shops. We just heard back from Benny's Pawn over at the Beach Mall."

I figured that Mike Salvatore probably gave him the information as opposed to him or his minions making any major investigatory effort. "Did you find out who tried to pawn the stuff?"

"I talked to Benny myself, but he didn't give me much. He said the guy was young and well dressed, but not much more."

"That's not helpful." Of course, talking to a cop probably wasn't high on the man's play list, so it was understandable Winters didn't get much. "Did he at least have a name?"

"He did, but when we ran the name through the system, he turned out to be a fake, as well as his address."

Surprise, surprise. "So, someone doesn't want to be known."

"That's to be expected, but if one of Salvatore's cameras showed up, maybe some of his other gear will start to make an appearance. If so, maybe the next broker will be able to give us more."

"Yeah, well, thanks for the info."

"So," he said, stepping closer still, "in the spirit of cooperation, since I gave you something, what can you guys give me that I don't already have?"

"What makes you think we have anything more? You told us to stay out of it."

Winters just stared at me. Forced to look at him, I tried not to blink first. Playing one of those stare games Ricky and I play, to see who winks first. In the end, he won. I'd have to give him something, so I gave up Mike Salvatore.

"So," he said, backing up a bit, giving me breathing room, "you talked with the victim's brother?"

"Today in fact," I said.

"We talked with him last week."

It took me a moment to register what Winters said. "Why didn't you say anything?"

Winters whined a little saying, "You and Manny

haven't been exactly cooperative. It's not like we are sharing critical information and have a working partnership."

"Come on, Winters, we've been square with you."

"Have you? Like telling us about Gloria Cruz hiding out in your laundry room?"

"What do you mean?"

"You can stop the charade, Moli. We nabbed her yesterday when she tried to get into her cottage. She's clammed up, waiting for a public defender to come in, but we have enough to keep her for a few days."

"Come on, Detective, Gloria is innocent."

"Is she? Well, maybe she is, but in the meantime, I let Lopez go. I just need one Mexican suspect locked up in the Cabana Bay town jail.

"Gloria's Puerto Rican."

"What-ever. She's enough to keep the mayor happy until we find the real culprit."

****

As soon as Winters drove off, I hustled to the laundry room. I found Manny reclining in the beach chair, reading the newspaper. I never understood how people who are hiding from the cops can relax so easily.

"Winters was just here."

"Oh?" he said, putting down the paper. "What did he want?"

"They picked up Gloria and locked her up in jail."

"So that's where she's been. I bet they grabbed her sneaking into her cottage. I told her to stay out of there. Well, with her behind bars it will be easy to find her."

"That's not all."

"What else?"

"Frank told me a camera belonging to Salvatore

showed up at Benny's over in the Beach Mall."

"How did they know it belonged to Salvatore?"

I explained to him all about Mike Salvatore and how Winters had been holding out on us.

"Well, that could shed a different light on things," he said.

"What?"

"Think about it. If Salvatore's stuff is showing up in pawn shops, what does that say about the perp?"

I paused for a minute before responding. Manny sat there waiting. I had the feeling this was like a test. I always hated tests. "Maybe whoever took the stuff needs the money?"

"Could be," Manny agreed.

"If so, we can take Colombo off our list of suspects. He may be a lot of things, but short of cash he's not."

After a brief pause Manny said, "Or our perp could have dumped the stuff somewhere, and someone else found it and is pawning the gear."

"In which case, Colombo is still on the list?"

"That's right."

"I hate to say it, but we're not getting anywhere."

"Since I'm stuck back here," Manny said, "you'll to have to take the lead on this."

"What about your security rounds?"

"You'll have to make the drive throughs, too."

"Me?" I laughed a little. "You're kidding, right? I barely know my way around the Cottages."

"You could make your way around blindfolded. You'll do fine."

"What about Ricky?"

"I'll meet you in the apartment about midnight and sit with him while you and the Dude make the rounds."

"One good thing about Gloria being stuck in jail," I said.

"What?"

"Since Winters now has Gloria, he didn't need Bob, so he let him go."

"That's good," Manny said. "We need him making tacos."

Back at the office I checked several texts from guests on the complex's information system. The family in cottage eight needed more towels. A couple in seven asked if they could take a golf cart off the complex to run to town, and a single in twelve asked if it was Taco Tuesday, when we charged half price on tacos for guests.

I dropped off some towels and told the family to never take the carts out onto the city streets because they weren't licensed for safety.

Back at the office I got a text message about a reservation change. I logged on the system and confirmed the change. While reviewing the next month's calendar, I noticed a reservation from someone named Jones, which reminded me of Chad Jones and the Doctor Jones family.

I had put my concerns about the handsome Chad Jones out of my mind, but now with the computer right in front of me, I opened a search engine, thinking I might chase down info on Chad's father. With the search window open, I realized I didn't have his name. In fact, besides the medical school story he told me, I didn't know a lot about Mr. Chad Jones.

After mulling over the situation for a minute, I typed in Doctor Jones and got about two thousand links, including a good many referring to Doctor Indiana Jones, who I was pretty sure had no relationship to Chad, although they resembled each other.

Realizing Ricky was due home soon, the Dude and I dashed out to meet him. When I claimed my boy, we took him back to the apartment. I got the two of them settled with food, and I spent the rest of the afternoon trying to balance accounts. Not for the first time, I wished Gloria was available to work the numbers.

My stomach started rumbling around five o'clock, so I visited the taco truck. Smoke from grilling meat and fish drifted out of the truck and made my stomach growl. Ricky and I could eat a half dozen tacos, but the Dude was always hungry enough to eat a dozen more. Since we ate free, I didn't mind, and I took advantage of the situation. The guys in the truck probably wondered how a little boy, skinny girl, and an old man could eat so much food.

After I placed our order, I was waiting in the shade of a stand of palms when Colombo strutted up. "Do you like them hot?" he asked.

"What?"

"Your tacos. Do you like them hot?"

"Oh, yeah, the hotter the better."

"Tacos or guys?"

"Now, that's something that's been bothering me, this flirting."

"You don't like to be hit on by guys?"

"No," I said, trying to meet his smirk with a steady stare. "I can take a hit, just not by married men."

He paused at my comment, a little less juice in his voice, "I told you I wasn't married."

"That's not what you told Gloria."

He paused again. His bright smile faded, replaced by a frown. "Okay, I'm married. You can't blame a guy for trying."

"That's where you're wrong, I can blame you for lying. Plus, if you're lying about being married, I wonder about what other lies are you telling."

"What do you mean?"

"Is your name even Colombo, I mean, Colombo? Did you get that watching TV?"

"Hey, that's a family name."

"Which family?"

"I've only got one."

"That's not what I hear?"

"What?"

"Someone told me your family has an interest in expanding down here."

A cloud of confusion crossed his face. Finally, a reaction. Maybe more anger than embarrassment.

A grimace settled around his eyes, and he said in a voice an octave higher than his normal, "I have no idea what you're talking about."

I wanted to drill him a little more, but he stomped off, without ordering any tacos.

****

After dinner, I put Ricky and the Dude to bed and made my way back to the great room to relax. I needed to get a little sleep before going out on Manny's patrol, so I locked up and stretched out on the sofa. I felt like I had just put my head back when Manny shook me awake.

"What are you doing here?"

"It's time for the patrols," he said.

"Where did you come from? I didn't hear you come in."

"I used the rear entrance."

"We have a rear entrance?"

"Well, in case you ever need it, there's a hidden door in my room. It's in the back of my closet and opens onto the inner corridor, across from the laundry room."

"So, that's how you've been getting in and out unnoticed."

"So, are you ready for your first patrol?"

"I don't know, Manny. I dropped out of cop school before I took the patrol class."

"Don't worry, Moli. It will be a piece of cake."

Chapter Twenty-One

Night Patrol

I woke up the Dude. I had to pull him outside but once he saw the Pirate Cove truck he perked up. When I opened the door, he quickly jumped in the passenger seat.

I drove through the North end of the campground and found no unusual gatherings or crowds. I figured a Tuesday night atmosphere called for the calm. I drove through the South side and had almost made a complete circle around the quiet grounds, when I found a group of four men and four women sitting around a fire pit alongside a big, and no doubt expensive, RV. Bottles of beer scattered the area, and the smoky aroma of grilled steaks hung in the air.

Though the campground's lights-out curfew had long since passed, the band of merry makers whooped and hollered about something, oblivious to the rules. I pulled straight up to them and the truck's headlights blinded them. For good measure, I flicked on the truck's search lights and directed both of them straight at the eight.

In unison, the people raised their hands to shield their eyes. With the light in their faces, I knew they couldn't tell who was at the wheel of the truck. I also turned on the flashing roof lights, hoping they'd recognized the security measures and comply quietly. If they thought Manny was in the truck, they might just break up the party without a fuss and climb into the RV.

No such luck. Two of the men stood and started toward me, cussing as they came. I didn't need to hear the specifics to know they were mad.

Tattoos covered one of the men's naked upper body. His bald head reflected the light from the spotlights. The other man was familiar, the assistant manager from the campground general store, Harry. Both kept coming despite all the lights.

When the men got within ten feet of me, I opened the truck door, and the Dude hopped over my lap. He hit the dirt ground beside the truck with a heavy thud and howled like the banshee, which was basically what he is. The dog walked out into the bright light where no one could see anything of him besides his giant black silhouette.

The other men and women panicked and scrambled to get away, but the two men in the group only stopped with a momentary hesitation, then kept coming. The Dude saw them and let out a blood curdling howl that would have scared the devil. Thinking better of their action, the two men spun around and ran. The Dude took aim at the lead bald-headed character. As the man twirled to run, the Dude clamped down on his rear end and tore a section of denim off his blue jeans.

One of the men who'd run off first, came out of the RV toting a long gun. I'm sure he didn't understand the Dude, and neither did I, for that matter. I mean what kind of dog differentiates trouble between loud obnoxious men and someone carrying a dangerous firearm?

The Dude, of course.

As soon as he saw the rifle, he closed the distance in three fast strides and launched himself at the man. He clamped his teeth down on the gun's barrel, and the dog's weight swiveled and slammed into the guy. The collision sent the man away in a somersault, but the rifle stayed in the Dude's jaws.

I was surprised at the sight of the long gun and jumped out of the truck. The campground had a prohibition against firearms, but there are always those who don't follow rules.

The Dude turned and galloped back to the truck where he deposited the rifle at my feet.

It was a standard Winchester, lever action, nothing fancy. I picked up the rifle and stepped out into the light. Then, someone in the RV turned on the vehicle's headlights. I guess they were tired of not knowing who was hassling them, besides the big dog.

"Well, well," Harry said when he recognized me. Taking a few steps my way, he said, "If it isn't the little *señorita*."

I still didn't like the guy. There was just something creepy about him. Then, remembering being mugged and how the guy referred to me then, I got mad.

I levered a round into the firing chamber of the Winchester and raised the rifle to a comfortable position at my hip. At the sound of the rifle loading, Harry raised both hands in the air and started to step back. I gave the rifle a jerk toward the RV, but he and his friends hesitated. When the Dude let out another howl, everyone raced to the big rig.

Almost immediately, the engine started up. The rig slowly rolled out onto the campground road and made its way toward the Cove's exit. When the camp site was quiet, the Dude jumped back in the truck cab, and I followed

I drove back to the Cottages and found Manny and Colleen sitting next to each other on the little love seat. I dropped the Winchester down on the kitchen island with a bang. When Manny turned and saw the rifle, he asked, "Did you have an interesting patrol?"

So, I told them.

"Which campsite?" Aunt Colleen asked.

"I'm not sure. It's in the back somewhere. I was kind of busy to take notice."

"Are you okay?" Manny asked, coming over and picking up the rifle.

"I'm fine, but I'll tell you something, someone trained the Dude right. I think he could probably patrol the grounds by himself."

Manny said, "Don't give my job away just yet."

"Just one thing, Aunt Colleen."

"Yeah?"

"Your assistant manager, Harry, was there, and he drove off with the RV."

"Well, I guess they'll need a new assistant manager."

"Another thing."

"What," Colleen asked.

"That guy who mugged me in the storeroom the other day. I think it was your Harry."

"What makes you say that?"

"Just something about the way he talked."

"If so," Manny said, "we are definitely close to something."

"Yeah," I said, "but what?"

Manny asked me if I wanted to skip the Oaks run

through, but I told him I didn't expect any rough stuff from a bunch of old people over there.

He said, "Don't be so sure." I think he was kidding.

I didn't need the Dude for the Oaks patrol, so I led him back to the bedroom where he took his place beneath Ricky. I didn't think he'd miss out on anything at the Oaks, so he didn't give me a tough time about being left behind. Before I left, I bent over and gave the big dog a hug. For my effort, the Dude slobbered all over me.

****

The Oaks security patrol cart didn't have the fancy lights like the Cove's truck, but since the Oaks's streets were rimmed with high intensity flood lights, they weren't needed. I doubted anyone could hide anywhere over there even if they wanted.

As soon as I got myself squared away, I hit the electric motor pedal and silently scooted into the night. The bar was empty when I passed at the late hour and the lights were off for the evening.

I circled the grounds clockwise and halfway around, drew up behind someone walking right down the middle of the street. I slowed down to a crawl. I didn't want to come upon someone and scare them, but I noticed the familiar stride of Chad Jones.

I figured he was headed to his parents' house. I was about to speed up to intercept him and offer a ride, but he swung off just then and strode down a side street. The direction surprised me. Only fifty-five to sixty-year-olds lived in the newest part of the complex. If Chad's parents actually owned a house in the Oaks, the unit would be on the northern side of the complex which was built thirty or forty years ago, when the first folks retired here. The average age of those retirees ranged from eighty to ninety, and that's where I would have expected Chad's parents to own a home, not with the fifty-five- year-old recent buyers.

I coasted to a stop and got out to follow Chad on foot.

I had to jog a little to keep the distance between us the same. A few houses down, he veered into a driveway at a garden home. I waited behind a thick crepe myrtle for cover. I expected the lights from the home to come on, but they didn't. A few minutes later I started to think I had gone to the wrong place. When another couple of minutes passed, I left my cover and crept up to the dark house. I got on the porch and put my ear up to the front door. Someone had a television on inside, but again, no lights.

I switched on my phone and when the startup screen lit, I used the light to read the name on the mailbox by the door. *'Ralph and Rebecca Swartz',* not *'Jones'.* I took a quick photo of the name plate, hopped off the porch, and jogged to the golf cart.

When I got back, Manny was snoring away on the sofa. An old war movie played on the television, but he had the sound dialed down, so Ricky wouldn't be awoken by bombs and artillery fire. I left the television on. If I had messed with the controls, Manny would have instantly awakened, so I let him sleep. I'd worry about him in the morning.

With my phone open to my photo library, I searched for Chad's parents through an online background source we use to check credit. There were a number of doctors named Swartz in Minnesota and an equal number in Wisconsin. Between the two states, it would be impossible to run them all down.

A better idea would be to just ask Chad about my questions. I mean, there could be a lot of reasons why he had a different last name than his father and mother, and I hoped he could give me a reason I could believe.

Chapter Twenty-Two

Wednesday

With Manny unavailable for the Wednesday night cookout, the day progressed from a morning of plain difficult to an afternoon of impossible. Thankfully, Aunt Colleen said she'd take over the cookout duties.

"Are you sure?" I asked after I explained what we were up against with Manny still hiding.

"I used to handle the department's summer get together. Now, you haven't lived until you've fed a hundred cops and their families. You get everything together and I'll jump in and do the cooking."

"Here, you'd better study," I said, handing her the menu. "You might want to know what you're getting into."

With Colleen on board, I rushed from one housekeeping task to the next, and even skipped lunch. I drove my truck through town and bought the groceries and other supplies we didn't typically have on hand for normal operations but needed for the cookout. I stopped at the convenience store where we got our propane for the gas grill. On the last stop, I parked in front of Geno's Bakery to pick up the ten dozen sesame seed buns big enough to hold the triple cheeseburgers on the menu.

Geno saw me in the crowded shop and signaled to me, pointing a finger in the air, indicating it would be a minute before the order was ready. The delicious aroma of baking bread floated over the place and since I was waiting, I ordered a coffee, and a custard filled zeppole. I scarfed down the pastry treat and gulped my coffee before Geno came out with my order.

After he helped me load our standing order of Wednesday buns, I checked them off my list and congratulated myself on getting everything on the list in record time.

I started up the old truck and headed down the drive that circled Beach Mall. I got to the end of the strip of retail stores and Benny's pawn shop. His sign above the building, *Sold on Old and Gold*, hovered like a vulture. Remembering what Winters had said about a Salvatore camera showing up there, I pulled to a stop in front of the shop.

I had only lived in Cabana Bay a few weeks when I found out about Benny's. The shop was known for paying low prices for people's old jewelry. Of course, that was only what I heard, but old people getting ripped off didn't sit well with me. I had a long way to go, but eventually I'd be an old person, too.

The shop had two brightly lit sidewalk display windows on either side of the recessed doorway. The extra light made the old, tarnished gold gleam like new, and the diamonds sparkle brighter. I frowned at the diverse collection of old wedding and engagement rings, necklaces, earrings, and other jewelry on display. Tears welled up in my eyes just thinking about old women coming in with their family treasures to pawn and sell for pennies on the dollar so they could raise a little money. It was money they probably needed to keep up with an inflation rate which outpaced their once adequate savings and pensions. I made a mental note that if I ever needed money, I could sell my old wedding ring. That was a hunk of gold I certainly didn't want anymore. I wondered how much I could get for it.

When I opened the shop door a little bell announced my presence, and I called out to an old guy behind a counter. "Benny?"

"Yes, ma'am," the guy with a rough beard said, maybe a little surprised that someone so young would even have any gold to pawn. "What can I do for you?"

Since I didn't have time to prepare a cover story of why I stopped in, I stuck with the truth, but with a smile. "Hi, I'm Moli Soto. Maybe you know my uncle, Manny Soto?"

"Oh sure, everyone knows Manny."

Surprise.

"Detective Winters told us about some stolen merchandise you took in, and we were wondering about that."

"Who is we?"

"Manny and me. You see, he provides security services to the Oaks and the campground and there have been a couple of break-ins over in the Oaks. Manny is in charge of recovering the stolen stuff, so we wondered if some of the things you have could have come from the Oaks, or the campground."

Benny's face squeezed up like he had sucked on a lemon. "I already told the cops what I know, which isn't much. It's hard to keep up with everything that comes in and out of here."

Which wasn't necessarily the case since these shops needed to keep detailed records for just such a purpose, but I didn't say anything.

"Detective Winters said you were cooperative."

"I want to cooperate with law enforcement," Benny said, his voice deep, like authoritative. "I'm a big supporter of law and order and always follow the law."

"Everyone appreciates that. We all value the vital role your shop plays in the community. Weren't you folks a sponsor of the Diabetes 5K Walk this summer?"

"Six years in a row."

"That's what I mean. You know, the Cabana Bay Cottages sponsored the race as well."

"Yeah, I saw that."

"As a fellow small businessman in the community, I hoped you'd talk to me about the man who pawned that stolen camera."

"I already told the detective everything I know."

"He shared with us what you told them, but maybe you recall something now that you didn't then."

"Like what?

"Well, let's see. You said he was young?"

"Right."

"Big guy?"

"A little taller than average and wide in the shoulders, with heavy arms, like he had worked hard all his life."

"How was he dressed, like a northerner, or like a local?"

"Oh, definitely a northerner. He wore a suit coat, fancy hat, and carried a cane."

"Did you notice anything about his hygiene?"

"What do you mean?"

"I mean, was he clean, or was he more like a homeless person."

"No, he was clean and healthy."

"Did he have an accent?"

"Oh sure, New York area, no doubt."

"Did he act like he'd pawned things before, or was he nervous about the whole thing?"

"No, I could tell he'd been through the drill before."

"How could you tell?"

"Because he argued about the price. In fact, he said if I gave him a decent price, he had other photography equipment he'd be willing to sell. So, I gave him a preferred customer price for what he had. Of course, that was before I found out the camera was stolen."

"Do you think he'll come back?"

"I hope he doesn't. I don't need to deal in stolen merchandise. There's enough legal old things in town."

****

When I climbed back into my truck, I realized I had wasted time trying to get more information on the man that pawned the camera. So much time that now we'd have to rush to get ready for the Wednesday cookout.

I drove faster than I should have but got the supplies Aunt Colleen needed back to the bar in time for her to start organizing. Chad arrived early to help, and I had asked two extra ladies from the shack crew to come in too. They both agreed because tips would be three times the normal amount and usually they all fought over the Wednesday night shift. Manny started off directing everything from the laundry room, but Colleen didn't like hearing it and closed the door on him.

A bigger than normal crowd crashed into the place. With a line of twenty or more waiting for the triple burgers, Colleen worked behind a cloud of grill smoke, flipping burgers and frying pub chips.

With the extra help on duty, we survived, and

everyone left happy. A couple of people said the burgers were the best they ever had. I made a mental note not to tell Manny about the feedback, although I did tell Aunt Colleen.

When everyone had cleared out and we finished cleaning, we all took a seat at the bar as the ladies cashed out, and Chad closed the register.

"Well, ladies," I said to the group, "thanks for the extra duty tonight. If business stays like this, we might have to put more people on the clock. No more surprising staffing changes. If any of your friends need part-time hours, send them our way."

By the time we finished, I could hear my bed calling for me. Chad said something half-heartedly about a breakfast, but when I didn't respond, he didn't argue.

Colleen and I found Manny sitting on the sofa with a WWII rerun on the television. He powered off the set when he saw us. "I took a quick peek at the crowd out there when I came to sit with Ricky."

"Yeah," I said, "what did you think?"

"You guys did such a good job maybe you should take over permanently."

"No," Colleen said, "you'll have to ride the monster you created again, as soon as you get out of here."

"Speaking of monsters," I said, "did you hear back from your man in New York on Colombo?"

"No," Manny said, "not yet. If he doesn't get back to me by the end of the week, I'll ping him."

"Yes, with the Doc out of the picture, we've only got Colombo left. If he doesn't pan out, we are all back to square one."

"What do you mean the Doc is out of the picture?"

Realizing we had never gotten around to telling

Manny about the Doc, Aunt Colleen gave him the news.

"You guys figured this out?" he said. "That's good police work. Winters would be proud of you."

"Okay," I said, "but that still doesn't get Gloria out of jail. What are we going to do about it?"

After we were quiet for a minute, Manny said, "We hope Colombo comes back dirty."

"Or" Colleen concluded, "we hope Winters is a better cop than you guys give him credit for."

Chapter Twenty-Three

Thursday

With Manny hiding out, Gloria in jail, and the busy weekend coming, I just wanted the Salvatore thing to end. I'd been ignoring my son, and even with the Dude's help, I fell short on my mom duties.

"Don't be so hard on yourself," Aunt Colleen said as she helped put out the Thursday morning breakfast.

She had told me the night before, when I finished the patrols, that she'd help me out when she could. With Harry, the assistant manager, gone, the higher ups made her a full manager over at the campground, so she could make her own hours.

That morning, she came over early to set out the breakfast and gave me a little more time to get Ricky ready for school. Even though the Dude makes a great bodyguard, he doesn't have a clue about little boy school clothes. After I got Ricky on the school bus I hurried back to the breakfast room.

"I can't help it," I told Colleen, when I shuffled back. "It's like I'm running this place single handed. Give me one good reason to keep going like this?"

"Because this isn't just a job," she said. "This is the family, and that's what you do in a family."

When we both got a coffee, we sat at a table in the corner. Guests were in and out of the room in a steadily flow. "What kind of family?" I asked her. "You and Manny separated. I'm divorced. Ricky is without a father, and his best friend is a big brown dog. What kind of a family is that?"

She smiled at me and gripping my hand she said, "The kind that loves each other."

I started to feel better about myself—until Frank Winters arrived.

He made eye contact with me and stomped straight across the room. "Where's Manny?"

"I'm not his keeper, Detective Winters, but I can tell you I haven't seen him this morning."

When Winters noticed Colleen, he said, "You must be Colleen Soto."

If Aunt Colleen was taken aback, she didn't show it. "That's right and you are?"

"I'm Cabana Bay Detective Frank Winters," he said, straightening to his full height. "I'm sure you heard that I'm working the Tony Salvatore case."

"And how would I hear that?" Colleen said, leaning back in her chair and looking up at the guy.

"Because when I talked to your former chief, he said that during his career, you were one of the smartest cops he ever had the honor to serve with."

After a pause, when Aunt Colleen didn't appear surprised that Winters had checked on her, she said, "That was very gracious of Chief Polaski. I consider him with as much high regard."

"Yeah, that's the thing, I can't understand why a nice white lady like you can get mixed up with someone like Manny."

"You mean a *Mexican* guy?" her tone of voice steady. Squinting at him she said, "Do you have something against Mexicans, Detective Winters?"

"No, I like Mexicans okay, but what I don't like is some guy trying to show me up. You're a smart woman. What do you see in Manny anyway?"

"Well," she said promptly, pointing her finger at the man, "Unlike most men, Manny has a great deal to like and after forty years of marriage, well, I've only grown to love him more for his faults."

"Aren't you two divorced?"

"We separated a few years ago before he came out here, but we never finalized the process."

"I should tell you that he's been seeing other women."

Colleen didn't skip a beat. It was like she'd been waiting all her life to defend Manny to a jerk like Winters. "When we separated, we suspended the marriage vows. After forty years, I figured he'd be hard pressed not to chase some women around. Manny is still just a man, maybe louder and bigger than the average, but still a man. A man I love."

"That's understanding of you."

"That's what love does."

"I wouldn't have any idea about love. My expertise is being a cop and you and Manny playing cops is mucking up my investigation."

Instead of denying it, she said, "We're just trying to lend a hand."

"Well, the Cabana Bay Police Department doesn't need your help. I told Manny and Moli Maid here, and I'm telling you, stay out of this. You're not a cop anymore and I won't tolerate any interference. Now, I haven't taken out a warrant for Manny, yet, but if he doesn't come in and meet with me and come clean on everything you've found out about this Salvatore thing, I will. That way he'll be in jail, and we'll have him where I can find him when I want to talk to him."

With that, Winters pivoted sharply and left us with our coffee. On his way out he stopped at the breakfast bar and grabbed a couple of donuts.

"Well," Colleen said, "what's eating him?"

I hesitated to tell her about Manny and Winters; things were dicey enough. But with my long hesitation I think she guessed.

"Oh, I see. Winters and Manny butted horns on a case?"

"A couple."

"That's okay. We've got more to worry about now, and our list of suspects is shrinking. I kind of like Winters, though."

That came as a huge surprise. "Yeah?"

"Sure, he doesn't sound like he cut Manny any slack. Sometimes that's what Manny needs."

****

I left Aunt Colleen to tend to the breakfast bar cleaning and hustled to the golf cart parking area to get the compound's maintenance cart. In addition to the bar area, all the cabanas, as well as the pathways, needed a good cleaning. I didn't think I'd have time to finish before Ricky got home, but I needed to try. Manny hates to see trash all over the place, and I've made the task to keep the complex spotless my personal challenge.

By noon I had worked my way around the facility, and the place looked spic and span, especially considering the number of customers the taco truck had served during the week. I was beginning to think maybe we should add another food truck. Maybe oysters which are big in the Sunshine State. Another truck would increase the complex's revenue stream. I'd have to get Gloria to run some projections—if she ever got out of jail.

I had just emptied the last of the ground's refuse into our dumpster behind cottage one when a big black SUV drove alongside my little golf cart and stopped. The service road behind cottage one is isolated from the rest of the compound, and I didn't like encountering a strange car there. But when the driver's side window lowered and Mike Salvatore stuck his head out of the window, I relaxed.

"You're a natural with a broom in your hand," the man said to me, smiling at his joke and shutting off the car's engine. "Like you're used to cleaning up other people's messes."

"I assume you're not talking about my janitorial skills, but my investigative abilities?"

"Something like that."

"So, did the family get here?"

"Yes, a big crowd. Tony has a lot of family, friends, and acquaintances."

"I guess that's good."

"Family and friends are good, not necessarily acquaintances. The line of work we're in attracts a lot of acquaintances. I think some people visited to see if Tony was going to make it. Ready to celebrate if he didn't."

"Celebrate?"

"Yeah, celebrate that if Tony died, whatever secrets he discovered would go to the grave with him. I'm sure a huge sigh of disappointment went up over Manhattan when the doctors told us Tony was going to make it."

"Tell me," I asked, broom in one hand and a dirty

scarf covering my hair, "with such a high-end business, what was your brother doing in little Cabana Bay?"

"I told you he just finished a job in Miami and came this way to work an unexpected new case."

"That's a lot of trouble. I'm sure he bought a round-trip flight from New York to Miami and back. But to change flights and get a rental car? That's expensive. It must have been an important current client. Not just any client. Probably a client important enough a big P.I. with other cases in the works would basically drop everything for and detour to little Cabana Bay."

After a pause he said, "You're very perceptive, Moli. You may be wasting your time in environmental services."

"That's what I tell Manny."

Mike Salvatore paused again. "Okay, listen, I talked to Tony about this. I'm going to meet with Colombo over in the Cove at eight. I've got things to discuss with him. I can't go into what things now, but I'll fill you in later and try to straighten out this mess."

"How are you going to get Colombo to meet with you?"

"I'm going to make him an offer he can't refuse."

Everyone has heard the Godfather movie cliché, but the way he said it was pretty funny.

****

After my conversation with Salvatore, I made myself a ham and cheese sandwich to stave off hunger. It had been a long time since my breakfast donut and coffee. Plus, this detective work is exhausting and made me nervous. And nervousness always made me hungry.

I made a sandwich for Manny. Then, after the Dude stared at me like he expected equal treatment, I also made him one.

Keeping in mind the local cops were still watching the compound, I used Manny's hidden closet door to the back corridor and slipped into the laundry room.

"Where've you been?" Manny asked when he saw me.

"I've been working. Sometimes I think you got yourself into all this trouble so you wouldn't have to work around here."

"I wouldn't do that. I love running this place."

"The sooner you get back to running things, the better I'll like it. In the meantime," I told him, passing him the sandwich, "eat up."

"Extra mayo?"

"Extra mayo."

"That's my girl."

I couldn't make up my mind if I should tell him about the proposed meeting between Mike Salvatore and Colombo. I figured telling him after would be better. One thing for sure, I wanted to be there. I needed support though. I wasn't worried about Mike Salvatore, but Colombo seemed capable of just about anything. I texted Aunt Colleen and told her to meet me at the head of the row of cabins just before eight o'clock.

****

I had paperwork to complete. With Gloria out of commission there were some money matters to take care of and bills to pay. No one had been to the bank to make a deposit since Manny went into hiding, so I added it to my list of duties to take care of.

After each task was completed, I checked the time on my phone. I just couldn't wait until eight o'clock. I just couldn't wait to hear what Mike Salvatore had to say. I just couldn't wait to see what Colombo would do when confronted.

But confronted about what? Trying to kill Tony Salvatore?

At three o'clock, the Dude and I walked out to meet Ricky. When we got there, I waved at the cop in the Cabana Bay Police cruiser parked out front, and the Dude barked. Don't let anyone tell you differently, dogs have a long memory. Or maybe it's just the scent they never forget. Like I never forget a name, Manny never forgets a face, and the Dude never forgets a smell.

Back in the apartment, I got the two buddies settled in front of the television, and I hustled to the bar and lost myself in the task of taking inventory of our supplies. With the massively busy week we'd had, I didn't want to run out of anything over the weekend.

When I checked in the laundry room, I found Manny sitting back in his underwear, a tip sheet by his favorite racetrack handicapper in his lap. After seeing Gloria in the same place, in her underwear and beautiful body, the sight of Manny jolted me. I prayed I'd be able to get the vison of Manny in his skivvies out of my head. If not, the scene might morph into one of those things that you never forget.

"I see you're trying to spend your time profitably?"

"Just trying to keep up with the latest odds," Manny said. "What's new with the case?"

I told him about the meeting between Mike Salvatore and Colombo and how I wanted to get close enough to hear what they talked about.

"That's too dangerous," Manny said. "I'd better come along."

"Besides the fact the cops out front will see you and

pick you up, you're not exactly the cat burglar. On the other hand, the good thing about getting picked up is you might be able to share a cell with Gloria."

"Nah, they house the males and females in different units."

"We can't show up in force like that; they might see us. Aunt Colleen said she can come along as back up."

"That makes the job more dangerous."

"Come on…"

"Hey, you're young and can take care of yourself, but Colleen's not the dynamo she used to be."

"Look who's talking. How about we take the Dude with us?"

"That will help."

****

For dinner, Manny snuck in through his hidden closet door. I warmed some leftover beef patties from the Wednesday night cookout and made hamburgers for Ricky, Manny, and me. For the Dude, I chopped up several patties and poured spicy sauce all over them. They were his favorite. Who said I couldn't cook?

With the big meeting between Salvatore and Colombo not for another hour, I slow played getting Ricky in bed and read to him. He usually goes to bed at seven, but with the meeting not until eight I read him a couple of extra books. I'd been anticipating the meeting all day and couldn't wait, so I was trying to fill the time until I had to leave.

I slipped on a pair of sneakers and changed into dark clothing, like the spies wear when on a mission. I pulled my hair back into a ponytail but left the Dude asleep under Ricky. Chances are he'd complicate the whole thing if I took him.

When I got out front Manny said, "Where's the Dude?"

"He can be loud, so I'm going to leave him."

"That's probably a good call. He can be like that bull in a china shop. What time's the meeting?

"Not until eight, but I'm going to go over early and stake out a spot."

"How about Colleen?"

"She's meeting me there."

"Okay then, you two be careful."

Although I didn't really feel that confident about the whole thing I said, "It's a piece of cake."

Chapter Twenty-Four

Cabana Moon

Since I had time, I meandered over to the campground and figured to beat Aunt Colleen there. I wandered across the Cove complex, then strolled up the beach path and approached Cabin Row. It was nearly dark, but I could make out the path between cabins and was looking for a spot to hide when Colleen jumped out of the bushes and scared me out of my shoes.

"Please keep quiet!" she hissed. "Are you trying to wake the dead?"

"Sorry, I was looking for a spot to hide in so Mike Salvatore wouldn't see me when he got here."

"You're too late. Salvatore got here a few minutes ago and tramped down the path."

"So early?"

"He must be anxious."

"How many cabins are rented out this week?"

"The four up here, next to the beach access, but none down at the other end by Mike's cabin."

"I don't like it. I expected a little more company down there. Aren't you a little afraid? Manny wanted to come, but with the cops on the prowl, I convinced him not to come."

"You convinced Manny not to do something?"

"I know, surprise, surprise."

"Well, let's get going."

It took us less than a minute to walk down the road. A fall full Cabana moon was out, just over the horizon, and lent an eerie atmosphere to the scene. Eventually we reached the end of the path. With none of the units at the far end rented, the whole area was in semi darkness, and the only sound I heard came from the male frogs in the nearby marsh, croaking out in the night for a potential mate.

The end cabin stood bleak and silent. I expected to see at least some light. I couldn't believe Salvatore would meet with Colombo in the dark.

"I don't like it," Colleen said.

"Yeah, the place gives me the creeps."

"Maybe I should go in with you?"

"No, you need to keep watch."

"What if you run into trouble?"

"Then you'll hear me scream."

"Be serious."

"I'll be fine. I'll just take a peek."

I crept up the short path to the screened porch fronting the length of the cabin. In spite of my bravado with Colleen, I started to sweat and not because of the humid night. A screen door stood ajar at the top of three wooden steps. I swallowed hard and waved at Colleen. Before going any farther, I got out my phone and pressed on the flashlight function to light my way.

From the stoop, I could see the inner door ajar as well, and I swallowed again and pushed through the outer door. Darkness engulfed the space beyond, like the beginning of a nightmare.

I stopped at the edge of the inner doorway, and I hoped I was close enough to hear conversation. Before I could get good and scared, a noise, like a thump, filled the room. That's right, a genuine thump in the night. I slowly stepped into the room and swept the phone light around and illuminated the fully dressed figure of Dante Colombo, getting up off the floor, with the body of Mike Salvatore right at his feet. Even from where I stood, I could tell the other Salvatore brother was in a bad way. Of course, the bloody hammer in Colombo's right hand may have played a role in the situation, then again, sometimes a person's vision plays tricks on you.

"Freeze, Colombo," Aunt Colleen said, coming into the room, both arms out and her hands wrapped around the handle of a Glock service weapon. She held a small flashlight beneath the gun, which she used to illuminate the form of Dante Colombo.

Colombo appeared in shock, first gawking at Aunt Colleen and blinking in the glare of light. Then he gazed at me, then looked down at the body of Mike Salvatore.

"Stay where you are," Detective Winters said when he stormed through the door, taking the same stance as Colleen, but on the other side of me, with a smaller weapon in his hand but a bigger flashlight.

Colombo squinted at Winters and Colleen, then looked down at the body of Salvatore.

"What's going on?" Manny said, joining the crowd. He had his old service revolver and a large flashlight. Not to be left out of the action, he raised the flashlight and his pistol up into firing position. "Will someone tell me what's going on?"

In the bright light, Colombo squinted at Manny, then looked down at Salvatore's body.

Then, someone behind us switched on the overhead lights, bathing the room in a glare, making everyone blink at the brightness. "FBI," Chad said.

Colombo looked at our latest visitor. I looked at our latest visitor. Chad looked at me. "Nobody move."

I don't think anyone was about to move with so many guns raised into a firing position, especially Colombo.

Two uniformed cops charged into the room last, guns drawn. I think they were a little disappointed they'd missed most of the action. I felt left out too because I didn't have a gun.

****

Colombo finally came out of shock and proclaimed to everyone holding a gun that he was innocent. He said he had come there for a meeting and when he arrived, he found the hammer on the door threshold. He said he couldn't see Salvatore's blood when he picked up the hammer because the lights were off. He said he had just gotten into the room and tripped over Salvatore and fell. He had just got to his feet when I came in behind him and lit up the space with my phone light. He said that was the first time he saw Salvatore stretched out on the floor.

Then Mike Salvatore groaned.

****

I finally regained my composure about Chad being an FBI agent. He had kept his secret from me and that ticked me off a little. I guess being FBI wasn't so bad. I mean, he could have been the one who tried to kill Salvatore.

Winters told the cops to cuff Colombo, read him his rights, and call the paramedics for Mike Salvatore. He told the rest of us to put the guns away and leave the cabin.

Once outside, with Colombo secure in a patrol car,

Winters asked me what I was doing there.

Without time to think of a good excuse I told him the truth, but with a smile, "Salvatore told me he was meeting with Colombo, so I decided I'd spy on them."

Just then the paramedics arrived and rushed into the cabin to tend to Mike Salvatore.

"How did you know about the meeting?" I asked Winters.

"The FBI asked for back up."

"How did the FBI know?"

Manny said, "I told them. Colleen sent me a message, said she was worried, and I made some calls."

"Do you know people in every governmental agency?" I asked Manny.

"Just a few."

"How did they respond so quickly?"

"Chad's on a case in the Oaks, a burglary cases, and he's FBI undercover."

I looked at Chad. "Who's bartending?"

Chad looked at me. "Who's watching Ricky?"

****

Full of ourselves over the role we played breaking the case, we all retired to the bar to celebrate. I checked on Ricky first, but with the Dude on guard I didn't have to worry.

Chad accompanied Winters downtown to question Colombo. With a real suspect in custody, Winters let Manny off the hook, so he didn't have to hide anymore. Thank God. Those night-time patrols were killing me.

Some of the long termers joined the crowd. Manny hugged the women and clapped the backs of the men. The only guests I didn't see were Lou and Marge Gigliotti and Colombo, of course, who was in jail.

Around midnight, with the crowd thinning out, Chad came in with Gloria at his side. "Mike Salvatore is going to make it," he announced. "They put him in a room with his brother. Together, they are making life miserable for the nurses. I talked Winters into letting Gloria go," Chad added. "She obviously couldn't have had anything to do with either Salvatore assault, especially since she was in jail when Mike Salvatore got whacked."

"How did Winters take it?" I asked.

"Since he has a real suspect behind bars, he's happy, and the mayor's happy."

"Anyone have a cigarette?" Gloria asked.

Just then a tall, handsome guy reached around Gloria to offer her a cigarette from a pack. I guessed Mr. Big was there to welcome her home.

When we closed, the ex-cops, Colleen, and Manny, me, and the real cop, Chad, settled on the stools around the bar and talked about the case. Gloria and Mr. Big had disappeared, I imagined heading off to make up for lost time. Man, do I have to be arrested to be so lucky?

"So," I asked Chad, "what did Colombo say?"

"He says he's innocent. Just like he said when we caught him with Manny's hammer in his hand."

"That's my favorite hammer," Manny whined.

"Forensics will have to go over everything and go back to cottage fourteen, Winters told me, but they'll find enough to tie him to the Salvatore attacks."

I asked Chad about his view of the case.

"Winters thinks Colombo was skimming from the condo project. That's why it's been in financial trouble. He figures once they run some numbers, they'll have the evidence and the reason the Salvatore brothers were sent down here and the motive for Colombo."

"What do you think?"

"It's their case. I try to stay out of the local police's way. Unlike some people I know," he said.

The three Sotos made no response.

Chad wasn't done. "Unfortunately, they'll have to close down cottage fifteen, until Winters can get the crime scene team in there." And before Manny could say anything he added, "Winters is mad as hell at you guys and the mayor is breathing down his neck, so don't expect any favors from the man."

I know Winters thought we'd been a drag on his investigation, but who knows what would have happened if we hadn't been involved. If Mike Salvatore hadn't come to town and started asking questions, maybe we never would have caught Colombo like we did. In fact, I still had questions about the whole case. Questions I wanted to ask. A lot of them, but with everyone celebrating, I decided my questions could wait.

Chapter Twenty-Five

Friday

Finally, we had a normal day. Gloria was back in charge of the bar and the shack ladies. Manny was back in charge of the night patrols. Aunt Colleen was back at her undercover job at the campground, and I was back in charge of Ricky and the Dude and environmental services.

Happy day!

Funny, about environmental services. That was what Mike Salvatore called it, making a joke. I liked the guy, but I couldn't ignore my contribution to the circumstances surrounding his attack. If I had fingered Colombo sooner, he wouldn't have confronted Salvatore, or Salvatore would have been more careful about meeting him in a dark place.

"Don't worry about that." Chad had told me the night before. "Colombo is a nut. You couldn't have predicted his actions."

The story on the Salvatore brothers broke the night before on late-night news and even got views on the internet and the morning paper. The morning news programs had the story as well. The Cabana Bay Cottages and Bar were prominently mentioned across all media, so Manny and Gloria spent the day preparing for a big Friday night.

Detective Winters tried to keep the Soto name out of the spotlight, but the story spread, and by that afternoon, the Sotos and the Cabana Bay Cottages went viral. With social media news spreading, I couldn't even imagine the crowd for tacos that night.

I spent the morning engaged in environmental services and in the office working on the reservation system. On the dot of noon, Chad arrived.

"Is your name even Chad?" I asked him.

"No, it's Jack."

"You're kidding? Like in Jack Ryan?"

"No, like in John Robert Davidson. All my friends call me Jack. And before you ask, yes, my grandfather and father are doctors, and I did get accepted to the Wisconsin School of Medicine, I just didn't go."

"So, let me get this straight," I said, rocking way back in my spring-loaded office chair, and pointing my pencil at him, "you chose a career in law enforcement over being a rich doctor with a second home in beautiful Cabana Bay?"

"Something like that."

"Why?"

"Why did you want to be a cop?"

"I never wanted to be a cop, but my parents expected us kids to follow in their footsteps. What's your excuse?"

"We've got enough doctors in our family. My sister's a doctor, too. They all do excellent work, but they work ER stuff. They work on people after they are hurt, and I wanted to stop the trouble before people get hurt."

I waited a minute, digesting what he said, but the logic thread was too much to wrap my head around. "I guess you won't be working in the bar tonight?"

"With my cover blown, I can't go back to that."

"Too bad. Manny said you had the makings of a good bartender. Speaking of Manny, did he peg you from the start?"

"It took him a few of days, but he figured it and promised to keep it a secret. He's a sharp dude. He puts on the lazy front with the flip flops and Hawaiian shirts, but he's still a tough old cop. He told me my secret was safe with him."

"That's our Manny."

We were at an awkward moment. At the big transition, the intersection, the fork in the road. Was Chad, I mean Jack, going to say goodbye when after, we'd never see each other again? Or was this the moment when we continue the dream, that maybe we have a chance together.

Maybe there was a future? I was torn between the two, even though I had supposedly given up on men. Instead, the door opened, and a familiar man dressed in a dark suit and wingtips entered. "Are you Moli Soto?"

"Who wants to know?"

"Me...Fred Salvatore."

****

At first sight, the man looked familiar, maybe a little older than Mike and Tony Salvatore, but he bore the same solid stature, broad face, and thinning black hair of the family.

"Who?"

"Fred Salvatore, Mike and Tony's big brother. We all work together."

"How many of you are there?"

"Why do you want to know? How many of us are you planning to put in the hospital?"

That hurt. Even in jest, it stung. "Well, I guess I'm

a little to blame for all that."

"A little? The cops won't tell me anything, so Mike said I should come talk to you."

"What do you want to know?"

"Everything."

So, I told him what we had been doing, what we found out, and what we assumed.

After I finished, he started to smile. At first, he started with a small smile, like just a grin, but his smile broadened, stretched across his face, like when Mike Salvatore smiled, showing big white teeth. Then, he burst out laughing.

"Tell, me," he said, when he quieted down a little and caught his breath, "there's no one's job or house on the line with this is there?"

"Why?

"Because you are all so far off on this, it will be a joke, and I don't want anyone to get fired."

"I don't work for anyone, but I'm not sure about Chad, I mean, Jack."

"Okay, listen up, Tony did come to investigate Colombo, but not for skimming off the condo project. No, you see, Dante Colombo is married to a granddaughter of the head of the Vincenzo family, in New Jersey. We do a lot of work for the family, so when Lisa Colombo, the granddaughter, told us she suspected Dante was cheating on her, she wanted us to investigate. That's what Tony was doing. Checking on Colombo's extra-marital affairs.

"When Tony got whacked, Colombo had no idea Tony was in town, much less investigating him."

"They were virtually neighbors."

"Tony is good at undercover work. He was secretly

tailing Colombo and can disappear into a crowd like nobody else. Plus, Dante worked long hours and wasn't expecting to be tailed. So, when Mike showed up, Dante was surprised to see him but agreed to meet. He didn't know the meeting was about things between him and Lisa, and he didn't know about Tony. The night Mike got it, Dante showed up to just go over a few details about family matters."

"So, you don't think Colombo wanted to kill Mike and Tony Salvatore?"

"No, Tony and Colombo go way back. Tony was Colombo's best man at his wedding. I think Mike is the godfather of Colombo's oldest son."

Now, I felt foolish about the whole thing. I had thought the pieces didn't seem to fit back when they arrested Colombo, but just not why. I wondered what Chad, I mean, Jack thought.

Chad, I mean, Jack asked, "Have you told Detective Winters any of this?"

"No, not yet."

"Why not?"

"Hey, what we do is confidential. The Vincenzo family is a private family. What goes on in the family stays in the family. Tony and Mike wouldn't tell the cops anything about this. That's why I'm here. Mike trusts you, Moli, and Jack and the FBI will keep this from the local cops, as long as no one is going to get hurt. So, that's why I told you what's going on."

"So, now what?"

"I can't speak for you guys, but I'm only staying long enough to make sure Tony and Mike are well enough to travel."

"What about Colombo?"

"Once the evidence is in, they'll have to let him go. We'll give them enough to set the record straight and the family will transfer Colombo someplace else. He's a nice kid, but he's not at the top of the dean's list, if you get what I mean."

He looks good in his underwear.

"What about the guy or gal who tried to kill Tony and Mike?"

"I'll let the local cops investigate that. It's their jurisdiction."

"So, okay then, do you need a place to stay?"

"No offense," he told me. "But I'm going to get a place downtown. I'm not much for the sun and sand."

****

Chad, I mean Jack, followed Fred Salvatore out the door, mumbling something to me about checking in with the head FBI office about everything he'd just discovered.

As he left, I wondered if that would be the last of Chad, I mean Jack. On the other hand, if he got fired for blowing the Salvatore case, maybe he'd stick around. We could always use him in the bar, but since I'm not into men anymore, I didn't care. Really.

I'd have to tell Gloria about Chad, and she'd have to set the record straight with anyone she told, and that could be a lot of people.

There was a lot to think about on this. Not the least was, since Colombo didn't try to kill the Salvatore brothers, who did?

Chapter Twenty-Six

Saturday

After talking to everyone about what Fred Salvatore told us about Dante Colombo, we all had a good laugh at ourselves, but had to start working and couldn't afford to spend a lot of time commiserating.

The Friday night crowd lived up to expectations, but we managed. With Gloria back in the bar, the place ran smooth as glass.

During the night, I snuck out of the apartment a couple of times, hoping I'd see Chad, I mean Jack, but he didn't show up. I had mixed feelings about it. On the one hand, who needed the complication. From my limited experience with them, I found men were more trouble than they were worth.

Even with not investigating an attempted murder or two, my life was full, so why did I think that adding a guy to the mix was a promising idea. Especially a government type guy.

Unfortunately, when I woke up Saturday morning, Chad, I mean Jack, and not Ricky, was the first person I thought about. What kind of a mother was I?

I didn't have time to evaluate my motherhood skills because I had a breakfast bar to arrange, people to check out, and cottages to clean before the afternoon check-in time.

People were standing in line to check out, even before the last person finished eating. When I finished checking out everyone, I started cleaning off the breakfast bar. I did a quick review of the breakfast inventory, and knew I would need to make a grocery and bakery run for supplies for the Sunday morning setup.

With my motel chores completed, I jumped in my truck and drove to town. I stopped at the party store for the paper goods, the farmers market for the fruit, and Geno's for the baked goods.

While they got my bakery order together, I stepped to the counter and ordered a coffee and sat because my feet were already throbbing from the day's activities. Halfway through my coffee a handsome man in a dark blue suit and tie strode through the door. His sunglasses hid his eyes, but I recognized Chad, I mean Jack.

"I stopped when I saw your truck out there."

"Whoa, what are you dressed for, a funeral?"

"Yeah," he said, coming over to my table and sitting across from me, "my own."

"What's up?"

"I'm flying down to Miami for a meeting with my boss in the Southeast Headquarters Regional Office."

"Are you in trouble?"

"I'm not sure. Could be."

"Well, I'm sorry if I was the cause."

"Actually, you're the one bright spot with this whole case."

I loved the way he always made me feel special. "We missed you last night."

"We or you?"

"We all missed you. They got slammed in the bar."

"I wanted to drop in, but I had calls to make and

email reports to send. I didn't finish up until late."

During a minute of embarrassed silence between us, the door opened, and Benny burst through the entrance, like in a hurry, and ordered a coffee and cannoli. When he saw me sitting there, he stopped and shuffled over to the table.

"Hello, Benny, do you come here often?"

"Yeah," he said to me, sitting in an empty seat at the table, "can't you see by this belly? You don't get this big by not eating. Who's your friend? Is he a cop?"

"This is, ah, this is Jack. Jack, this is Benny, from Benny's Pawn Shop."

"Oh, I've seen the signs, *We're Sold on Old and Gold.*"

"Do you like that? I came up with that fifty years ago."

"Cute."

"Yeah, I think people remember the service when they see the signs. I mean, think about old folk. What good does an old gold ring or gold necklace doing for you? When you're old, your fingers get thin, or you get arthritis, so you can't wear your rings anymore. What's the use? Your neck fills up with wrinkles, so you wear a scarf to hide them, and no one can see the gold necklace. Better to sell your gold stuff and take a trip somewhere, or maybe you buy your grandkids some nice things."

I said, "How about you give your gold things to your grandkids?"

"They don't want that old stuff. We end up melting down most of the gold things we buy and sell the bulk weight. It's sad but getting old is sad. I'm actually providing a service for old people."

Chad…I mean, Jack, said, "That's one way to justify

it."

"So, what are you two young kids up to today?"

"We're not so young, Benny," I said, recognizing that Chad and I were actually pretty young.

"I don't know, to me you are. Anyone younger than me is young."

"Well," I said, "we were just discussing the future."

"Your future, like together?"

Embarrassed I said, "Maybe."

"Well," he said getting up to leave, "if I learned anything living for eighty years, it's, you're only young once, so enjoy it."

After Benny left, Jack and I sat through another moment of embarrassment, he finally said, "Moli, I've got a plane to catch, but I'll be back tomorrow morning. Maybe we can meet for lunch?"

"Okay, I'd like that. I'd like to hear all about what happens at your meeting."

"Nothing dramatic. I mean, they might transfer me to another region, like maybe to Alaska."

"I read the glaciers up there are beautiful."

When he got up, I turned my cheek to him, like I was offering it for a kiss. When he leaned in, I spun quickly and planted one on his lips.

Jack left the shop, and I wondered again if that would be the last time I'd see him. I didn't know how the FBI did things. Maybe they'd put him on a plane and fly him straight to Alaska from Miami? I wondered if my old truck would make a trip to Alaska. I might have to get better tires.

I paid for my stuff and with my arms full, I shuffled out to the truck. I found a spot on top of everything in the rear seat of the crew cab and carefully arranged the bakery goods where the croissants wouldn't get squashed. I got in the truck and started to drive out of the shopping center.

Between Geno's at one end of the center and Benny's Pawn Shop at the other, Beach Mall housed a variety of shops owned and operated by locals. I loved the entrepreneurial spirit of the community and supported the neighborhood businesses when I could.

Benny's signature sign, *Sold on Old and Gold*, hovered over the North end of the center, reminding people of their advancing age. Benny didn't shy away from his business model. If you're old and have gold things then sell them to Benny, no questions asked. I mean, when people got old, did they need their gold?

I'm sure some people think of their gold things as a form of savings. For others, sentimental reasons make them hang onto their gold. The oldest member of my family, my great grandmother, who had her ninetieth birthday that summer, wears gold. She is still spry and ageless, like Benny. Despite his rationale, I couldn't envision her getting to the point where she didn't want to dress in her best, including wearing her gold rings and necklaces, no matter what her age.

Besides his penchant for preying on the old for their valuables, Benny had a positive take on aging. What did he say, everyone his age or younger was a young person. When I talked to him about the person that pawned one of Tony Salvatore's cameras, he said the guy was young.

Was he young? Or was he just younger than Benny?

I slammed on the brakes and skidded to a stop, scattering baked goods everywhere. Sliding the transmission stick to reverse, I backed up to Benny's shop. Getting out, I entered his place, and the little bell above the door announced my arrival.

"You again," Benny said from behind a display case. He still had his coffee out and the remnants of the cannoli dotted the countertop.

"Yeah, so Benny, last week when I asked you about the guy who pawned the stolen camera."

"Now, I told you, that pawn was legit."

"Right, but you said something about his age. You said the guy was a young guy. Did you mean a young guy, or did you mean he was just younger than you?"

"Any guy younger than me is young."

"I get that, Benny, I do. But in this case, how old do you think this guy was? If you had to guess."

"Oh, probably in his mid-sixties. Why?"

"I think you told Detective Winters the same thing, right? That he was a young guy?"

"Like I said…"

"Right, any guy younger than you is a young guy."

So, based on Benny's description of the guy who sold that camera, Winters and the police force had been pursuing a young guy. Not someone just younger than Benny, like someone in their sixties or seventies. Not someone young, like Colombo.

****

"What's the difference," Manny said to me when I told him what I found out from Benny. We were in the storage room putting away the supplies I just bought. "Does who is hocking Tony Salvatore's stuff really matter?"

"I think it matters if the guy pawning Salvatore's valuables is the man who tried to kill him."

"Someone old, like in their seventies? How can a seventy-year-old take down a guy like Salvatore?"

"You're in your seventies, Manny."

"But you've seen those Salvatore brothers. They are built like tanks."

Manny was right, The Salvatore brothers were pretty fit. Could a seventy-year-old man take down the Salvatore brothers? How could that even happen? Well, he'd certainly would have to had surprised them. So, how does that happen? In the case of Tony Salvatore, he was hit from behind. So, how did that happen in a small room? How would the man have gotten in the room if not invited, and if invited, how did he surprise him?

As much as I hated to admit, the whole scenario was hard to imagine, and just thinking about it gave me a headache. At that moment, I didn't think I had very much of a head for detective work after all.

****

Since it was Saturday, I rushed to the office and started to check people in for the week. The eclectic group contained a mix of singles, couples, and small families. Based on my experience, a varied group was best. The hardest was a complex full of couples. They always partied the hardest and longest, making my job as Moli the maid harder.

Unfortunately, I'd completely forgotten that Winters had closed down cottage fifteen. When I checked, the reservation system had assigned a small family, two adults and two toddlers, there. With no cancelations, I was in a bind, but I texted Colleen and told her my problem and she said she had a nice unit available on Cabin Row.

–Not the one where Mike Salvatore got whacked?– I texted.

*–Nope, Winters closed that one–*she texted back.

When the small family arrived shortly after five, I broke the news to them but explained our policy for overflow. They were a little hesitant, but I put them all in our biggest golf cart and chauffeured them over to show them the layout and they were happy with the arrangement. The little cabin was actually bigger than our cottages, so they liked that, especially since they priced them the same. To top off the service, I left the golf cart with them, so they could scoot around both complexes with ease.

By six o'clock, I had everyone checked in.

For the first time in two weeks, I fixed Ricky a dinner of franks and beans. The meal may have come out of a can, opposed to take out, but I tried. Even the Dude ate a helping.

On her way to the bar, Gloria stopped in to say she had a full crew for the night, and I wouldn't have to fill in anywhere and I could take the night off.

Lucky me.

"Who's on the back bar?" I asked.

"Mr. Big."

Happy days all around!

After I cleared the dinner plates, I took Ricky and the Dude to play on the beach with the sun, sand, and salt. Ricky wore his swim trunks and played in the water. The Dude followed him, wading along the shore and Ricky rode on the dog's back. There were other kids from the campground in the water and they all took turns riding on the Dude's back, and he loved it. A few parents appeared apprehensive about the dog's size, but with Ricky playing and hugging on him, they relaxed a little but stayed alert.

With the sun setting it was cool enough to play for a

couple of hours. At the end, Ricky and the Dude were exhausted, and I dragged them back to the complex. I stopped at one of our outdoor showers and washed the Dude and Ricky down. I dried Ricky off with a towel but gave the Dude about a ten-foot space so he could shake off, sprinkling water everywhere, including on our row of golf carts and Manny's truck parked nearby in our private guest and staff lot.

I was going to make popcorn for everyone, but when I started to put Ricky's PJs on him, his head drooped, so I put him straight to bed. He was asleep in a minute, with the Dude not far behind.

I left them to their dreams and slipped out into the living area to pour myself a glass of wine. I was going around the room closing blinds and through the South windows I saw that Señora Martinez's cottage and Lou and Marge Gigliotti's cottage were dark. I wondered where the old people were on a Saturday night.

****

I fell asleep in front of the television but woke up when Manny toddled in. He looked exhausted, so I volunteered to make his security patrol rounds for him. I didn't have to ask him twice. He tossed his key ring to me and disappeared into the back of the apartment.

The Dude fought me when I called to get him up to ride shotgun with me, but when I jingled the keys in front of him, he perked up and ran out to the truck.

The campground was quiet, and the Oaks was quiet too, like the dark of night, which it was.

When I got back to the apartment, I could barely keep my eyes open. The apartment's parking lot door was locked, so I got out my master key to open it, but it wouldn't work. So, half asleep, I used the door's duplicate key and let myself in.

Now extremely tired, I brushed my teeth and climbed into bed. In the dark I heard the Dude snoring away. Just before I nodded off, I wondered if Chad, I mean Jack, snored in his sleep, and I wondered if I'd ever get the chance to find out.

Chapter Twenty-Seven

Sunday

The next morning, after the busy day and Saturday night frenzy, my legs felt like lead. Someone banging around in the kitchen had woken me. The Dude was missing, but Ricky slept soundly, still worn out from yesterday's afternoon in the sun, sand, and salt.

When I stumbled out to the sitting area, Aunt Colleen was in the kitchen, working on the breakfast bar prep.

"You need to stop coming over and helping like this," I told her. "You're going to spoil Manny and me. Don't you already have a job?"

"It's the least I can do with you folks working late last night."

I helped her get the rest of the stuff out and when the first of the guests started coming in, we took the window seat that Lou and Marge Gigliotti always took.

When we sat down, I said, "We might have to give up this table if Lou and Marge come in to eat."

"Why?" Colleen asked as she got situated with coffee and a donut.

"Because this is their table. At least it's been their table since I've been here. Habits are hard to break for old people."

"Well, they'll have to fight me for it. At least until I

finish this Boston creme."

We talked about the Salvatore case for a while, being careful not to talk too loudly so we wouldn't be heard by the guests. It was still a mystery about who wanted to kill Tony and Mike Salvatore, but we had reached the point where we were tired with the whole affair. Gloria and Bob Lopez were out of jail and Manny was off the hook, so what did we care? We still had the Pagan drug thing going on in the campground, but as long as we got back to full capacity in the Cottages, we'd be happy.

After an hour of sitting and talking, the breakfast bar closing time came, so we cleaned.

"Thanks for helping, Colleen," I told her as we carried leftovers to the back.

Manny, Ricky, and the Dude were sitting in front of the television watching cartoons when we plodded in with our arms full.

"I've got breakfast, if you want it."

"Mom, are there any donuts?"

Even though I shouldn't have, I said, "Chocolate, just the ones you like." What kind of a mother was I?

After Colleen left, I searched for my housekeeping cart. I hoped Chad, I mean Jack, would actually come back for lunch, but I couldn't just sit around waiting on the guy. I mean, what kind of woman just sits around waiting on a man? I had important things to do. Like clean toilets.

Since it was the weekend, I started cleaning the South wing cottages of the long-term renters, beginning with cottage three. I was always careful with personal items when cleaning the cottages. For a couple of renters, these places are their only homes, so I respected their privacy by not snooping in drawers or peeking into closets, except for Doc Murphy's that is.

Señora Martinez was probably in church somewhere, so when she didn't answer my knock, I let myself in with the duplicate cottage key and started cleaning. She had the usual mix of to-go boxes and bakery bags. From the bags I found it appeared she favored a Cuban bakery in town over the heavily sweetened confections we stocked in our breakfast bar. Señora Martinez kept her figure trim and neat. Probably the result of avoiding the American diet of three basic food groups: sugar, salt, and carbs.

When I swept out the kitchen area, I gathered a pile of her clay work particles. Playing a game, as I always did, I surveyed the room to see which of the varied plates and cups on her shelves was her latest creation. I decided, since we were approaching the holidays, the red and green Christmas decorated coffee mug was the most recent addition to her collection. At least I hadn't remembered seeing it before.

When I finished, I locked the place and wheeled my cart next door to the Professor's cottage. I knocked but he didn't answer. Maybe he attended church in search of redemption. I let myself in with the cottage's duplicate key.

I had missed cleaning his cottage the week before, so the place was a mess and took longer than I planned but finished up. When I was done, I closed up the unit and made my last stop, next door.

I hadn't seen much of Lou and Marge Gigliotti over the last few days. I noticed their big old Buick was in and out of the parking lot, but I hadn't seen them since Thursday. They frequented the senior center during the day and took advantage of the scheduled activities there, but not seeing their car at night was a new habit for them. Of course, it was none of my business what they were doing.

I knocked on their door and when no one answered, I let myself in with the duplicate key and started by changing all the linen. Marge wasn't much for cleaning, and I didn't blame her. After a life of working and keeping house, she was enjoying her retirement, and cleaning was not part of that equation. That was one reason they switched over to the Cottages.

When I swept out the rooms, I was surprised to find a mess of clay particles under the kitchen island, just like I found in Señora Martinez's cottage. The clay surprised me because I couldn't picture them making funny mugs or bowls, and there were no results of their work on display on any shelves.

After cottage one, I dumped the trash from the three cottages into our dumpster and headed back to the office.

I checked my watch as I rolled the housekeeping cart. I calculated, if I hurried, I'd have just enough time to shower and make myself presentable, just in case Chad, I mean Jack, showed up for our lunch date. I wasn't counting the minutes or anything, but I was anxious to hear if he was going to be transferred to Alaska.

****

"You smell good," Ricky said when I came out of our room.

"Wow," Manny said, sitting at the island, reading the Sunday paper. He had already showered and dressed, wearing a pair of chinos and shoes, to go along with a fresh Hawaiian shirt. "What are you up to today?"

"I might be going out. If I do, can you watch Ricky?"

"Okay, but he'll have to go with Colleen and me to church."

"Church?"

"Don't worry; he'll be fine. They have a children thing for the kids."

I hesitated. I was delinquent with my own church responsibilities, so I should have b0een happy if Ricky got in a little of the Holy Gospel. I mean, his soul needed saving as much as any. Right?

"We'll go for lunch after."

"Okay, Ricky?" I asked my boy.

"Can I get ice cream for dessert?"

By the time Colleen came, I had Ricky ready.

Colleen's hair had returned to a natural shade of soft brown with streaks of gray, which suited her. She and Manny were natural together, too.

I followed them to the door and the three squeezed into Manny's truck and off they went. The Dude let out a whimper, but I told him not to worry. Ricky was going to be okay. I mean he was off to be with God and all, right?

As they drove out of the parking lot, a nondescript dark sedan pulled in and up to the door. "Hello," Chad, I mean Jack, called out, as he climbed out of the vehicle.

"Hello, stranger," I called back, and since I couldn't wait to hear, I asked him, "So, when do you leave for Alaska?"

Jack took off his sunglasses and closed the car door behind him. "Well, I've got good news and bad news on that."

"What's the bad news?"

"The boss didn't like the way the Salvatore case ended."

"No?"

"He said I wasn't assigned the case, and I needed to stick to my priorities and not blow my cover on a case that wasn't ours to begin with."

"Ouch, that's bad. So, what's the good news?"

"They are going to reassign me."

"Why's that good," I asked, feeling that news in my stomach and visions of Alaska in my head.

"Because they are reassigning me from Miami to the Tampa office."

"Oh?"

"Yep, I'll still be around a lot."

"Well," I said, and I'm sure he could see my blushing face. "That is good news."

****

We drove to the Venice Marina Grill, sort of like an anniversary trip to the location of our first date. Just like the first time, I couldn't tell you what I ate but I had a wonderful time.

When we got back, we changed clothes, and when Ricky came back from lunch, we trekked over to the beach. Ricky and the Dude played in the water all afternoon, but not to be out done by a dog, Jack played with Ricky too, even letting him ride on his back. I think the verdict is still out on who won that competition, as far as Ricky is concerned. For my money, Jack won the day, and not just because he speaks English.

Later, we ordered beef tacos from the truck, Ricky's and the Dude's favorite, and ate in the bar. The crowd was light as expected on a Sunday afternoon, but with a football game on, the bar stools were full, and Gloria ran back and forth serving drinks. When the sun set in the west, everyone paused and applauded.

While eating, Ricky started nodding off, and with school the next morning, we stopped for the day. Unfortunately, I bummed out a little. Since Jack wasn't on a case, he wouldn't be staying over in the Oaks.

"You mean, your mother and father don't actually have a house in the Oaks?"

"They have one down in Naples, but that's a little far to drive."

"Where are you going to stay?"

"Colleen fixed me up with a cabin in the Cove, until I can find something more permanent."

"Oh?"

Well, maybe I will find out if Jack snores.

Chapter Twenty-Eight

Monday

The next morning, I woke up to the Dude, holding his leash in his mouth and staring me in the face. The only good thing was, with the leash in his mouth, he couldn't slobber all over me.

I took him for his morning tramp out on the sand, and when we got back, the Monday morning calamity started. Breakfast for Ricky, breakfast bar for the guests, school bus for Ricky, clean up, clean out, new linen for a kid accident in cottage nine, more towels for cottage six, business in the office, and a quick shopping trip into town for bar and breakfast supplies in the afternoon.

I came back just in time to meet Ricky's school bus. The Dude beat me there.

When we got to the apartment, Ricky showed me his surprise present, a clay plate. Starting with a block of clay, each kindergarten kid flattened the hunk into a plate-like form and impressed their handprints into the soft surface. Once dry, they painted the imprints, and the parents got a keepsake of their kid's little handprints, showing each hand including each of the delicate fingers.

"When did you make this?" I asked my future artist.

"We started last week but had to wait for the clay to dry before we could paint them. When the paint dried, they stuck them in a big oven over the weekend."

"Well, I love it, Ricky. Now, I'll always have a mold of your hand to remind me how small and young you were. You know, one day you'll grow up and be a young man."

"Mom," he said, "can I not grow up too soon?"

"Okay, Ricky, you can take your time. In the meantime, I'm putting your plate on the counter to use as a key holder. This way, every time I grab my keys to go out, or every time I come in and put my keys in it, I'll think of you."

He smiled at me and gave me a big hug. It made me feel like maybe I was making headway in this mommy thing.

****

After dinner and checking in the bar to see how Gloria was doing, I drove the golf cart to cottage five to deliver a bundle of extra towels to a family. The couple in there had a five-year-old, a three-year-old, a toddler, and an eight-month-old, so they were going through a lot of towels.

We usually couldn't cater to large families since we only had one bed in each cottage bedroom and a fold-out sofa in the living space. But with small families and a portable crib they could fit in. At night this family was putting the three-year-old and five-year-old in the fold out, the toddler in the bed with them, and putting the baby in a portable crib. That plan worked with families with small kids, but you couldn't do the same with teenagers. The last family we had that had three teenagers only lasted half a week and ended up moving to a cabin in the Cove, where everyone had extra room.

I maneuvered around screaming kids to gather all their soiled towels and stuffed them down in a laundry bag. To help out some more, I grabbed the trash spilling out of overflowing trash cans in the bathroom and the kitchen. I dropped the laundry bag in the back of the cart and hoofed it up to the dumpster behind the Gigliotti cottage to toss the trash bags before they burst open.

When I passed cottage one on my way back, I noticed Marge and Lou Gigliotti still weren't in. Worried now, after not seeing them for a couple of days, I knocked on their door a couple of times. When no one answered I got out my master key to open the door. Once again, the key didn't work. I found the duplicate cottage number one key and used it to open their door.

"Hello, Lou. Hello Marge?" I called out, opening the door just a crack in case they were there and in bed or sleeping in front of the television.

When no one answered I pushed the door open and entered. In the dim light everything seemed in place and undisturbed. I even checked the bathroom, and the toilet still had the strip of paper I always stretch and attach across the bowl, indicating I had done my job, and Marge and Lou hadn't been home since I cleaned.

I retraced my steps and locked the door on my way out.

When I got back to the apartment, I dropped my keys in the key holding plate that Ricky made for me and rounded him and Dude up and put them to bed.

I put on my pajamas, slipped into my slippers, and sat down at the kitchen island with a glass of wine. When I saw my keys down in Ricky's clay plate, I took out my key ring and separated my master key. At least three times during the past week I had unsuccessfully used my master key, so I slid it off the ring and inspected the cuts. I could see a couple of cuts and warding on the key were caked with mud, like I'd been using the key to dig a hole somewhere. No wonder the key wouldn't work.

I got a steak knife from a kitchen drawer and used the pointed end to pick the key clean of the dried muck. I used a little olive oil to wipe the blade clean. To see if the cleaning worked, I slid the key into the lock on the side door of the great room, and when I twisted, the lock clicked open.

The trouble with the key began the week before when this whole mess with the Salvatore brothers started. The first day I tried to open Gloria's door for Winters and his crew, and my master key didn't work. There was also the time at Manny's shop when the key didn't work, then at the side apartment door, and just now at the Gigliotti cottage. Until Gloria's door, the key worked fine. Something happened to the key just before this whole mess started.

I put the key back on the ring and dropped the set of keys back onto Ricky's clay plate. Now, I've never been described as dense. No, many of my former teachers described me as bright. But as I sat there with Ricky's plate in front of me, I finally saw the connection between my malfunctioning key and clay.

Apparently, I had gotten clay or some mud on that key that kept it from functioning properly. I couldn't imagine how. I could have dropped the ring I mused, but around the beach that would have put sand on it, not clay. Or someone had pressed that key into clay on purpose. If so, the only purpose I could think of was to make a mold of the key, just like Ricky pressed his little hand in a slab of clay to make a mold.

I couldn't imagine what was involved. I wasn't a machinist or anything, but I was sure I saw an old movie where the same scenario played out. I didn't have any real-life experience with metal, or clay for that matter. Was it probable that a mold could have been used to make a duplicate master key which gave someone access to all the cottages and buildings on the complex. Since nothing was missing, I assumed the duplicate wasn't used to steal anything. If not, what?

Oh, yeah, how about to try to kill Tony Salvatore. Someone could have used a duplicate key to let themselves into Salvatore's cottage and then waited for him to come home. They could have hidden behind the door and when Salvatore comes in, whack him over the head with Manny's hammer, in complete surprise. No one would have expected to be hammered like that. Then they lock the door behind them when they leave. At this point, we had assumed Salvatore knew his assailant, but in my key mold scenario, Salvatore could have been surprised and smacked by anyone who had access to my keys.

Wow, so my carelessness with my keys led to someone getting nearly killed. And since I leave that keyring hanging on my housekeeping cart, anyone who booked with us would have had access and used that knowledge to make a duplicate key.

But who thinks of that kind of thing? Not me. You'd have to watch a lot of crime shows on cable to pick up on something like that or read a lot of mystery books. Either that or you are a professional. But no professional would be hiding out in the Cabana Bay Cottages.

So, a guest or an observant killer. Not Colombo, which was laid to rest by Fred Salvatore. But who else would want to kill a Salvatore and why?

When Manny finished his patrol, I was reluctant to

tell him about my findings. If I was right, well, I could be blamed for a couple of near fatal attacks. That was something I didn't want to own just yet.

I climbed into bed for the night, hoping to dream about Chad, I mean Jack, but instead, I stayed awake for a long time, thinking about Tony and Milke Salvatore in the hospital.

Chapter Twenty-Nine

Taco Tuesday

In the morning, after I got Ricky off to school, I found Winters in the breakfast room with a cup of coffee and one of our cinnamon buns. Several of our guests surrounded the donut tray, including Lou and Marge Gigliotti. "What a surprise," I said to Winters, filling a paper cup with coffee and gulping down the caffeine. "Any special reason for your visit?"

"Some of Salvatore's photography stuff made an appearance in Sarasota."

"Oh yeah?" I said, gulping more coffee.

"Yep, apparently there are a few honest pawn shops down there."

"Same perp?"

"No, this time an old guy. Three separate places reported taking in the stuff, but bad addresses and phone numbers again."

"An old guy, huh?" I stopped slurping long enough to pay attention to this new information. Viewing the *old guy* description with greater clarity since hearing about old age from Benny I asked, "So, what do you think?"

"I think Colombo dumped the camera equipment and someone else found the stuff. Now, they are selling the junk off."

"I don't know. Why would Colombo take the stuff

if he's just going to dump it?"

"I told you all back when this started, I thought it was a robbery. A robbery gone bad."

"Did he confess to that?"

"No, and now he's got a big shot lawyer from New York down here. He's making a lot of noise, the lawyer, not Colombo. Colombo hasn't said a word. So, the mayor wants me to follow up and make sure we have the evidence to hold Colombo."

"He was kind of caught in the act with Mike Salvatore," I said finishing my coffee, crushing the cup and tossing it into a bin, "wasn't he?"

"Exactly, but the mayor is being cautious. Anyway, we're done with the cottages. You can have them back."

"Great," I said and rubbed my hands together, just raring to go. "I'll have them booked by the end of the week. For both Manny and me, thanks."

"You're welcome. I'm sorry we took so long."

"Say," I said, remembering some details of the case, "did the pawns in Sarasota give you anything more on the pawning customer?"

"They all said the same thing, he was an old guy, but tall, fancy dresser, and limped and used a cane. Do you recall anyone that fits that description?"

"Here in Cabana Bay?" I smiled at him. "Only about half the male population."

Winters plodded to his car and for some reason I waved goodbye to him. When the breakfast room emptied, I cleaned up.

****

Later in the day I had an emergency call from the family in cottage six. Apparently, their toilet was stopped up and possibly overflowing. I'd unstopped a hundred toilets during the year, so I hurried there before the water belched out and did some real damage.

Luckily, the water had barely breached the bowl's rim, and I was able to clear a roll of toilet paper one of the kids had tried to flush before any damage. I used a coat hanger I had previously fashioned into a big hook for just such occurrences and fished the blob out. I put the whole mess down in a garbage bag and mopped the floor dry. When I left, the mother was trying to explain to the kid that she couldn't flush so much toilet paper at once. Something every mother should convey to every offspring.

When I got outside, I wheeled around south toward the dumpster to toss the bag. I saw Marge Gigliotti quickly enter her cottage, like she was trying to avoid me. Which was unusual, as most every other time she would stop and say hello and invite me in for a cold drink.

"Marge," I said to her when she showed at the door to answer my knock, "how are you? I haven't seen much of you two the last few days. Where have you been?"

"We were visiting a friend in Sarasota," she said, standing firmly in her doorway, trying not to make eye contact. "She's been under the weather."

"Oh, that's too bad. I took the time you were away to give your place a good cleaning."

"Yes, dear," she said, still averting my eyes, "I noticed. Thank you so much."

"You missed some excitement around here. They arrested Dante Colombo for attacking Tony Salvatore and his brother Mike Salvatore."

"Yes," she said, finally glancing at me, "that's what Señora Martinez was saying."

"Can you imagine," I said, "someone like that was living right under our noses."

When we both stood there for a minute with nothing more to say I asked as a courtesy, "Well, I'm on my way to the dumpster. Do you have any trash?"

Not one to pass on an opportunity to have me do one more thing for her she held a finger up and said, "Well, we do have a couple of bags."

I wondered how she would have any trash at all since I had just gone through their place and had already taken out the trash. When she left me at the door I stepped inside the cottage and glance around at the place.

Something looked different about the place, but I didn't have enough time to study the scene.

"Here you are." Marge said, interrupting my snooping and handing me several heavy trash bags, and ushered me out.

On the way to the dumpster, I resisted the temptation to peek in the bags to see what they could be throwing out since I emptied their trash the day before. I hated being nosy, but I did get a whiff of garlic, so figured she had been cleaning their refrigerator.

When I got back to the office, Manny had left me a note to meet Colleen and him in the food court in the Cove. I washed up and took a golf cart over and joined them at a wooden picnic in the shade, at the far end of the shelter.

"What's up?"

"Have some hot wings," Colleen offered as I sat down on the picnic table across from them.

Manny said, "Colleen got a report back from the shack ladies on the reservation list."

"A report?" I said, looking at the greasy pile of

chicken.

"Yeah, real professional," Manny said, showing me a stack of papers, "even typed."

"What did they discover?" I asked with a wing in my mouth.

"The ladies ran the numbers on all the spaces and found several potentials."

"Potentials?" I said, licking my fingers.

"Yeah," Colleen said, "two adjoining midweek overnight spaces that were blocked out the same day, every month, for the entire year. It's different days and different weeks, but always a midweek day, and there are several pairs that meet the parameters.

Colleen said, "The whole thing is unusual. To reserve a midweek overnight, they lose the whole week, because no one wants to stay only part of a week. Most people want the whole week. So, you lose money if they are renting the space for only part of a week."

Manny said, "But if they don't care about making money on the rental?"

"Then they must be making money another way," Colleen said.

"Wow," I said, and wiped my hands on a wad of paper towels. "Those ladies deserve a raise."

"Don't get crazy," Manny said.

"Now what?"

Colleen said, "I'll research who owns the lots. When we find out, we can keep an eye on the spaces."

"A stakeout? I want in on that."

"You've got work to do cleaning cottages," Manny said. "You won't have time for a stakeout."

"Come on, Manny, I think I've proved I can do a little more than clean cottages."

"Which reminds me," Manny said. "Señora Martinez is out of town all week, so she wants her floor stripped and waxed."

"I can get to it tomorrow, but what about this stakeout."

"Okay, I'll let you…"

"Wait," I interrupted him, holding up my hand, like a cop at an intersection, "when did Señora Martinez tell you she'd be gone?"

"She told me last week on Thursday night when I was talking to her in the bar. She left Friday for Miami. She'll be there for the week to visit her daughter."

I started to get a funny knot in my stomach, and not because of the hot wings.

"I think Lou whacked Tony and Mike Salvatore."

"What?" Colleen said.

"I talked to Marge an hour ago. She said she heard from Señora Martinez about Tony and Mike Salvatore and Colombo. But she couldn't have. Marge and Lou have been gone for a couple of days. Marge and Lou didn't get back until last night. By the time they got back here, Señora Martinez was already gone. You said she left Friday morning."

"That's right," Manny said, "but how does that say anything about anything?"

"She lied to me about that. She couldn't have known about Mike Salvatore and Colombo unless Lou or her were there."

"She's just old," Manny said. "Both Lou and Marge are old. Maybe they heard about it online or on the news."

But it was coming together for me. Right out in the sand and salt.

I said, "Señora Martinez does these craft things at the senior center. Well, I bet I've swept up left over clay from her pottery projects every week since I've been here. She must have fifty of the things around her place."

"So, she's an artist," Manny said.

"She is that, but Marge Gigliotti isn't, and I found similar clay remnants on her kitchen floor. But there are no examples of clay art in their cottage. They've been doing something with clay, but not making coffee mugs."

"What have they been doing?" Colleen asked.

So, I told them about my theory of a clay mold of my master key.

"Wow, that's quite a theory," Colleen said. "What do you think, Manny?"

"I don't know…iffy at best."

"Why?" I asked.

"For one, just because someone makes a clay mold of a key doesn't mean they have an actual key. You couldn't use a clay key in a lock. No way."

"How about the stolen camera equipment being hawked up and down the coast. The pawn person could be Lou Gigliotti."

"Lou? No way."

"He fits the description, old guy, tall and broad, fancy dresser. If he was in a line up, I bet Benny could pick him out."

"You'll need more to get Winters to put him in a lineup."

"I don't know," Colleen said. "We might have to check this out."

"What, you too?"

"Manny," I said, "I may be wrong, but if we want to

ask Lou and Marge anything we need to hurry. I just spoke to Marge, and I got the impression they were getting ready to run."

"What makes you think that?"

"I know how a person acts when they are about to run, and from what I saw, Marge is getting ready to bolt. Plus, they had several bags of trash to throw out, like they were clearing out their place."

"Manny," Aunt Colleen told him, "I think we better go up there and talk to Lou and Marge, just to make sure."

Once Manny agreed we climbed into our golf carts. Manny in his Oaks patrol cart, me in the Cottages cart, and Colleen in a Cove cart with pirate decals.

We pulled up in front of Lou and Marge's cottage and the three of us got out, but at their door, no one answered my knock.

"Better open it," Colleen said.

"What if they're in there," Manny said.

"They are not there, Manny," I said. "They ran."

"Okay, okay," he said, "let's see."

I opened the door with my now functioning master key. While I stayed in the living area, Manny checked out the bathroom, and Colleen checked the bedroom.

I stayed out front but there was something different in the room. Marge was always redecorating, so I couldn't be sure what she'd done to pique my interest.

"There're gone for sure," Colleen said from the bedroom. They cleaned out their closet."

"I've seen them putting stuff in their Buick."

"Yeah, you may be right," Manny said from the bathroom. "Their toiletries are gone, and the medicine cabinet is empty."

"The refrigerator has been cleaned out," I said from the kitchen. "That's Marge. She's too fussy to have left a mess in there. She would have worried if the next guest found rotting leftovers."

We gathered in the front room.

"Now what?" I asked the two ex-cops.

"Let's not jump to conclusions," Manny said. "I'm still not convinced Lou and Marge had anything to do with the Salvatore brothers."

"Why did they run off then?" Colleen asked.

"Maybe they were skipping out on their rent."

I said, "They are paid up for this month."

"She lied to Moli about Colombo," Colleen said.

"She could have heard about the Salvatores anywhere and was just confused."

"What about the clay and the key," I asked him.

"Look, a clay mold doesn't get you a metal key. You're missing a couple of steps there to get to a functioning metal key."

"Like what?"

"Like someone would have to use the mold to form a key out of metal. Then they'd have to work the blank of metal to match the mold and the key's cuts. Not just anyone could do all that."

"How about someone that used to be in the United Machinist Union," I said, standing in front of the group of shelves in the cottage, finally noticing what was different in the room…the shelves were half empty. "Someone like that could work with metal like you describe, couldn't they?"

Manny and Colleen joined me in front of the bookshelves.

"What are you getting at?" Manny asked.

I pointed to something they didn't take with them and said, "It's a certificate awarded to Giuseppe Gigliotti, for thirty-five years in the United Machinist Union of New York. This has always sat right here, partially hidden behind other stuff, so I never got to read the inscription, but they left it behind."

"I'll be…" Manny said, "but where would he get the equipment to work a metal blank?" Scanning the small space he added, "He'd need at least a metal grinder and maybe more."

The answer came to me quickly. "The Senior Center is located right next to the community college, and they have a full automobile workshop. Would an auto shop have what the senior center didn't have to form a key?"

"Maybe, but why attack Tony Salvatore?"

"They relocated over here because they couldn't afford the Oaks. Maybe they needed money?"

"They attacked him for his cameras?" Many said. "How much did they get selling those? A couple of hundred dollars? And why attack Mike?"

"He needed to get rid of Mike to cover his tracks," I said.

Then we heard a howl from the direction of the office.

"That's the Dude," I said. "I forgot all about the time. Ricky must be home from school and is in trouble. What kind of a mother am I?"

I was the first outside and jumped into the Cottage golf cart. Manny followed in the Oaks cart, and Colleen came next in the Cove cart, with the pirate decals.

When I approached the office, I drove right to the entrance and slammed on the brakes and slid the last ten feet to the door. I jumped out and banged through the doorway and found Ricky sitting at a table in the breakfast room, sipping from one of the half pint cartons of chocolate milk we keep in the countertop refrigerator with a glass door.

The Dude bellowed out again from across the room, behind the reception desk, in front of the office door.

"Are you okay, honey? Are you hurt?"

"No, Mommy," he explained to me as Colleen and Manny rushed in. "I was thirsty, so I came to get milk. But the Dude saw some people behind the counter, and he chased them into the office. They're still in there. They closed the door on the Dude. I think he's mad at them."

Manny rushed over and grabbed hold of the Dude by his collar and dragged him back to sit near Ricky where the dog slobbered on my kid. The dog had torn most of the sheath facing off the hollow core office door trying to get in. Through the ripped-out gaps in the door, we could see Lou and Marge Gigliotti cowering inside the small office, their eyes wide.

Lou had used the community college's machine shop to make a duplicate cottage master key. They used the key to get into the motel's office where they thought they would find some cash and used the key to get into cottage fourteen. I could have told them that breaking into the office was a lost cause since hardly anyone used cash anymore. Most people use cards.

The couple had been planning to run, but when they heard Winters telling me about an old guy selling Salvatore's camera equipment in Sarasota, they jump started their getaway. They knew I'd figure out what was going on sooner or later. *Hey, how about that?*

And as much as we coaxed them, they refused to come out of the office until the police came and got them.

Chapter Thirty

The Dude

Winters showed up and locked down cottage number one. He threatened to close the whole place down, but when Manny begged him, he relented and settled for just cottage number one. Since cottage one stood at the end of the row of units and near the dumpster, they could cordon the place off by itself.

I think arresting Lou Gigliotti for attempted murder and Marge for being an accomplice was enough for Winters, even though the couple were on the old side.

"Hey, *amigo*," the detective said as his crew draped yellow crime scene tape all around cottage one, "I guess I should be thanking you and Moli for your role in all this, but I'm not sure the good you did outweighed the bad. So, I'm going to say we are even."

He never mentioned our help in any official comment the town made on the case. But I didn't care because I put the story out on Instagram, along with photos of the Dude and little Ricky. By the next morning the Dude had ten thousand followers.

If the site drew a few more followers, we might set the Dude up with a YouTube channel. If we attracted some dog food sponsors it might make enough to pay for the boy's college education. Of course, that was thinking way ahead since Ricky was only in kindergarten, but don't financial advisers say to plan ahead? Who said I wasn't a good mother?

When they showed the Salvatore brothers a photo of Lou Gigliotti, they couldn't identify him because they had never actually seen the man, since the case they were working didn't involve him. Lou had been able to attack Tony from behind. As I figured, he got into Tony's cottage with the duplicate master key he made and hid behind the door until Tony showed. He whacked him with Manny's favorite hammer, which he also obtained by using the key.

Before the incident with Colombo, Lou heard Mike and me talking about the meeting when he took some trash out to the dumpster. He figured he could get there ahead of Mike and whack him in the dark, and when Colombo came, he'd get the blame.

There were a few hours of panic in the mayor's office when the town attorney pointed out that there wasn't a clear motive for the crimes, but Aunt Colleen's contact finally got back to her from New York. Apparently, Lou Gigliotti had been injured on the job and the union let him go. They had planned to retire down to the Oaks and believed they were going to get a big cash settlement, but they only received a fraction of what they expected, and they were mad. They had already signed a contract on the garden home, so when they left New York, Marge transferred a hundred thousand dollars out of the union account. She'd been in charge of the books and hoped to hide her tracks in the accounting. They reasoned they were due the money anyway. When that money ran out, they moved over to the Cottages.

When we passed the info along to the town police,

they confirmed the case against Lou and earned Winters another black mark in the eyes of the mayor and cemented our role as amateur investigators.

When Tony Salvatore first showed up in Cabana Bay, Lou and Marge saw him sneaking around and were afraid he had come down there to investigate them and they panicked. So, Lou whacked him. They took his equipment to sell since they needed money. After pawning the first camera at Benny's, they went out of town for the other stuff, which is why they were down in Sarasota.

Mike Salvatore was just another obstacle they needed to get rid of to cover the theft. Marge said it wasn't personal.

Later that evening, the Salvatore brothers left town on a private charter. We all went to the airport to see them off, except Winters.

I told Mike how sorry I was about everything, but he told me to forget it. On the way out, Fred Salvatore told me to give him a call if I ever decided to go into the business. He said I had a head for that kind of thing, which I was happy to hear since up until then, I figured a career in environmental services was all I had to look forward to in my future.

That night I got tacos for everyone including a dozen steak tacos for the Dude.

I was sitting at the kitchen island with my mouth full of fish when I looked up and Chad, I mean Jack, and Marco Valente, walked in.

Oh, oh, double trouble.

A word about the author...

Ruben was born and raised in East Los Angeles. After college he was with the Peace Corps and spent two years teaching elementary school in a small African village by day and reading and writing by candlelight at night. Ruben's first published work was by the BBC for world broadcast. After the Peace Corps, he moved to North Carolina. Ruben was an entrepreneur for many years owning his own business. He began working with the City of Winston-Salem in 1997. Before he retired from the city, he was Director of Business Development. Now he writes full time and teaches part-time with the local community college system. Ruben has published other books in the mystery genre, but this is the first where the main characters are Latinx.

www.rubendgonzales.com